John Brason wa[...]n-
ing as a painter at the Royal Co[...]ed
for 27 years in the film industry. In 1962 he began writing
for the screen, entering television in 1971. He was
principal writer for the BBC television series *Colditz*
(for which he scripted an award-winning episode), and is
script editor of *Secret Army*.

JOHN BRASON

Secret Army

British Broadcasting Corporation

The BBC–1 television drama series *Secret Army* is devised by Gerard Glaister and Wilfred Greatorex. The main characters are played as follows: Albert, Bernard Hepton; Brandt, Michael Culver; Curtis, Christopher Neame; Dr Keldermans, Valentine Dyall; Kessler, Clifford Rose; Monique, Angela Richards; Natalie, Juliet Hammond-Hill; Yvette, Jan Francis. The producer is Gerard Glaister and the directors Kenneth Ives, Viktors Ritelis and Paul Annett.

First published 1977 by the
British Broadcasting Corporation
35 Marylebone High Street
London W1M 4AA

ISBN 0 563 17400 5

© John Brason 1977

Printed in England by
Love & Malcomson Ltd
Brighton Road, Redhill, Surrey

This book is sold subject to the condition that it
shall not, by way of trade or otherwise, be lent, re-sold,
hired out or otherwise circulated without the publisher's prior
consent in any form of binding or cover other than that in which
it is published and without a similar condition including this
condition being imposed on the subsequent purchaser

CONTENTS

Introduction 9

'Lifeline': The Beginnings 23

Evaders: The First of the Many 79

The Way Back 185

For Nicholas

The action of this novel precedes the episodes of the BBC Television series.

I have been fortunate in hearing so many stories and personal recollections of RAF evaders, and these tales form the background to the book.

All the incidents related herein happened to someone, even the unlikely chain of events which I have attributed to Sergeant Barry Parks occurred to (several) actual persons during their evasion. I have stretched a point in letting one person get away with it all, but I am reliably informed that *not one* RAF person managed to evade capture and return to the UK without assistance from the evasion lines.

It is a matter of record that the evasion lines returned over three thousand Allied Air Forces personnel to the UK, there to continue the fight against Nazi Germany.

No small achievement.

My special thanks are due to Group Captain W. S. O. Randle CBE, AFC, DFM (Chairman of the RAF Escaping society) who acted as Technical adviser to the television series and gave unstintingly of his time, his recollections, and his enthusiasm.

J.B.

Introduction
1939

31 August, Upper Silesia: *The two trucks turned onto the Tarnowitz road and drove straight at the dull red sun above the radio-mast of the transmitting-station. In the cabin of the truck the SS Sturmbannführer felt a sense of smug achievement as he was jogged and jolted along the dry, pitted surface of the road.*

7.45 on a summer's evening in Upper Silesia, just inside the Polish border on the German side, was usually appallingly dull. The unit had been here for only two weeks yet it already seemed a lifetime of boredom and frustration. Twice their mission had been called off; twice reinstated and delayed. But there was no stopping it now.

In the tarpaulin-covered truck, five trusted and experienced SD men, dressed as Polish Infantry, joked quietly. They were about to make an attack, using lethal weapons, and leaving dead behind them, but they, too, showed neither tension nor fear – indeed their joking revealed genuine high spirits. They were about to make an unprovoked attack against unarmed persons, create noise and mayhem, and leave some dead bodies behind. They had brought the dead ones with them. They were in the second truck.

At the same time two other separate contingents were a short distance away heading for their own objectives – the Forestry Station at Pitschen, north of Kreuzberg; and the Customs Building at Hochlinden between Gleiwitz and Ratibor.

They, too, took their dead with them.

Biem. Belgium: It had been a quiet birthday for Lisa Colbert. There wasn't much to do in Biem – even on a birthday – but her father had insisted upon inviting his brother Gaston, who journeyed from Brussels with his wife for the occasion. Together with their neighbours, the Musins, Lisa had invited her closest friend, Avril.

Then, of course, there was Pieter, and it was thoughts of Pieter that had taken the edge off the whole birthday.

Lisa was in love. Simply, naïvely, devastatingly in love. Like all romantic girls brought up and fed upon the saccharine diet of American movies her understanding of love and sex bore little relation to actuality, so that when urgent animal pressures began to make themselves felt she was both excited and repelled. It was disturbing.

Now there was only the evening meal left of her day, and Pieter was still absent. He had neither sent a message nor telephoned the Musins, next door. It was unlike him to be so thoughtless – especially on her birthday. Lisa was feeling the first pangs of that nagging fear which besets lovers and she was taking it badly, when at last the young man put in his shamefaced and tardy appearance. Relief was the first emotion to sweep over her. There was time enough for irritation and remonstrance.

Pieter Coecke, twenty-seven and fair haired, attractive rather than handsome, had an air of assurance and responsibility at variance with his vacant but willing grin as he made his excuses to all, and lastly – more humbly – to Lisa herself. She forgave him, of course, and sat down to the meal content and 'complete' at last. Her day was not going to be a total write-off.

Brussels: Albert Foiret glanced quickly round the restaurant-bar. It was tatty. Not much doubt about that, but an experienced eye could see what a bit of shifting around, a decent coat of paint, and some new light-fittings would do to the place. Roomy enough, yet intimate . . . Not at all bad, in fact.

He squinted at the agent.

'What's out the back?'

The young assistant detailed to show a prospective customer round a property after hours was obviously not the top man in the agency. A pimply, bespectacled youth in a cheap, mass-produced suit, he was almost certainly giving up part of his evening – unpaid – and wouldn't say 'Boo' for the inconvenience and imposition. By the time he found the typewritten particulars of the rear of the premises Albert had seen for himself. Kitchen, storeroom, back-parlour, a bottle-store-cum-still-room, and an outside lavatory.

'How do you get down to the cellar?'

'It's under here, sir. Under the stairs . . .' Grubby, eager fingers fumbled with the catch, and then offered the open door. Albert switched on the light and descended the wooden stairs. The cellar was a good one with pavement access. Cold and dry, and obviously extending over a larger area than implied by the freehold particulars. Albert sized up the area mentally, and quickly paced the length.

'Was the shop next door once part of the restaurant property?'

The lad looked vacant.

'I . . . er . . . don't really know, sir.'

Albert knew already that he was going to take it. He sensed it as he first saw the restaurant area. It felt right. The cellar only clinched it. He turned with an air of decision.

'You can tell Monsieur Bodart I'm interested. I'll drop in and see him in the morning.'

'Don't you want to see upstairs, then?'

Albert eyed the astonished youth quickly. Obviously if the lad had turned out in his own time he wanted it to be to some purpose. Albert smiled.

'All right. After you.'

They clattered up the uncovered stair-treads, narrow and without benefit of a stair-head window, and into the room on the right.

Upper Silesia: *The engineer liked to start his shift with a cup of coffee. It was his proud boast that he consumed at least eight cups during the late shift, and his locker at the end of the corridor held the tin of coarse-ground beans that he favoured. He was on his way to get that very tin when it all happened.*

Out of the corner of his eye he saw five men – uniformed men – with what appeared to be guns of some sort making from the station engine-room up the stairs to the broadcasting-room. He swung round, still kneeling, and was about to shout out that they were 'on the air', but the words stuck in his throat as he recognised the round object immediately before his face, the tip of the muzzle pressing into his newly-shaven cheek. It was a nice, new, shiny Walther Pistole ·38, and it was very close.

The Sturmbannführer kicked open the door, shouting orders in his newly-learned Polish. The broadcasting-staff gaped as the 'Poles' clattered about and made as much noise as they could, wrecking and overturning, yet careful to avoid anything that might hamper or break off the broadcast. The Sturmbannführer found the storm-microphone as detailed, and held it strategically to pick up both the sounds of wrecking and shooting, and his own barked, thickly-accented Polish. The station staff were quickly handcuffed and carted off to the cellar.

Four minutes later it was all over.

Last to leave, Schanführer Ludwig Kessler glanced round the entrance and the small area inside the wire perimeter. Three men wearing Polish uniforms were lying dead, judiciously placed to give credence to the raid and the splendid fight put up by the station staff. He bent over the one by the gate and rearranged him to one side.

He thought that the corpse looked excessively stiff for someone newly dead, but after all it was not his province. He'd done his job, and quite enjoyed the doing of it.

From Pitschen, from Hochlinden, and from Gleiwitz, the trucks withdrew in a hasty, cowardly, jocular, dusty spurt, and disappeared down the various roads. The dust settled, the dull, red sun slowly sank behind the yellowed purple of the Silesian plain.

Just another, quiet, summer evening.

Biem. Belgium: It wasn't much of a walk – out of the town on the road to Bree, first turning on the right beyond the old church, no longer in use, and two kilometres past dirty, scrubby fields where the old pit winding-house slowly fell to dust amid the rubble of yesteryear.

There was a place by the wall – the only piece of wall undamaged by the vandal heels of small boys – where they frequently sat and looked over the plain, with its pit-shafts and slag-heaps, its factory chimneys, and all the grim figuration of the industrial landscape. In late evening, especially in the autumn when the sun hung heavily in the firmament, something seemed suddenly to stoke up the furnace in the sky. It grew deeper and redder, and flooded the landscape with an engulfing glow that sent long shadows wriggling across the terrain, black fingers poised to clutch the earth in a still, possessive grasp. That was when it became exciting – infernal. That was when the marvel and the terror of nineteenth-century industrialisation asserted its claims upon the hearts of the young.

That was really why they came up here so regularly. Pieter loved it. He drank in the challenge and the drama Lisa had not even seen it until he opened her eyes to look beyond the obvious. It had been to her no more than a disgusting defoliation of nature – a never-ending dump upon which the less fortunate of mankind spewed out the earth's innards, and scurried amongst the offal like so many rats in a rubbish tip.

Then Pieter came. He made her see beyond the pock-marked face. He instilled into her a sense of his own vision and purpose. An engineer, about to sit for his finals, Pieter had grown up in the area as Lisa herself had. Her own nature warmed to the gentler landscapes, the easy, cultured and friendly towns of Ghent, to the throbbing excitement of Brussels, and left her dissatisfied and anxious to escape from the black, scarred horror she had known as home. But he delighted – even exulted – in the grime, the sweat, and the roaring, belching, smoking vitality that was, to him, home and heaven.

'I'm sorry I was late, Lisa. Really – I couldn't help it.'

Pieter was so blatantly contrite that Lisa flung her arms round his neck and kissed him on the jaw-line of his cheek. She rather liked doing that. There was something curiously satisfying about the youthful shaven cheek – like fine glass paper – that hinted at the man emerging from the boy. But Pieter was abstracted, and did not respond. Instead he held her away from him so that he might look earnestly into her eyes as he spoke. Her heart sank a little. He was going to be serious.

'Listen, Lisa. This is important . . . please listen. I was late because the Reservists have been called to report for active service. Something's happening. Now! I'm not sure what, but I think there really is going to be a war. Listen . . . please!'

Lisa wanted to interrupt, and make foolish poo-pooing objections to the serious turn the night had taken. She did not want this. She had not planned this. She wanted him to explore and caress her body again. That was why they had come out into the late summer night, and trudged miles away from places and people. But Pieter would not be sidetracked. Sometimes he infuriated her, he was so desperately callow.

'. . . and I shall be sent up to the border with the rest. France has sent more men up to the Maginot Line, but the Germans are shaking their fists at Poland, and Captain Broek says he thinks it will all burst into another war whatever we do . . .'

Lisa stared at him unheeding. Why didn't he do anything? She tried so hard to look attractive for him today. Everything had gone wrong today.

'. . . Lisa! You aren't listening. Darling, I'm serious! I leave at six. I wanted to ask you . . .' Pieter became even younger, and lost his grown-up look and confidence. She didn't much like that.

'Will you marry me, Lisa? Will you? Not now, of course, but when it's all blown over . . .'

Senlis. France: The big house on the edge of the town was built of warm grey-brown stone, with a high wall facing the street and small square. Behind the huge, wooden gates *La Laitière* stood silent and calm. The warm evening glow caught the chimneys and roof-tops, and glinted momentarily through the tall trees on the west side of the house. The lawns, dry for lack of summer rain, bore the ornate, white-painted, cast-iron table and chairs which, in turn, carried the remains of peeled pears, some peach stones, and, tucked into the ornamentation of the back of one chair, a half-used ball of knitting wool – all quietly listening to the evening sound of the grasshoppers.

Senlis, a charming country town some forty kilometres north of Paris, situated in the ancient Forest of Chantilly, retained much of its old-world charm despite the week-end encroachments of the Parisians and their cars and bicycles. The road to Amiens lay ten kilometres to the west, and left Senlis mercifully free of noisy, uncaring through-traffic. Had it not done so the quiet Place de la Laitière would scarcely have known about it, tucked away – almost secreted – as it was. Apart from the big house the delightful little Place was formed by four eighteenth-century houses of charm, with a sense-of-place that two later, ostentatious, brick piles failed to destroy.

La Laitière had been the gift of a certain nobleman to a young demoiselle of undoubted charms whom he kept at a discreet distance from the great Château, and visited from time to time. Long since, the house had come to the Chantals, and was now occupied by the two remaining members of that highly respected family. Mesdemoiselles Sophie and Madeleine Chantal, both now over seventy and unmarried, would be the last of the line.

Sophie's high-pitched voice carried on the evening stillness.

'Berthe, I seem to have mislaid a ball of wool. It's probably on my chair in the garden. Would you mind, dear?'

Berthe – only ten years younger than Mademoiselle Sophie – muttered and grumbled as she clopped down the stone passage to the rear door of the house. She had earned the privilege of grumbling by faithfully serving the two spinsters for forty-three years. Not that they ever treated her as anything other than a servant. They would not. They could not. They were aristocrats of the Third Republic – mercantile to be sure (but so was the Republic) – without a single drop of blue blood coursing their frail bodies. Yet these two enormously dignified gentlewomen held sway over Senlis and its environs in a way not seen since the feudal days of the Counts of Chantilly. Mademoiselle Madeleine had only to draw herself up and purse her thin lips for the entire community to hold breath and tremble.

The gentler, vaguer Sophie would sit and knit for

hours on end, or crochet countless table-mats for non-existent guests, and silently suffer her sister's tight and trivial tirades against the community's civic conscience and the cheating of tradesmen. Sophie had almost married once – a long time ago. From time to time she looked back on what might have been and smiled to herself, then regarded her few married acquaintances with their impossible and vulgar spouses, and mentally lit a candle for the happy escape. Madeleine, as far as anyone knew, had never been asked. Her estate was not inconsiderable, but one glance was enough to intimidate any suitor. The fortress remained unassailed.

When their father died there was no one else. The property and its incomes came to them as a matter of course. As did the fealty.

'The doctor's coming down the front path.' Berthe grumbled as she handed over the ball of wool and clutched the peach stones tightly in her other, blue-veined hand. 'I suppose you will want the Armagnac.'

Neither sister saw fit to reply, merely stiffened already straight backs, and looked expectantly in the direction of the door, hands folded upon their laps. Doctor Nitelet paused at the half-open door, and gauged his welcome.

'Good evening, Sophie . . . Madeleine.' Sophie beamed.

'Good evening, Doctor. Such a lovely day it's been! I've sat in the garden shamelessly all day, done a little knitting and a lot of dozing. Old age is creeping on.'

'Spare us the platitudes, Sophie. Armagnac, Doctor?' Madeleine stiffly and solemnly handed him an exquisite cut-glass goblet, none too clean, and chipped in the foot, but generously filled with what Nitelet knew to be a superb 1905 Armagnac laid down by the discerning parent.

'Well? To what do we owe this visit? You haven't

tramped all the way from that wretched hospital to sit with two old women, and sip a glass of brandy. Something has happened. I can smell it.' Madeleine drew herself up before Doctor Nitelet, and waited.

Nitelet knew them both very well, their charm, their idiosyncrasies, their extraordinary feudal posturing, and their gentle undemanding kindness to every living thing in the community. But he stretched the moment as he found himself a chair, and silently savoured the magnificent spirit on his tongue. Sophie waited half-smiling, half-expectant. Madeleine fixed him with an imperious stare that was fast showing constraint.

'Mussolini has offered to act as mediator in a conference. Daladier has turned it down.'

Madeleine's fingers whitened as their entwined grip tightened, and she sharpened her nose.

'I never liked that man, but for once he is right. I suppose that fool Bonnet wants to clutch at the straw.'

'I heard something to that effect, but all is now clamped down. Utmost secrecy. Nothing at all coming out of Paris. The next thing we will hear will be a Declaration of War, I fancy.'

'Heh! You amaze me, Doctor. I should have thought experience would have shown us all that one more "Munich" is all we can look for.' Madeleine's disgust and shame was obvious.

Sophie perked up hopefully, and sought to lighten the tension in the room.

'Mister Roosevelt and Queen Wilhelmina have both sent pleas for peace. So has His Holiness.'

'And a fat lot of good that will do!' exploded Madeleine. 'Why isn't there a M A N in political life these days? That nasty little Austrian almost deserves to get away with it. Oh! if only Father were alive! He would go and see Marshal Pétain and get somebody to speak plainly to the British and make them see what is happening.'

The doctor glanced at them both quickly, then focused his attention on the elder.

'What will you do – if the worst happens?'

'I don't understand what you mean . . .' Sophie genuinely did not, but Madeleine turned away in silence, and walked to the window where she stared blindly across the dark lawn. Nitelet addressed her again.

'I mean – what will you do if the Germans advance towards Paris, as I believe they will. Will you remain here?'

'But . . . surely the Maginot Line will stop them doing that! Isn't that what it's for?' Sophie's bewilderment spoke for at least half of the French nation, and Nitelet's reply could not conceal the bitterness of innocence betrayed.

'Yes, my dear Sophie, that is what it is for, but only a fool or a geriatric Commander-in-Chief now believes it will fulfil its function.'

Madeleine turned slowly, and spoke with a quiet firmness and dignity, as was her way in all matters of importance.

'We will stay at *La Laitière*. It is our home. We will do all we can to help France and fight the Boche. I would rather die fighting than submit to those strutting brutes. We are still seigneurs of Senlis, and we shall become the bastion of our little community, Doctor. It is our duty and our privilege.'

The subject was closed.

1 September 1939: *The morning headlines of the* Volkischer Beobachter *and other national newspapers shouted the news in bold lettering:*

POLISH INSURGENTS CROSS GERMAN FRONTIER

and told of how detachments of the Sicherheitspolizei on frontier duty had opposed the intruders, and how fierce fighting was still continuing in certain unspecified places.

The German press delighted in the reportage, and showed several of the photographs they had been encouraged to take of the dead 'Polish' soldiers. Someone commented on the shaven heads of the dead men, and how like concentration-camp victims they were. Later, in a speech to the Reichstag, Hitler screamed his righteous indignation and announced retaliatory measures against Poland, precipitated by several border incidents – three of them serious.

The Master Race had unleashed its Aryan hounds-of-war five hours previously, but, then, nobody worries about chronological detail at such a time. And nobody did, as their beloved Führer sealed the outbreak of the Second World War.

But it was a curious thing. No one ever really questioned. No one – anywhere.

'Lifeline': The Beginnings

1

1940: During the night of May 9th the German Army invaded Belgium and the Low Countries. Army Group 'B', under General von Bock to the north with twenty-eight divisions; Army Group 'A', under Von Rundstedt, giving the main thrust to the south between Aachen and the Moselle. Within hours the roads westward were blocked with fleeing refugees dragging, carrying, or pushing their pathetic belongings out of the range of German guns, Panzer tanks, and the exaggerated villainy of German rank and file. The memories of the First World War, distilled by time, brought anger to the minds of those old enough to remember; apprehension fostered terror in those who had not yet experienced invasion but had learnt the embroidered truths at their parents' knee.

Within hours the bridges across the Meuse had been dynamited, but two had been left across the Albert canal, and that omission was exploited to the full by the triumphant and apparently invincible Wehrmacht. The Luftwaffe, with lessons in technique perfected in Poland after their initial experimentation against Basque towns, supported the German advancing armies with straffing, bombing, and screaming Stuka attacks.

By 6.45 on the morning of May 10th General Gamelin ordered the long prepared French High Command's Plan 'D' into operation, and Lord Gort moved his BEF forward into Belgium, beside the million-strong French Armée under General Georges.

It was to no avail. The German advance continued, laying waste the border lands. The wretched inhabitants either braved it out in cellars and shelters, or packed a few belongings onto whatever was to hand, and fled ahead of the advancing Boche. Sometimes they ran from the Stukas; sometimes they died from their bombs and bullets.

'Golden-dwarf. Toffee-castle. Saucepan-man. Golden-dwarf. Toffee-castle. Saucepan-man. Golden-dwarf . . .'

Lisa kept repeating it to herself as she stumbled along the road – over and over again, like some mantra that became hypnotic in its repetitive effect. It was to her a magic formula, a tenuous link with a world of innocence, childhood, warmth, and gentleness which saved the last vestige of sanity from fleeing the mind already shattered by the events of the last thirty-six hours. The words enveloped her like a protecting cocoon into which she mentally crept and huddled while the world of actuality staggered and shook about her – the real world, the vile, hateful, unbelievable, terrifying world.

She knocked into the woman walking ahead who clutched her sleeping child to her. His tiny mouth was stupidly open, breathing with adenoidal snoring, and one thin and dirty arm hung, apparently lifeless, out of the small blanket. The child was exhausted, drained by constant fleeing, and fear that was the more frightening for being totally without understanding. The woman did not notice the accidental nudge. She, too, was moving in a zombie-like trance down a road packed with prams, carts, horse-drawn cars, and just footsore and weary travellers. Refugees. One small tributary of the great European river of fleeing humanity flowing towards the great sea to the west. West. Away from the soldiers, and the planes, and the bombs, and the screeching dive-bombers, and the machine-gun bullets. Away from the Germans.

No one seemed to be aware any longer which way they were going, or even why. No one remembered what their original plan of salvation was. They just moved together. Away from the Germans.

Lisa had lost count of time, knew nothing of where she was, or how she had come there. A stray, tight, little thought kept recurring . . . escape . . . somewhere to the west. Away from the Germans.

'*Golden-dwarf, Toffee-castle. Saucepan-man. Golden-dwarf. Toffee-castle. Saucepan-man . . .*' It came from some childhood memory – a book from the nursery shelf – and now a pathetic incantation to retain her hold on sanity and gentleness.

Suddenly there was a muffled cry and a scatter. People ran, and dived for the ditch down the side of the road. Lisa went with them. Automatically. Instinctively. A moment later, and the drone of the aircraft grew in intensity as it dived towards the road. Hands covered ears. Arms wrapped themselves in a contorted knot over heads, and limbs trembled, kicked, and shook with mortal terror as the noise increased and approached. But there were no spurts of earth about the road, no raucous chatter of machine-guns, no bombs bursting and maiming in a pattern along the macadam-patched cobbles. Heads glanced up quickly, and gasped their relief as the *Hurricane* showed its red-white-and-blue markings as it swept overhead. A few feeble hands clapped, but most people just scrambled to their feet, formed into the endless, slow-moving crocodile, and continued on their way. Away from the Germans.

Hours later the bedraggled tributary entered St Truiden. Lisa felt she had come to the end of her energy. Unseeing, she drifted away from the throng, down side streets into a small cul-de-sac she later came to know as the Rue Cherain, and she went to sleep.

St Truiden: Eulalie Moreelse sat in her tiny café, bloated and mildly drunk. Her hair askew, her face puffed and blotched, and her feet encased in faded red bedroom slippers, down at heel, and split at one side to accommodate the swollen ankles. Pieter Pynas stood behind the counter and wiped glasses that had not been dirtied for three days. Why he wiped them he didn't know. It was something to do. Pieter was no more than five feet tall, a curtailment due in part to a deformity which had hunched his back in childhood.

One more tribulation to add to his unprepossessing stature . . . his pallor . . . and his sickliness. Now – at the age of fifty-eight – the pallor was deathly – like someone from the grave. The skin like waxed parchment, bleached under a stone, and stretched over bone structure not quite even on both sides. Now the thin wisps of white hair, and the equally white stubble on his cheeks caught the last of the day's light as he peered over the top of the counter, watching his companion of fifteen years as she slowly chuckled and sank into alcoholic bemusement. Neither said anything.

Eulalie sighed from time to time, and interspersed the sighs with chuckles. Pieter limped round from the counter and picked up her empty glass. He moved with the stiffness of a puppet, his baggy, grey trousers held up by striped braces over his yellow-grey, short-sleeved woollen vest. Pieter's eyes were sad as they caught and held the puffed stare of the woman. Eulalie's eyes were sad too. The eyes of a fundamentally happy sot suddenly sad with a deep sadness. Pieter's were more than sad. Playing around the thin-lipped mouth was the same expression as in his grey eyes . . . fear. Fear so heart-felt you could smell it.

Pieter shuffled back behind the high counter, and washed the glass in a bowl of water indistinguishable in colour from the beer he served.

It was when Pieter took out a crate of empty bottles to leave by the door that he found Lisa. He stared but said nothing, then quickly returned to the café bar, and limped towards the crumpled bladder in the red, flower-print dress and bedroom slippers.

'Eulalie! Eulalie. – Wake up . . . wake up, you old bag. Eulalie!'

The old bag jerked into awareness, and peered through the twin, puffed slits at the little man.

'Wha'sit . . . wha' ye wan'?'

With a curious little hop he reached the bench in time to stop the flesh-filled red flower-print from falling to the floor like a sack of potatoes. He moved his tiny misshapen body from side to side as if the rocking could make him take the decision Eulalie was incapable of giving. Then he turned and limped back to the open door where he stared at the sleeping Lisa. Distant rumbling brought back the realisation of what was happening not so far away, and Pieter gnawed his lip before bending to shake the young girl on his doorstep . . . or rather – his mistress's doorstep, for it was Eulalie who owned the impoverished and dilapidated café.

'Hey! Hey! Mam'selle! Wake up . . . please, wake up. Mam'selle. Hey!'

Lisa opened eyes still heavy with sleep, and closed them just as quickly. Within seconds she was sliding her shoulder down the wall of the building, and only Pieter's little hop-movement stopped a total collapse to the cobbled street itself.

It was two weeks later that Lisa learned she had been taken into the little café and put to bed, had developed a fever and become delirious, crying out loud and screaming for 'Papa', before, lapsing into total silence accompanied by body shivering and perspiring. Throughout she had been cared for by the strange pair. Pieter had fetched a doctor to attend her, but he had come only once, and the tablets he left had long since run out.

Two days after her collapse, she learned, the main body of Belgian and British Expeditionary Forces had retreated through the town; less than an hour later the first German troops and Panzer tanks appeared. They had passed through, and the town as yet saw little of their conquerors apart from staff-cars, and dispatch-riders, who sped noisily through the streets at all hours of day or night.

Eulalie sat on the edge of the little bed, and fussed over her as she related the events of the last few days. Lisa listened in silence. Her grief had become numbness. Her pain lay buried within her. Nature reacted to the shock treatment received with an inbuilt defence-mechanism that blotted out detail, and gave her no opportunity to examine chapter and verse. Only the situation remained. Only the bare facts seemed relevant. Her father and mother were dead. Pieter Coecke was dead. Her Pieter. The man who loved her, and she loved – was dead. Her parents had died, in Biem, under the German advance. Two gentle civilians caught up in a war they knew little about. Pieter had been killed in the first hours of the advance . . . that much she had learned from the dazed and shaken stragglers who retreated through Biem before the advancing Aryan hordes.

Eulalie's chat washed over her – she had her own thoughts, but it was evident that the plump, little woman sitting on the bed did not really expect answer or comment. She was talking to herself.

The door opened a few inches, and Pieter Pynas' head appeared. He entered with a limping shuffle clad, as ever, in baggy trousers, vest and braces, and bearing a small enamelled tin tray on which was a bowl of soup.

'Eulalie!' The constrained voice grunted.

'The soup'.

Eulalie's face looked up and beamed as little Pieter limped towards the bed with the tray.

'Here you are, my dear. Try some nice hot soup. You have to eat something, you know. Not that there'll be much to have soon, what with the Boche and no deliveries and everything . . . Come along now, sit up and taste my soup Pieter Pynas has brought you.'

Lisa stared at the bowl, then turned to stare at the curious little hunchback standing breathing heavily in the manner of asthmatics, and staring at her with his frightened grey eyes. Lisa turned back to regard Eulalie – a face she knew well from having discovered it beaming down on her several times in the last few days when she woke momentarily.

In the great world outside the guns roared and pounded as the two opposing sides faced each other in and around Leuven, with the lazy Dyle flowing between them. Seventeen divisions of the German Sixth Army, together with two Panzer squadrons, attacked and pressed forward against the remainder of the Belgian Army and the BEF, both holding very much better than the French Armies flanking them to north and south. Liège, Namur were both in enemy hands. Antwerp was under siege. Brussels only eighteen miles behind the lines. Names familiar in their war context were being voiced in communiqués once more – Mézières, Montmedy, Sedan, Charleroi – like echoes from the past. Sad, doomed names.

The French, Belgian and British air forces were taking a battering from the Luftwaffe. The RAF had already less than half its force serviceable, and much of that outmoded.

Later that morning Pieter stood on a small box behind the bar and reached up to the shelf to switch on the brown bakelite radio. Once its oval shape and rising-sun speaker-grill had been considered smart and à la mode, now the battered old thing, with dark, sticky circles of grease round the milled knobs, had to be coaxed, even kicked and thumped, into performing its function. Pieter fiddled and twisted through the squawks and static until a piercing heterodyne whistle gave way to an urgent Flemish-speaking voice. Pieter's anxious, frightened expression never changed as he turned and placed his yellow hands atop the counter, and stood on his good leg to listen.

'. . . the German attack and the retirement of the French divisions to the south are forcing the British to divide their forces and make a defensive flank against new attacks from this region. Otherwise the British and Belgian forces are still repelling the German advance towards Brussels. In the north French forces are falling back west of the Scheldt. The islands of Walcheren and South Beveland have already been evacuated by military units, leaving only the civilian population.

'It has just been heard that the struggle in Holland has come to an end. The Dutch High Command capitulated at 11.0 this morning. It is understood that the Royal Family and some of the High Command have fled to Britain, but news is, at the moment, sketchy and unconfirmed. There will be further news bulletins as they are received . . .'

Pieter stared at Eulalie sitting in her usual place on the wall bench, and growing puffy by the minute. His sad, graveyard pallor looked even paler in the morning light which forced its way through the unwashed window panes. Slowly he lowered his chin onto his vest, the rubber buttons pressing into the white stubble, and great, glistening tears rolled down his waxen cheeks. Eulalie just studied him stupidly and emptied her glass.

2

September was warm and stretched the summer out. St Truiden wore the fading flowers sadly, though life had quickly returned to a semblance of normality once the occupation was complete. People even went about their business without hindrance or restriction. Neither the civil authorities nor the occupying military had time to consider or organise such things as papers and permits – not until the third week, when it became obvious to everyone that the Boche were not to be thrown back . . . neither now, nor, possibly, ever.

Shutters that had been closed for upwards of two weeks were thrown open once more. Women were to be seen beating their mats against stone walls, and old men scuffed fitfully in the top-soil of gardens. German soldiers off-duty commenced to appear in public places. They entered the cafés and attempted to buy drinks for the locals – drinks downed with either scorn or fear, but downed none the less. The Germans were well behaved, and treated the populace with deference. Curfew-passes were issued and the civil authorities put up notices about future rationing, identity-cards and travel-permits, but nothing seemed definite or imminent.

Lisa seldom ventured out of the café, and never waited there in the evenings when German soldiers might be abroad. It was not that she feared molestation – the Germans were under strict instruction to respect the Belgian girls. It was only that the mere sight of the field grey uniform sent her into a fit of trembling that she was unable to control.

Gradually it eased, and she was able to walk about the town, and control her fears and recollections. Soon she was looking after the household chores. Eulalie and Pieter began to regard her as one of the family. They asked no questions and she offered no explanations. They were all content to let it remain so. They were each reassured by the presence of the other and wished to let the boat remain unrocked.

Then came Tuesday the twenty-second.

Lisa had spent an hour in the hot, dusty square, sitting without thinking, watching people come and go from the depleted shops, and local motorists attempting to plead with the garage for even a half can of petrol – without success. She felt a slight chill about her shoulders, and decided to return to her new home. The café door was open.

Eulalie sat in her place on the bench, slowly leaning forward as if eventually to fall. She was staring at nothing through the puffed lids, and the cigarette in her mouth was no longer alight. Her beer glass was empty and the overspill on the wooden table-top had dried like shellac. Obviously she had been sitting like that for hours.

Lisa went to her and put her arm round the older woman's surprisingly narrow shoulders. Eulalie seemed to sense the contact rather than feel it, and very slowly looked up at Lisa. She smiled weakly.

'They took Pieter.'

'When, Lalie?'

'I don't know.' She shook her head as if to clear it. 'Some time – hours ago. I don't know. They said terrible things about him. They said he was repulsive and disgusting. They said he should never have been allowed to live. Pieter Pynas, who never hurt anyone ...'

'But why did they *take* him?'

Eulalie lowered her head and it shook from side to side while she muttered to herself.

'Pieter Pynas found a British airman outside the town

one night last week. He brought him here and kept him in the cellar. He didn't tell me . . . not even his old Lalie . . . He was like that, my Pieter Pynas. He didn't talk very much, you know . . . He gave the airman his food . . . we didn't have much . . . Why did they say he was a revolting human being? Because he had a hump? Poor little Pieter Pynas.'

Lisa fetched a bottle of beer from under the counter where Pieter kept Eulalie's favourite brew . . . now in short supply. She poured it into a fresh glass and gave it to Eulalie, who sipped almost without noticing it was there.

'Lisa' . . . Her voice came deep and strong.

'They said Pieter Pynas smelled.'

Lisa hurried through the side door up to the bedroom where she fell upon the bed and tried to cry. Tears were needed and, in a way, wanted to come. But they simply would not.

For the next two days Lisa did everything she could. First with the intention of confronting the German authorities, perhaps pleading with them to obtain the poor little man's release. What harm could the wretched little hunchback do to the might of the German military?

It was not long before she found that not only was she not going to secure a release for Pieter Pynas – she was not even going to find out where he had been taken. No one knew, or confessed to knowing. It was not that she met obstruction. That would have been something. It was like trying to grasp a large grey cloud. There was nothing there. Only evasions and excuses, and pretences of not knowing. Not, that is, until someone let slip the sibilance of Terror – 'SS'.

Instantly she knew it was no good. Pieter Pynas might as well be marooned on an island in space for all the chance she had of reaching him. Lisa returned home to

Eulalie and tried to comfort her, but already the second wave of fear and misery was sweeping through her. She was ready to cry, and even hide, at the sound of a gutteral German voice. There was again the need to move, to go away. Away from the Germans.

3

In the large back garden, next to the Prefecture, where the Germans had built a three-metre mound of earth against the house to accept stray bullets, they had also planted four wooden stakes, three metres apart.

It was bright and sunny when Pieter Pynas and two others were brought from the cells into the light, which made them blink and half-close their eyes momentarily. The trees, the sunny day, the twenty or thirty people, men and women, who stood around and chatted and smiled, made it all seem like a ghoulish garden party. The three men had no doubt of why they had been surfaced, nor were they disabused of the knowledge when they saw the wooden stakes and heard the tramp of soldiers' feet on the garden gravel.

Little Pieter Pynas limped forward through the standing cocktail-party grouping of civilians. Belgian civilians. His face bore the expression he had worn the greater part of his life. Wary, frightened, but puzzled. His wide, grey eyes stared about him as if to try and fathom why life was like this, and what it all meant. He had been dealt a rotten hand at birth, and the game progressed without trump cards. One by one he had lost his doubtful, uncompromising hand. First, being dropped – which gave him his hunchback. Then chronic anaemia – which lent him that waxen pallor. Then the slip in the snow which broke the pelvic girdle and gave him a permanent limp. Then there was his asthma, of course, and his ugly hands and feet.

The wooden stake was nearer now. Even his limp could not keep it away. He noticed that the grass round the base of the stake was worn away.

The thirty-eight Belgian civilians who stood around might have been waiting for tea to be served. They chatted, and the Belgian men pretended not to notice the three Belgian prisoners who had been brought out and were now being tied to three Belgian tree stumps. Several Belgian women, in their flowered print dresses, watched in fascination and clutched their handbags under their arms tightly.

The men to be executed had their hands tied behind them, then were roped to the stake across the chest. At last a blindfold was put across the eyes. Pieter Pynas shook his head. He wanted to see – to look with puzzlement at this final affront by his fellow men. The SS officer-in-charge strutted in his elegant and superb black uniform. The women awaiting the entertainment, or warning – depending upon how one looked at it – eyed him as he strutted. Why did their own men not look like that in Belgian uniforms? These fine-looking young men simply radiated virility and unabashed sex-appeal. All conquerors were not unwelcome.

Orders were barked, and tension filled the back garden in St Truiden. Eyes flickered for a moment, then held the slightly-closed stare focused upon the three men at the stakes. Women's mouths relaxed in contrast to the men's, where tightening was general. Their lips parted in anticipation and held. Breath was held too.

For the men at the stakes time stood still. Breath came in great gulps and gasps, with the effect of internal spasm.

Behind the blindfolds thoughts and imaginings ran riot. Little Pieter Pynas turned his head from the firing-squad at the other end of the garden and looked at the civilians grouped to either side. One woman was short and plump . . . like Eulalie, a little. Pieter smiled with his colourless lips, but the solemn, wondering expression froze in his eyes as the shots rang out.

One moment of silent, stomach-turning tension, then the soft gasp of relief, followed by nervous chatter as the watchers regrouped and continued their converse where it had been interrupted. One or two men, in grey trilby hats and overcoats, ambled across towards the stakes where German officers were examining the men now hanging with their full weight upon the enfolding ropes. One offered a cigarette from a silver case to the Hauptmann presiding, and accepted a light from a slim golden lighter in return. Casually, even interestedly, they regarded the drooping men who had been alive fifty seconds earlier, and talked about the difficulty of obtaining coffee.

In the middle of the garden, unlike the other two, standing quite stiff like an uneven puppet against the stake, there was a funny, little man in a greyish-yellow vest, with baggy, grey trousers suspended from braces. It was noticeable that he had a hunchback, and looked ill and colourless. He had ugly hands, too.

Something about the braces holding up the roomy, ill-fitting bag of grey flannel on this little, misshapen creature was highly amusing. Several pointed to him and laughed.

The expression in the dead man's eyes was one of sadness, and puzzlement. Even the glazing of death could not change Pieter Pynas.

4

It was October when the notice was served. Lisa had twenty-eight days in which to find herself alternate accommodation and leave the little café and her room with the striped wallpaper, faded and torn in two places. Since the death of Pieter Pynas and the mysterious disappearance of Eulalie, Lisa had continued to use the room and the café as her home. Every effort she made to trace or help Eulalie had been blocked and discouraged, until she was blatantly told that the poor woman had been removed to a 'resettlement' camp in Eastern Germany, and it was useless to pursue the inquiry.

A self-seeking neighbour had put in a bid for the café property at the Hôtel de Ville. It had been approved by the Kommandantur, and he had become the new owner of the café. There is always someone anxious to profit by another's misfortune. Lisa knew him by sight.

The evening after receiving the notification she went for a walk outside the town. The curfew had finally been imposed by the Kommandantur but it was lenient, as they intended it should be, and permitted the customary opening of cafés, cinemas, dance halls, and the relatively late movement about the streets even after dusk She walked into the countryside and blankly ruminated about her situation – a state devoid of much purpose, and without even a determination to stay alive. The loss of her parents and Pieter had weighed heavily upon her. The care and human concern of the two people who had given her undemanding shelter had healed the wound considerably. Now they were gone. The same Behemoth had destroyed them.

But something was changing inside Lisa. She no longer

merely accepted, meekly and fearfully. A hidden steel was being quietly bared. This further affront and pain in the loss of Eulalie and Pieter Pynas was too much. The reaction inside her was fermenting, waiting only for the moment when hate could find outlet in positive action.

'Mam'selle . . . S'il vous plaît. Mam'selle!' Lisa turned to see who spoke to her. She was near the edge of town with only a small garage, closed because it was evening, and two shuttered houses without signs of life. The road at her feet was tarmac-covered cobbles in front of the buildings, then pot-holed concrete at either end. She remembered noticing that the tarmac was ridged with caterpillar-track marks from the advancing Panzers. Later, whenever she recollected that first encounter, the picture that crossed her memory was of tarmac and tank tracks. She peered into the gloom by the side of the house. A shadowy figure could be discerned, flat against the wall. Lisa was not nervous. She was no longer alive enough to be nervous. She crossed to the man who had spoken.

'M'sieur?'

'Parlez-vous Anglais, mam'selle?'

'Yes . . . I speak English . . . a little.'

'Thank God for that! Please, miss . . . I'm an RAF navigator. I was shot down and I'm trying to get back home. Can you help me . . . please?'

Lisa stared at him, then replied flatly.

'Yes . . . I think so. Come with me.'

The navigator had a dirty, old raincoat over his uniform. In the dusk the latter was not particularly noticeable. Together they walked down the street and into the town. Few people were about, but it was impossible to get to the café without crossing the small square in front of the church. Lisa turned to the airman.

'We have to go across the square. You'd better hold

my hand. People will think we are sweethearts. Let me talk if we have to.'

He took her hand nervously and smiled in a rather embarrassed fashion. She led him across the square, exactly as one leads a child. He followed her, and trusted her with the same unquestioning confidence that a child would have shown. Something about the contact and the sense of responsibility touched her, and immediately a sense of purpose returned, if only for a short time. For those few minutes Lisa lived. She was alive once more ... with reasons, purposes, and a place in mankind.

There were no incidents. The café she had not locked when she left it, and now she led the way back into the interior. Before switching on any lights she closed the shutters and drew the blackout curtaining. Once light flooded the room she examined her 'child' more carefully. English, and obviously so, with a close-cropped, short back-and-sides favoured by the military of most nations. Little more than a grammar school boy, he seemed excessively young, pink, gauche, and more than a little scared. His eyes never left her, questioning perhaps how much he could trust ... how much he needed to watch. Apparently reassured he smiled.

'I was jolly lucky to find you. I could have been turned in to the Jerries. I hope I won't get you into trouble.'

Lisa stared at him as at a being from another world.

'If they found you here, Sergeant, I would not be "in trouble". I would probably be shot.'

'You mean ... just for taking me in? But you haven't done anything.'

Lisa ignored the pathetic ignorance of what life was like in Europe now, and moved towards the kitchen.

'You must be hungry. I'll see what there is ... Come.'

He followed her into the kitchen, and she gave him what little there was. After the meal he produced some cigarettes and talked quickly, expansively . . . almost anxious to unburden himself of his background. Lisa listened with half an ear. It wasn't that she was uninterested in what the young man said; it was the all-pervading sense of futility that was taking toll of Lisa Colbert and had already extracted a down-payment in demoralising and enervating the house it chose to occupy. If the RAF sergeant thought anything he probably assumed that she was simply nervous, and reluctant about the whole thing, and wanted him out of her house at the first moment.

Lisa lay in bed that night with a collection of thoughts that pummelled her reason unmercifully. The momentary glow she had felt while she actively participated in helping the evader had impressed itself upon her and restored a semblance of survival sanity. As she watched the dark ceiling, or tossed and turned, unable to quiet the thoughts and dispel the growing agitation within, one message came through loud and clear. She, Lisa Colbert, needed help fast – the sort of help that no well-meaning person or medical practitioner could give. It was necessary for her to rejoin what was left of the human race . . . and the RAF sergeant asleep on the bed once occupied by little Pieter Pynas, in the house once owned by Eulalie Moreelse, had given the answer.

When morning came she rose early, still unclaimed by sleep, and prepared and packed some food for them both. It was after eight when she went to waken the navigator. He was sleeping like the grown-up child that he was, exhausted after three days of wandering and fear. Over bread, jam, and coffee Lisa told him what she had decided. Very simply it was to take him from St Truiden to Brussels, there to take a train to the border – or, better still, across the border all the way to Paris. There she would speak to some friends she knew who would advise her whether to make for 'free' Vichy France, or skirt the unoccupied zone and travel down to the Pyrenees and into Spain.

Sergeant Tom Wetherby gawped at her, his cup of coffee in mid-air before him as she calmly stated her intent.

'You mean . . . you'll take me all the way to Spain? You can't do that. I mean . . . what about your life, your job, and family and things . . .?'

'There is no job, and no family. And I think I need to help you more than you need my help. Please don't ask questions or try to protest. I have decided. We start in half-an-hour.'

Tom finished his breakfast in silence, not quite sure if his helper was an angel in disguise or a raving maniac. He had been told to watch out for congenital idiocy in rural areas of the continent, just as he had been warned not to drink the water, nor have intercourse with the disease-riddled whores of Europe. Ideas of dipping his wick had so far not occurred to Tom Wetherby. He might have thought about it once or twice back home in an idle moment and wondered what it would be like, but his virginal mind was rather too preoccupied with surviving the Aryan hordes of Nazi persecution to bother about whether the water was drinkable, or whether 'les girls' might give you a dose before you could say 'Hitler'.

Tom, like most of his companions in the squadron, was fresh from grammar-school to the recruiting-centre. Selection at Padgate, followed by what was now a crash course . . . literally, in rather too many cases . . . led straight into active service, and he, and his friends, were gauche, unworldly, rather naïve, and basically nice, un-assuming, young men whose very existence, until operations began to take their toll, gave no possibility for growing up or acquiring the veneer of sophistication that took away the stigma of 'school-boy'.

Lisa returned with some men's clothing, once the property of Pieter Pynas, and hopelessly out of size for Wetherby. But worn loosely under the dirty raincoat he already possessed they might just pass casual scrutiny. Papers were the problem. In the first weeks of the occupation a certain laxity in these matters was permitted because it had been too sudden to allow much else. Now that identification, ration, curfew had brought the administrative genius of Germany to work, and passed on the enforced enthusiasm to local, civil authority, papers and forms abounded.

Somehow, somewhere, Lisa had to obtain papers for her sergeant, or the crossing of the Belgian French border would not be easy, and the journey across France, particularly through Paris, would be hazardous indeed. She had already heard of the 'lotteries' in the Paris streets, where squads of German soldiers suddenly roped off an area of street, and held a spot-check on civilian papers. They had picked up hundreds of deserters and malcontents already, and it was proving so successful a ploy that the authorities had decided to retain it as a permanent institution. Without papers Paris could not be risked. Without using the Paris terminal running south, the Gare d'Austerlitz, the journey would be long, tedious, and dangerous. Instinct already told Lisa that the express train was probably the safest and quickest way of crossing France clandestinely. At least they would try.

They reached Brussels without incident. Lisa had a teacher-training college friend living in Melsbroek on the outskirts of the metropolis. It was just possible she would have contacts who could help with both papers and advice. It was worth a try.

Her friend, Avril, turned out to be an inspired thought.

She had a friend who knew someone who could get passes and things, and the day after Lisa made her contact and presented her case she was given a complete set of papers for her evader and a travel-permit for herself. Thus armed she and her charge set off for the Gare du Midi and France.

The journey was instructive. Lisa learned how to behave, what not to do, and by careful observation of her RAF charge, who by now regarded her with a mixture of awe and disbelief, mentally decided that the next evader she helped would have to unlearn habits and mannerisms peculiarly English, would have to let his hair grow rather more than Sergeant Wetherby, and would greatly benefit from at least a smattering of French. Perhaps the most important thing would be to acclimatise the English evader to his surroundings; let him become used to mingling with foreigners and, above all, the person of the enemy. Only that way could they possibly avoid acute nervous reaction when confronted with the field-grey uniforms that made their movements and behaviour unnatural.

Lisa had decided what she was going to do with her life.

5

Berlin: 'I am sorry, Erwin, but you are being grounded. It is for your own good. Now, you must not take it too badly. Many would give their limbs to have such a thing happen. You have been fortunate. You are also being promoted to the rank of Major.'

The words still rang in Brandt's ears as he returned to his hut. It wasn't exactly a death sentence, though it felt rather like one. Flying had been Erwin Brandt's life since he was a boy. He had graduated from a youth corps – a bunch of glorified boy-scouts – to a gliding-club near Wuppertal. There, together with dozens of keen young men, he had trained to fly. It didn't matter that it was unpowered. They learned to fly. When later their hero and Führer broke every agreement by which his country was bound, and the Luftwaffe was properly born, the transition to single-engine monoplanes was painless and quick.

He had seen service in Spain, in Stukas, enjoying every moment of it until the nature of their bombing targets gave him second thoughts. It was about the same time that, following his father's death and funeral, he had drawn closer to Admiral Canaris, his father's old friend, and Head of the German Abwehr. Canaris took him under his wing, and introduced him to his own circle of close friends . . . perhaps not solely for his father's sake. Canaris was reputed to be without friends. What was meant, of course, was that he was without friends *in the party*. The Admiral was not only a dyed-in-the-wool, old-school German, he vehemently disliked the Nazis and everything they stood for. It was not long before Erwin Brandt himself perceived the cracks in the surface of the regime.

Disenchantment was swift, but fought with a natural loyalty to his Fatherland. The war came and doubts had, perforce, to be sublimated. Even Canaris put political thoughts behind him for the moment, and was seen to be closely associated with Reinhardt Heydrich (though this last ploy was little more than self-preservation to keep the Abwehr out of the greedy hands of the SS).

Brandt served in Poland, again in Stukas, but no

longer with enthusiasm. His mind revolted against the Blitzkreig tactics, effective though they certainly proved to be.

After the fall of Poland his drooping spirits were revived when Sturzkampfgeschwader 79 was transferred to the western front, and war became active and real in the more acceptable, if sad, attack upon Belgium, France, and the Netherlands.

Brandt, like everyone else, felt the surge of power and triumph as Germany swept all before it. The Glory of Arms affects most men in some degree. Erwin Brandt was no exception. The Reich was invincible, and everybody likes to be on a winning side. Now England would sue for peace, and the war would be over. Balance of Power would be properly restored, and honour redressed. The Third Reich would flourish for its thousand years, and people could get on with living. After all, Britain had ruled the roost for long enough. Despite the fact that he knew and liked England, Brandt was not wholly sorry to see her humbled and forced to sue.

But England did not sue for peace. With bulldog tenacity and unimagined stubbornness Albion proved unpredictable to the end. At least that was what the majority of his countrymen believed. Tighter, better informed circles had known from the beginning that Britain had no intention of surrendering and, indeed, would never do so. It was not in the character of the people to capitulate. To run and fight another day, was one thing. To give up outposts of Empire was another. But to surrender one inch of the homeland was quite a different matter. Had the German High Command been better advised, had they understood anything at all of the British character, had they spent one day in the humble home of an English family they would have learnt one simple fundamental truth: The British could not lose this war because it never occurred to one of them that there was even a possibility of doing so. Britain did not lose wars. It was as simple as that, and centuries of history jingoistically dinned into generations of school children reduced to nil the possibility of such a thing happening.

Canaris and his friends knew this. Brandt was beginning to learn it. One day, over the channel, six weeks after the Battle of Britain had decided the course of the war once and for all, Brandt found himself a little too near anti-aircraft bursts. The blast had not only crippled his plane and forced an immediate return to base, it had given him substantial head injuries and shattered his right eardrum.

Now, what he had to show for his years of service was in the small top drawer before him. Iron Cross, First Class (1939); Iron Cross, Second Class; War Merit Cross, First Class; Honour Cross for the Spanish Campaign, Second Class; a Wound Badge, and a Long Service Medal, and the Operational Flying clasp. He also had a scarred mind that was no longer at peace with his conscience.

The following week he received his posting as General Staff Officer at HQ Belgium/North France Luftgau in Brussels. He was attached to the local Army Commander as Air Liaison Officer to the Wehrkreis.

6

The Chaussée de St Jean Baptiste runs roughly north/south through Ixelles, midway between St Gilles and

Etterbeek. Number seventeen belonged to Gaston Colbert and his wife Louise. They had lived there for twenty-two years, ever since Gaston had taken a position with the Brussels Bank and they moved away from Liège, which had been their home since their marriage. An unpretentious house, comfortable, and well situated for moving to and from the centre of Brussels. A tram to the Bourse was easily obtained. On clement days one could walk the distance in twenty minutes. Gaston enjoyed the walk, and the exercise did him good. The park was no more than five minutes away, and the Forêt de Soignes but half-an-hour on foot, seven minutes by public transport.

It was not until returning from Spain in late January that Lisa decided to make 'Brussels' her base and asked her Aunt and Uncle if she might live with them for the time being. They were overjoyed to see her, having believed her at least to be missing, possibly even dead. The bodies of her father and mother had eventually been found under the rubble, but no one seemed to know anything of Lisa. Louise wept copiously, and hugged her to her bosom. Gaston preserved a calm that could not wholly conceal the lump in his throat.

The first week passed without incident, and without her being urged to relate her experiences. Little by little Louise's curiosity got the better of her, and she endeavoured to press Lisa to give them details of how she had lived, where, and what – if anything – had happened to her during the German advance. At first she was silent and refused to answer, and Gaston changed the subject. She was, indeed, trying to put the recollection of those days behind her, but it would not leave. Two or three nights each week she would awaken in a cold sweat of terror, and lie weeping in the darkness. If Louise noted the damp pillow-slip in the morning she said nothing.

Lisa made her own bed and kept her room tidy, yet it developed no personality nor held any clue to the nature of the occupier. It remained a dormitory and nothing more. If Lisa had ever had a personality of her own there was no sign of it now. She came and went and used room, and house with restraint and in almost total silence. Gaston, being out at the bank most of the time, seemed unaware of this abdication, but Louise watched and wondered, and was deeply sad that it should be so.

Sometimes in the night Lisa called out in her dream-tossed sleep. The odd name – 'Lalie', 'Pieter', and cries for her parents. Gaston and Louise gave up going to her, and let the torment spend itself. Days ran into weeks, but the nights remained as a great hollow cave into which she was reluctantly drawn time after time after time. That venturing, however involuntary, became a search. She entered the silent labyrinth and moved through it as the sounds from all around increased – cries, explosions, screams, the chatter of machine-guns, and the shriek of dive-bombers. Pale and sweating with the never-to-be-laid fear she moved through her tiny hell searching for the answer. But the Minotaur, whose voices barked and bellowed around her, never revealed itself. No silver thread led her back to waking, only emotional exhaustion suffered her exit . . . until the next night.

Initially she accepted the inevitable and attempted sleep in a stoical sublimation of her subconscious to whatever was to come. But, as the weeks passed, she stayed up later and later. Frequently she stayed long after her aunt and uncle had gone to bed and fell asleep in the high-backed chair.

Once or twice she caught her uncle regarding her with gentle inquiry in his kindly eyes, but Gaston bided his time, and hoped for her to capitulate and seek help and reassurance from her new 'parents'.

One evening after supper it came. Louise had announced the last of her stock of coffee and suggested that they might take tea instead. Gaston agreed, as of course he would, despite the fact that he disliked tea and would probably rather have done without. Then, to their surprise, Lisa asked if she would mind waiting before making the tea, as she had things she wanted to say.

In quiet anticipation they looked at the tense, small girl before them, fighting within herself to bring out the knot of vipers which had nested in her heart and was slowly destroying her. She began, faltering . . . then stopped and recommenced as if she was relating history to her class in school . . . She told them of her flight, her breakdown, and of Eulalie and Pieter Pynas. She explained her recovery and the second collapse after her two friends were taken. But she did not tell them about the evader.

As the time passed Lisa involved herself with outside activities unknown to Gaston and Louise. There were other evaders . . .

No questions were asked. It was right that she should enjoy as much young life as the troublesome time permitted. Once or twice she exceeded the curfew hours, and Gaston fretted until she was safely returned. Then the time came for her to take a short holiday . . . or so she said. A college friend had apparently written to her asking her to spend a few days in St Jean de Luz near the Spanish border. It meant crossing the border into France. The friend's name meant nothing to Gaston, but he asked no questions.

When the Vichy government had made its peace with Germany, Europe settled down to a period of relative calm. Restrictions relaxed and a certain amount of travel was permitted between neighbouring nations who now basked in the Pax Germanica – but a travel permit was required. Gaston, many of whose friends were persons of status in the Hôtel de Ville, implied that he could possibly help with a travel permit, and was, indeed, as good as his word.

Lisa apparently enjoyed her brief sojourn, and an open invitation was extended to repeat the visit as often as she could find the time and the train fare.

Neither Gaston nor his wife questioned the frequency of such visits. They were only too glad to have her enjoy herself and resume something like life. It seemed to do her good. She returned from each visit quieter in herself, and showing a sense of personal calm that was both encouraging and gratifying. It was after such an excursion that Louise decided to attend to some of Lisa's clothing, in particular one jacket which showed a button missing from the sleeve cuff. Louise decided, after replacing the button, to send the jacket to be cleaned, and, in emptying the pockets found two reserved-seat stubs for the Paris-Biarritz journey. The fact that there were two disturbed her, and she confronted Gaston that evening when he returned home.

'Gaston . . . Lisa had *two* reserved seats on the train to Biarritz. Surely, if her friend lives in St Jean she would not be travelling from Paris? You don't suppose . . . I mean . . . she isn't, well, going away with a man, and doesn't want us to know?'

'If she is she will tell us when she is ready.'

'Oh! How can you sit there and say such things! She is a daughter to us. We must think what Marie would have done. What would your brother have said if he found his daughter was going away with a man?'

'My dear . . . we do not know that she is.'

'Surely it is self-evident. Why else would she say nothing about it? I want you to speak to her. You must act as if you were her real father.'

'I will do no such thing . . . and I ask you to remain silent yourself. Lisa is twenty-one, Louise. She has the right to do as she sees fit with her life. If she has found a man to love then I am humbly grateful. I was frightened that the shock of Pieter's loss would have prevented her forming any relationship for a long time. I hope that she *is* enjoying herself, and behaving like a healthy young woman. Please, my dear, try and understand. She has been through a great deal. She needs every worthwhile human experience she can get in order to restore her to some sort of normality. If it is serious she will tell us when she is ready.'

That evening Lisa did not go out and talked animatedly with Gaston about the new civil regulations for the Brussels citizenry. She also requested his advice about certain matters and gradually began to pump him about his childhood. Both Gaston and her own father had spent the early part of their lives – up to the age of thirteen – in the small township of Genly, some seven kilometres outside of Mons, and about five kilometres from the French border. She questioned him about the place, his friends – had he kept in touch with any of them? – and asked him many things about the landscape, the railway running from Mons to Mauberge, even the river Sambre which crosses the border between Jeumont and Soire. Gaston enjoyed the reminiscence, and if his suspicions were aroused he did not say so.

Two days later he returned home from the office with his brief-case bulging, and extracted two elderly books on Hainaut and the border area for her to read. It was in her room later that she made the discovery which was to influence the rest of her life.

The following morning she determined to confront her uncle with her suspicions and play it by ear from there.

7

It was shortly after ten when Lisa entered the bank and walked to the desk of the Chief Clerk.

'Can I assist you Mam'selle?'

'I wish to speak with M'sieur Gaston Colbert. Would you tell him it is his niece.'

'Of course. One moment, please . . .'

The short clerk scurried off towards the door at the end of the banking-hall and disappeared within. Three seconds later Gaston emerged looking highly worried. Lisa joined him.

'My dear . . . is anything wrong? Louise is all right?'

His concern was touching, and Lisa smiled her reassurance with great warmth of feeling.

'Everything is all right, Uncle . . . really. I just wanted to see you about something. I couldn't talk about it at home. May I come into your office?'

Once they were inside, with the door closed, and both seated at the desk, Lisa delved into her handbag and brought out a small packet which she handed to Gaston without comment. He unwrapped the packet slowly, but his face betrayed that he knew the contents. Three ration-card forms were revealed . . . uncompleted. Gaston sighed and then looked up at her.

'Where did you find them?'

'They were between the two books you lent me . . . I think you did not see them.' Gaston was silent at his appalling carelessness.

'Uncle . . . please tell me about them. I want to know . . .'

'There is nothing to tell. They are ration forms, nothing more. Why do you wish to know about such things,

Lisa? It can be of no interest to you. I must ask you not to mention this to anyone . . . especially your aunt . . .'

'I was not intending to say anything. Whatever it is you do, Uncle, I respect it deeply. I have come for your help. You see . . . I too am involved.'

'What do you mean?' Gaston's face showed shock, even outrage.

'Don't look so startled, Uncle. You are not the only person concerned in trying to do something for the war and against our German masters. I have been helping RAF evaders get back to England. You are managing to obtain papers and rations . . . for whom I can only guess. Is it not time we spoke to each other of such things? We could be mutually useful, you know.'

Gaston regarded his niece solemnly for some moments then walked round his desk and took her in his arms.

'My dear child! How little we realise about our friends and our families! We must talk, but not now. Tomorrow . . . about three I will expect you here again. Come straight to Emile Verhearen, the Chief Clerk, who you spoke to a few moments ago. He is discreet and has some sense of procedure . . . though he knows nothing of any of this. Please say nothing in front of your Aunt . . . she would be most distressed if she guessed . . . The fewer people who know the better.'

'Uncle Gaston . . .', Lisa looked up at her uncle's care-worn but kindly face. 'I love you very much.'

Gaston smiled his pleasure in the warming confidence, and patted her hand between his own.

'Your trips to St Jean . . . were they to do with your work?'

Lisa nodded. 'How did you guess?'

'Like me, my dear, you were careless. You left *two* reservation stubbs in your pocket. We must learn to be more expert . . . more thorough, or we shall not survive long enough to be of any real help to our cause.'

They kissed fondly and Lisa left. In the late morning sunshine, quickly dispelled by grey cloud and a slight breeze, Lisa walked through to the Boulevard Anspach and decided to while away some time by window shopping. The windows had long since ceased to be much of a show. Goods were becoming noticeably scarcer and, although no one could yet claim deprivation and shortage, there were the unmistakable signs of tightening up, and, the reverse of the coin, a quickening of black-market activity.

But it depressed her to look into shop windows and see only fripperies at inflated prices. She decided to wander behind the boulevard, and look in the antique shops and smaller boutiques away from the main thoroughfare. The old theatre looked empty and forlorn, and the shops without life. Few people were about, and the German soldiers did not frequent the area much. They liked the red light district round the Bouchers, or the Rue de Pelican. It was on the corner of the small square, where it is met by Rue St Michel, that she felt she was being followed, and turned to see a young woman looking at her furtively. As soon as she realised she had been discovered the young woman overcame her reticence, and approached Lisa.

'Are you the one they call "Yvette"?'

'Yes. Who sent you?'

'No one. I just heard about you. There's one of "them" ... he's been hurt.'

Lisa was taking a chance, and she knew it, but the Germans had not seriously got round to deviousness as a method of trapping resistance and evasion workers. She followed the girl. For almost twenty minutes she was led through streets, and back alleys, towards an industrial area with warehouses and factories dating from the turn of the century, and showing every conceivable sign of collapse and neglect.

'He's in there.'

With that simple remark tossed at her, almost as a hot potato, the girl turned and ran. Lisa was about to call after her but thought better of it and entered the warehouse. It was no trap. There was a young RAF sergeant lying semi-conscious against the back wall of a disused office, with a dirty, torn blanket draped over him. His head was supported on a folded old raincoat, shining and stiff with the dirt and grease of two decades. The young man was obviously badly wounded and in need of medical attention. That was the immediate problem. She did not know a doctor whom she could trust enough to put this man's life and freedom into his hands, together with her own. The mistake could only be made once. It must not be left to chance. She made the Sergeant as comfortable as she could, and returned later with hot soup and bread. But he needed a doctor's attention not her ministrations.

She decided to seek advice. But from whom?

The following afternoon when she entered the bank promptly at three, the Chief Clerk rose to greet her, beaming, and with every suggestion of deference.

'Mam'selle Colbert . . . your Uncle is expecting you. Please come with me.'

She was taken to the office door and admitted after a respectful knock had brought the command to enter. Inside the office Lisa, to her surprise, found Gaston seated at his desk, and before him another man turning to regard her.

'Come in, my dear. I want you to meet a good friend of mine and a business associate who may be useful to you. M'sieur Albert Foiret . . . my niece, Lisa Colbert.'

Lisa examined the newcomer closely as they shook

hands and sat before the great desk. A rather unprepossessing man in many ways, Foiret relaxed in the chair, and returned her examination with evident suspicion.

'Your Uncle tells me that you have helped some RAF man to evade capture, and would like to help us in our work... can you tell me a little more?'

'Not strictly correct, M'sieur Foiret. I have taken *eight* RAF evaders through our country and ensured that they reached the British Consular authorities in Madrid. I do not believe in doing things by half. And whereas I would be happy to help you with your work, I was actually hoping that you and your organisation would help *me* with *mine*.'

Albert Foiret stared at her for a moment, Gaston looked vaguely embarrassed, but Lisa held herself calmly and returned Foiret's stare. Slowly a chuckle emerged from his throat, and a suggestion of a smile flickered in his eyes.

'Have you really got eight out? That is four more than we have... double, in fact... and there are seven of us. Good girl! Now... let us talk business. You are Gaston's niece, and he vouches for you, otherwise you would be very carefully screened...'

'That will be our first difference, M'sieur Foiret... I would have you – and me – thoroughly screened whoever vouched for us. If we are to work together and set up an organisation the way I intend, then our security will be tighter than that of the Germans, and they are highly efficient. We can afford not one single mistake. You are trusting me because of my Uncle. That is a mistake! You, Uncle, lent me two books which just happened to have those papers caught between them when you were bringing them out of your brief-case. That was a mistake! I left ticket stubs in my pocket. Each of those could have cost *us* and everyone in the organisation our lives!'

'No one would have betrayed the others, Lisa . . .' Gaston looked horrified at the thought.

'You would, and I would, and everyone else would once the Germans had got to work on us. That is the first thing we have to learn. Everyone breaks under their tortures. Why do you think they bother? Because they are sadistic beasts? They may well be, but that is not the point. I have seen what they do, and what they *can* do to people, and it is terrible. We have to assume there are no exceptions. Our security must be so good that the right hand simply does not know what the left hand is doing. There is no other way to ensure continued success.'

'You care so much for these men's lives? You will risk all that? Lisa, my child, I do not know you at all. How can you think . . .'

Albert Foiret was regarding her with half-closed eyes, and held up his hand to silence Gaston.

'Lisa . . . Why do you do these things? What motivates you to involve yourself . . . risk your life? Why? Is it patriotism, or do you have political motives? I need to know.'

Lisa turned to regard him full in the eyes.

'M'sieur Foiret, patriotism is a very fine thing, but I am never sure how deep it goes. It is a poor sort of person who does not love his country, and who does not rise up in righteous indignation when his home is invaded, especially once again by a hereditary enemy . . . but that is not enough. To work for a bright new future and a changed order of things argues that one must be very sure that one knows that the changed order will be better than the old. I have no such convictions, and I doubt if many Belgians have. I certainly do not propose to hand over my country from one invader to another . . . even if they come in sheep's clothing. That, too, is not enough. For me it has to be deep-rooted hatred of the German and everything his disgusting regime stands for. Preferably a personal hatred, with scars that even time cannot heal. I want people who can kill those beasts with their bare hands if necessary, and have the courage to kill their own friends and neighbours if there is danger of betrayal. This is not a game to me . . . any more than it is to the German.'

Both men stared at the small, lovely, young girl as if they were seeing her for the first time.

'Lisa!' Gaston's face was one of mild horror and pity, but Albert Foiret was regarding her with considerable interest and just a touch of admiration.

'Tell me about the way you operate, Lisa. I think we have a great deal to talk about. I have no objection to working with you – even *for* you, once you have convinced me that you know what you are doing, and that you are not merely trying to get even with the Boche to settle an old score. There is no time for personal vendetta in this war . . . but it is good to have hatred in your belly.'

'She is only a child, Albert, a slip of a girl, and she is my brother's only child, now mine. We cannot expose her to such things.'

'I doubt if there is anything we can expose her to which is not water off the duck's back, Gaston. Something tells me that Lisa is older than both of us. I want to know the way her mind works, and see if she's as good as I suspect she might be. Come to my café one day, about six. We can talk there. Don't give your own name to anyone . . . not even me.'

'I had no intention of doing so. My evaders knew me as "Yvette". I will keep the name.'

Albert gawped at her.

'*You* are Yvette?'

She nodded and smiled.

'Do I understand from your expression that you have heard something of me, M'sieur Foiret?'

'There are at least three persons of some importance in Resistance circles who are very anxious to know "Yvette". There are several who have mentioned the name to me, but no one had the remotest idea who this girl was. We were even beginning to doubt if she existed at all.' He nodded approvingly. 'Yes, my girl, I think you really do know what you are doing. You left no trail behind you whatsoever. That is good.'

'It is not so difficult to remain unknown and untraceable if you are alone, Albert Foiret. Not so easy when there is an organisation. But if I am to do anything in sufficient numbers to make an appreciable difference to this war it cannot be done by one person working alone. I don't intend to rest until I have not one, but one thousand airmen back in England who will return to bomb the Germans again and again. Then it is worth doing.'

Before the meeting broke up Lisa decided to seek immediate assistance from her new acquaintance.

'Albert . . . I need some help at this moment. I will tell you nothing except that I need a doctor who I can trust. Do you know of one?'

Albert eyed her coldly then spoke with calm and clarity.

'Pascal Keldermans. Rue de la Tulipe. Ixelles.'

Their eyes met once again, and Lisa knew she had found her right hand, just as Albert Foiret knew he had found his 'angel', his GOC, his inspiration – in this petite, lovely, slight girl, whose name was now 'Yvette'.

8

The big house stood back from the road. Between lay a small courtyard large enough to permit a vehicle or carriage to draw up outside. A covered way led to the entrance where a fine solid door gave even greater substance to the impression created by the imposing house. Lisa rang the bell and waited. After some moments the door opened revealing a tall, elderly man with a small, greying beard. His aspect was commanding though his eyes were kind.

'What can I do for you? Is someone ill?'

Lisa summoned her courage, and looked him straight in the eyes.

'You are Dr Keldermans? Pascal Keldermans?'

He nodded, but just a trace of wariness passed over the eyes.

'I need your help. Someone is injured. He is a British airman.'

Doctor Keldermans showed no sign of shock, or even of disturbance. He regarded Lisa keenly for a moment as if summing her up. Then, very matter-of-fact, reached for his coat hanging just inside the door, and his doctor's bag similarly placed.

'I was just about to go out to visit a patient. She can wait. Take me to your "visitor".'

Keldermans closed the door behind him, and indicated Lisa should precede him.

They arrived at the warehouse as dusk was settling in. Lisa glanced swiftly down the street in both directions before letting herself in through the small side door. Keldermans followed. They had not spoken during the journey. In the deserted office Sergeant Logan was lying apprehensively, and fighting off the unconsciousness creeping upon him. He showed little reaction, or even fear, as the two arrivals entered the room and bent over him. Keldermans was simple, quick, and efficient in his examination.

'The ribs are badly broken. I suspect there may be lung damage, and internal haemorrhaging. There is nothing I can do for him here. Go to the nearest café and ring this number. Say that Doctor Keldermans has a new patient and needs the ambulance immediately at this address. Tell them you can't remember the name of the fracture, but it is the same as birds get in their wings when they are damaged.' Lisa looked at him squarely. He smiled.

'Get the message right, my girl. "A fracture – the same as birds get in their wings . . ." They will understand.'

Fifteen minutes later Logan was being carried out to the small civil ambulance drawn up in the street by the entrance. Keldermans turned to Lisa.

'Do you have a curfew-pass?'

'No. I'll get back all right. Don't worry.'

'But I do worry, my dear. It is an affliction of doctors and old men. We are, therefore, both wary and devious. Come with me.'

Lisa was bundled into the ambulance, and a nurse's cap stuck into her hands.

'Put that on. The cap is enough.'

The ambulance sped through the city. The driver was good, and obviously used to driving such a vehicle.

Keldermans turned to the communicating-window and knocked. The panel slid back.

'We are getting into difficult territory here, Jacques. Let us use the claxon and warn them of our approach.'

Sure enough, not two streets away a German patrol blocked the road, and signalled to the ambulance to stop.

Keldermans quickly got down from the rear, and attacked the German private who was approaching.

'You must let us through quickly, please. This is an emergency. I have a patient haemorrhaging, and must get him to the operating-theatre quickly. Sergeant . . . kindly tell your men to let us through . . . Please, this is urgent.'

Keldermans flashed his papers before the Germans, who only glanced at them before approaching the ambulance. One peered inside at the nurse bending anxiously over the blanketed patient, with a stretcher-bearer in attendance. It seemed enough. He waved them through, and the ambulance continued on its way, the claxon making all the din it possibly could. Once safely back in the doctor's house Lisa was dispatched to the waiting-room to rest and fortify herself with cognac generously dispensed by the tall, taciturn Keldermans. The RAF man was taken into the surgery and with the assistance of one of the stretcher-helpers, operated upon.

Lisa woke to find Keldermans gently shaking her shoulder.

'Wake up, my dear. We have some talking to do.'

Lisa sat up and arched her back to relieve the stiffness. Keldermans passed a small, firm cushion.

'Put that behind. It will help. – Now, why did you come to me? Why not another doctor?'

'Someone told me you might be sympathetic and discreet. I had to chance it if I was to save that man's life.'

'Not as dramatic as that, young lady. There was a tiny lung puncture from the splintered rib. Not as bad as it sounds. But that is not the point. Your Englishman will be perfectly all right. We can stop worrying about him. There are things nearer to home we must look into. First . . . *who* told you to come to me?'

'Just someone. I am not saying, doctor. There is no point in pursuing it.'

Keldermans regarded her solemnly, but there was the merest suggestion of a smile playing about the corners of the eyes.

'So. Do you work with some underground organisation, or are you only involved because of a chance find?'

'A chance find, as you put it. I could think of nowhere else to take him. He was done-in, and in a lot of pain. I could not chance taking him through the centre.'

'You acted quite correctly, and used your brains. I should, of course, hand him over to our German masters ... There is no need to look so aggressive. I am not going to do so. I merely said that I should. He can stay here for several days until he is well enough to be moved. Then he must be taken to one of the evasion-lines who look after this sort of thing.'

'An evasion-line? Such things exist already formed?'

'Oh yes ... in rather rudimentary stages, I'm afraid, but now that the British are stepping up their bombing-raids on Germany our Conquerors will no doubt become aware of what is happening to the downed enemy air-crews, and they will step up security. At the moment it is not so difficult. Germans are not too thick on the ground away from the coastal areas.'

Keldermans eyed her shrewdly. 'What is your name?'

Lisa did not answer for some moments.

'They call me Yvette.'

'Where do you stay in Brussels?'

'My parents were killed in the advance. I am staying with relatives. I'm sorry, but I can't tell you who they are.'

'Quite right, my dear. You are wise to trust no one. Not even one who is already compromised by you. So. Have some more cognac. It will do you good. It is a present from a high-ranking German officer who is a patient of mine.'

Lisa's reaction brought a chuckle from Keldermans.

'You need not be alarmed. I treat human beings, whatever their race, creed, or nationality. The Hippocratic oath I swore when I became a physician was not taken lightly. But it does not influence my personal sympathies, Mademoiselle Yvette. I like to think of myself as a patriot. You can trust me.'

'Thank you. You are a good man.'

'Will you be a good woman, and visit our patient during the next day or so? Once will be enough – just to reassure him that he has not fallen among thieves, and will be coped with when he leaves this house.'

'Of course. I can come on Saturday.'

9

'Glad to meet you, Brandt. If we are to work together we might as well be friends.'

Brandt sized up the man before him. Of average height and neat in his Allgemeine-SS uniform, with rank of Obersturmbannführer and therefore, comparatively, Brandt's superior. He seemed agreeable enough though Brandt had long learned to suspect anyone associated with the SS. The handshake was encouraging, however. Most of the SS, if they offered to shake hands at all, held out a limp paw, and withdrew it immediately upon contact. Gundel's grip was firm and manly, and his smile looked genuine enough.

'I imagine you are reluctant to be stuck with a desk

job. From your appearance, and the incomplete record they sent me, I imagine that you have seen a great deal of action, and served with distinction. We are honoured.'

'You are too kind, sir. But correct about the desk job. I wanted a service posting, not a policeman's office.'

'Well, before you settle down to comfortable obscurity I will disabuse you of one thought. You won't find it quite as much of a desk job as you imagine. Throw your coat on top of that filing-cabinet and sit down.' Gundel called out in the direction of the door. 'Janowitz . . . bring in the cognac and some glasses. Schnell!'

He offered his cigarette-case as Brandt seated himself, taking one for himself after Brandt declined.

'You will find that there is more going on here than you imagine. Very little ruffles the surface, but Resistance is building up throughout the occupied territories, and one day will become a real force unless we nip it in the bud . . . believe me. You, I gather, are to concentrate your energies upon the fast-growing band of RAF evaders who slip through our fingers.'

'I have read the reports that were sent to me. Surely it is not that serious!'

Gundel chose not to answer the remark until the orderly had departed the room after depositing the cognac and glasses on the desk.

'My dear fellow, what is in those reports represents less than half the truth. Do you imagine anyone wants Berlin to know exactly how many Allied airmen are getting back to England to fight again?'

'Surely it is not significant enough to merit such concern?'

'Decide for yourself. Your Luftwaffe background will give you a pretty shrewd idea of the time and cost involved in training aircrew personnel. For the moment Britain is not without raw materials, and is very rapidly increasing her manufacturing output in all spheres. That was to be expected. If we cannot destroy her factories, if we cannot eventually cut off her supplies, we have only one course of action . . . destroy the trained personnel who fly their aircraft until the demand far exceeds that supply and they become increasingly helpless, for it is a progression towards defeat once it is started.

'We are shooting down a very fair number of RAF bombers, surely. My figures are encouraging, if not exactly enough to merit a national holiday. Reichsmarschal Goering has expressed his approval of the flak results, and our night-intercepting is improving week by week.'

'It doesn't matter, my friend. Those planes come down in occupied territory where the greater part of the populace are sympathetic to the Allies, if not actively engaged in undercover resistance. The aircrew are concealed, then make their way across country. Three months ago we picked up four out of five of them – or they surrendered, semi-starving and half-dead with exposure. Now the figure is about two out of four . . . and in another three months time it will be one out of five, unless we do something. I don't envy you your task, but at least you work for superiors who make allowances. My masters will replace me shortly, I imagine. My record is none too good, and the SS don't like failure. I doubt if they will shoot me for it, but the Waffen-SS is being built up, and there are always vacancies in suicide regiments for people like me who have to prove their devotion to the Fatherland by dying for it. That's life. Drink up, old man.'

Brandt warmed to Gundel quite quickly, and the first few days of service in Brussels brought the men closer together. Brandt studied every available document, every report, every transcript, and familiarised himself with Gundel's private dossier.

The Oberst was right. Many more evaders were getting through German fingers than had been reported to Berlin. Canaris had hinted that such might be the case when he saw Brandt briefly at the Tirpitz Ufer before his transfer to Brussels, but clearly Luftwaffe HQ was not fully aware of the size of the operation.

On the Tuesday following Brandt was poring over the latest batch of evidence and report from Antwerp and Liège, on which seemed to centre the main collecting areas of RAF personnel shot down on the way back to their bases in the north and east of England, when Gundel entered, and placed a manilla folder before him.

'Have a careful look at this report . . . then compare it with the one from Neidlinger in Antwerp. So far we think there are three evasion-lines in Belgium that cope with the bulk of the RAF personnel. One which seems to operate from round Huy, and takes their people over the Ardennes down towards Switzerland. I have reason to think that they are politically oriented . . . communist, in fact. Another one, out there somewhere not far from Liège, specialises in Jews. What they do with them I cannot imagine. So far we have not even a trace . . . not even one capture. The third one crosses the French border, probably between Valenciennes and Mauberge, goes through Paris, and then down into Vichy France just east of Tours. Their idea is to get as many as possible across the sea to North Africa or Gibraltar. The French are being cooperative so we manage to pick up quite a few . . . but that is not really your pigeon, Brandt. Leave that to Barrault in Strasbourg. He's coping.'

'But if you look at these papers you'll find there is every suggestion that a new line is operating. I suspect through Paris down to the Spanish border. Not much to go on so far . . . but you'd be well advised to dig into it.'

'Thank you, sir . . . you are very helpful. I appreciate it.'

'That is not all, my friend . . . not by any means. We have been asked to vacate our premises. Don't look alarmed, I have found us something much better. Come with me and inspect them . . . tell me what you think.'

A black Mercedes took them across Brussels, first to the Kommandantur on the corner of the Boulevard du Régent where Brandt waited in the car until Gundel emerged laughing with a city official, then out to Ixelles.

The Avenue Louise runs more or less from the great Palais de Justice to the Bois de la Cambre, flanking Ixelles before it reaches the park. It is a pleasant, wide, fashionable road, taking the air, as it were, in the high ground above the city centre. Major Brandt descended from the car first and looked about him. A tram clanked past bearing few passengers, and the streets were relatively quiet of traffic. Gundel joined him and together they regarded the new modern block before them. It was clean, tidy-looking with good window space and balconies and a discreet entrance supervised by a concierge. Gundel grinned good-humouredly.

'You see. What did I tell you? Much better than the Rue de la Loi. You're away from everybody. Come and go as you like . . . and it'll save you money. Come. I'll show you.'

Gundel rang the bell which brought the woman concierge immediately. She opened the door for the two tall Germans and stood back subserviently to admit them.

'You remember me. I was here before. I want to look at the building again.'

'If the Colonel will follow me, please . . . Madame Heubeek has been informed that the building is to be requisitioned. She leaves on Sunday.'

Gundel grunted satisfaction, and led the way down

the carpeted entrance hall to the staircase and lift.

'You'll see for yourself. Each floor is self-contained, with bathroom and kitchen facilities. We can make coffee, cook . . . even entertain, eh?' He laughed and nudged Brandt with conspiratorial involvement as they stepped into the lift.

'We start at the top and work down.'

It was indeed highly satisfactory. Luxurious even. Two floors for the Luftwaffe police . . . four for the Gestapo and general Security Services personnel.

10

Within the month Lisa was taken to the café owned by Albert. To her surprise one of the men she was taken to meet was the doctor who had assisted her previously – Doctor Keldermans. The older man beamed at her as they were formally introduced.

'I was right, was I not? She is just as lovely as I said she was. Welcome, my dear. Albert tells me you wish to speak to us.'

'Yes. Thank you for coming. May I ask now how you propose to explain yourself if we should be raided in the next few minutes?'

Keldermans eyed her appreciatively and nodded. 'You think quickly and sensibly, my dear. Yes, I have a reason to be here. Albert may have told you that his wife is an invalid and confined to her bed. I am her doctor, and visit her from time to time. Will that suffice?'

Lisa smiled at him. 'Perfectly, I should think. Forgive me for not assuming such a thing, but I do not propose to assume *anything* in what we are about to organise. It is too important and too dangerous for mistakes.'

At that moment the barmaid Lisa had noticed as she crossed through the café came into the back room, followed by two men and a young girl. The latter was pretty, exotic-looking, and probably considerably younger than Lisa herself. Albert introduced them.

'This is Monique, who helps me in the café . . . Natalie . . . and these two oafs are Jacques, and Alain. Both have contacts with the Resistance groups of Brussegem and Hamme. Alain is a radio-operator and has his own set. It could be useful to us.'

Lisa looked at them all, one by one, without saying anything, just as they in turn scrutinised her. At length she spoke, calmly, but with authority.

'Albert knows my name. There is no reason for anyone else to. I am known as "Yvette". That will be my name in our organisation. If you decide to work with me, as you have with Albert in the past, I shall be very pleased. But if you do you must work for no one else. You, Jacques and Alain, must sever your connections with the Resistance. Once we are operational there will be no time for divided loyalties, and no time to hold up our own progress while you run about doing sabotage that does little good and equally little damage. We will hit the Germans hardest by returning Allied airmen to continue their bombing of Germany. Alain . . . is the radio your own property?'

Alain, a farmer's son, grinned widely. 'It is now, Yvette. It used to belong to the Germans . . . it is a good one, and parts are easy to replace.'

'You agree to contact England only for us?'

'Well . . . I don't know . . .'

'That is a condition of working with us. We will call our organisation "Lifeline". And you, Jacques . . . how do you feel about a single loyalty?'

The man Jacques had limped slightly as he came in, and now rested his weight on the table edge as he weighed up the girl talking to him with such dogmatic command. Lisa remembered him as the driver of the ambulance.

'I accept the need for that. I agree. What is it you want me to do?'

'You will, for the moment, coordinate our collectors and see that their charges are brought to us safely and speedily. Albert, can you and Doctor Keldermans make it your business to select and scrutinise safe-houses in and around Brussels? I will visit them myself once you have them shortlisted, and see that they are suitable. You are Natalie Chantrens I think?'

The young girl nodded and looked squarely into Lisa's face. 'What am I to do?'

'You and I will be the principal guides. We will take the evaders down the line from safe-house to safe-house. We will act as Guardian Angels right from Brussels down through Paris, to the Pyrenees, and if necessary take them over into Spain. You and I alone will know the entire route, and all the safe-houses. Everyone else will know only his own area, and the contact from whom he receives, and to whom he passes. That way there is maximum security.'

'What about me?'

The barmaid looked squarely at Lisa, clearly expecting a rebuff, or at best a cold evasion, but Lisa smiled warmly at her and said:

'You will help *me*, Monique. I need someone I can rely upon to act as liaison within the group. Someone who can move about easily, and at the same time have sound reason to remain here and hold the fort at all times. We will see how it works in the next two or three weeks, and cut our teeth on the two groups now coming in from Antwerp. Doctor, can you possibly house two of the men until we find a substitute house?'

'Yes. But I must stress that I have many German officer patients. Patients I don't particularly want, but they are useful cover, and frequently talk more than they should.'

'Keep those, please. They could prove invaluable for more reasons than one...'

Lisa stopped in mid-sentence. She and others glanced up at the ceiling as a firm and pronounced knocking was heard from upstairs. Albert looked embarrassed and moved towards the staircase.

'It is Andrée... my wife... she must have heard the talking and wonders who is here. Excuse me. I won't be a moment...'

Once he had left Natalie chuckled quietly and glanced at Monique who showed a solemn face. Jacques broke the silence.

'Poor Albert. One day he will strangle her, and it will be the end.'

Monique rounded on him. 'It will also be the end of Albert. I hate that damned woman, but he needs her right now to give himself an excuse for being a martyr. It is a sort of flagellation.'

'Why? I don't get it.' Alain's blunt directness spoke for more than himself, and it was Doctor Keldermans who answered in his calm, reassuring, deep voice.

'Monique is right, you know. Albert needs his wife at the moment just as she, poor creature, needs him. He blames himself for the accident, and no one can convince him otherwise.'

It was later in the day, long after the meeting broke up, that Lisa walked back towards his surgery and home with Doctor Keldermans, and brought up the question again.

'I don't mean to pry into something that is none of my

business, Doctor, but I think I need to know a little more about Madame Foiret's condition. It may become important to "Lifeline".'

'Strictly speaking I am bound by medical confidence not to impart anything to you without the permission of the patient, but Albert has already given me permission to tell you. Indeed I think it is right that you should know. Exceptional circumstances call for exceptional procedures. You must call me "Pascal" by the way. I have an inbuilt objection to attractive young ladies regarding me with awe and deference because I happen to be a doctor and older than I would wish.

'Andrée is suffering from what we usually refer to as GPI, or General Paralysis of the Insane. Not a happy title nor strictly accurate, and blessedly uncommon these days, though many a fine life in the nineteenth century was cut short by the appalling disease. The paralysis and insanity are caused by the effect of the syphilis bacteria on the central nervous system. Had Andrée been treated in the early stages there would be no need to expect the worst. As it is she does not respond to any treatment I have been able to give her. Eventually her mind will be affected . . . she could even go blind, or deaf. She herself is not aware of the possibilities, and I see no purpose in giving her the information. Albert knows, of course, as he is – indirectly – responsible. Poor man, he was not aware she was suffering from such a thing, but now that he knows his sense of guilt and personal blame is growing by the remorse on which it feeds. I doubt if anyone can do anything for her. She has passed through the secondary stage and it may be some time before any further manifestations occur. As I said, the car accident of two years ago advanced the final stage by providing a physical reason for a paralysis that would have come of its own volition anyway.'

'How terrible for them both!'

They continued walking in silence for some minutes before Keldermans turned to her.

'I think it would be wise for you to become my assistant. Your uncle can prepare papers providing you with a reserved occupation and certain qualifications as a physiotherapist. You will then automatically obtain a curfew-pass for all areas and conditions, and will have your own reason for visiting the café, and meeting me in the surgery.'

'I'm afraid I have to earn a living, Pascal . . . I could only take the job part-time.'

'My dear, I had every intention of paying you an adequate salary, and I shall expect you to learn something of the work and assist me from time to time. You may well find it useful . . . even interesting, and I shall certainly be grateful for the company, if nothing else. An old man gets lonely, you know . . . whatever they say about being crusty and separatist.'

11

Major Erwin Brandt was not impressed by Soudon. It was one of the least inspiring of Belgian small towns, which put it very low on his list of favourite places. The quarters were crude and obviously uninspected by anyone in authority. They were simply inadequate. There the complaint stopped. With what was there the officer-in-charge had done his best. The quarters were neat and clean, disposed as well as circumstances would permit. The unit was probably efficient and well run. The men were probably keen and champing at the bit of administrative inefficiency, or, what was worse, total HQ disregard.

The Feldwebel of Volksgrenadier held himself well, and was both courteous and properly turned out as he led him to the CO's office and knocked.

'*Herein!*' A crisp, young voice. The Feldwebel opened the door and announced him.

The young, clean-looking officer behind the desk shot upright, and greeted Brandt with both dignity and correctness, and both men sensed an immediate rapport. Brandt settled down to survey the working routine of his prime squad, examine the thinking of its officer, and endeavour to see how the efficiency of the unit could be improved. An hour of thorough examination indicated that he was fortunate in his officer and the unit generally.

Their problem was bad and tardy communication coupled with antiquated transport. Brandt had eleven such units spread over the entire area of Belgium, with Brussels and his own office as the nerve centre. But it was hitherto a nerve centre without a brain to coordinate and express impulses to the system. Leutnant Schippers was direct and forthright in his assessment of the system and the lack of proper directive, but by the time Brandt left Soudon both Schippers and the unit were in revived spirits, knowing not only that they had a commanding officer they could respect as an officer and a gentleman, but one who would not rest until he had his command adequately equipped and housed. For once the Volksgrenadier NCOs and the infantrymen did not complain of their lot in being stuck under some bloody Luftwuffe pricks, who didn't know their arse from their elbow, and why didn't they get back to their bloody Messerschmitts, or Heinkels, or whatever they called the bloody things.

Within three weeks the folding-bikes were replaced by

motorcycles, and two brand new Opel *Blitz* 3-ton trucks arrived in Soudon, together with an almost new Volkswagen Type 82 '*Kubelwagen*' for officer use. Nobody asked to have back the old Krupp *Boxer*, so they hung on to that as well.

Within four weeks they had captured eighteen RAF crew, a considerably higher average than they had ever achieved hitherto. Brandt had insisted upon immediate telephone information with map references of downed *terrorfliegers* being sent to his units at the same time as his own office was informed. It cut the initial alert by three to four minutes, and his orders were then transmitted to already-alerted-and-ready motorised units. On one occasion the Soudon unit arrived at a crashed and burning Wellington in time to assist the burnt and injured navigator to drag the unconscious body of the pilot from the conflagration before it exploded.

Already one Englishmen owed his life to the efficiency and improvements of Major Erwin Brandt.

By Easter Brandt's Luftwaffe Police was working more efficiently than had hitherto been thought possible. The number of British and Allied aircrews picked up greatly increased, but, as Brandt was the first to recognise, that was really only because the whole bombing of Germany had been stepped up, and ever increasing formations of aircraft left Albion's shores almost every night for targets in the Ruhr, German ports, and industrial centres deep inside the Fatherland.

The evasion-lines were quickly becoming highly efficient, with an ever-increasing territorial embrace that seemed to almost scoop the parachutists and crashing aircraft out of the sky.

The most successful of the lines was new.

It was run by a young woman.

Its name was '*Lifeline*'.

Evaders:
The First of the Many

1

Somewhere in Belgium: There wasn't a damn thing to see as he sped down through the cold night air. He hadn't had any practice jumps to prepare him. Very few had. There just wasn't time. Now all he knew was that the downward movement was faster than he had imagined. The restraining drag from the harness comforted but it didn't much help with the preparation for the bump he knew was inevitable and getting closer every second. If only he could see something! How in hell can you prepare yourself for the landing if you can't see the bloody ground? *Let the knees absorb the shock and roll over with the drag . . .* or something. Why hadn't he paid attention? Why? Because it wasn't going to happen to him. Other people got shot down – not Barry Parks. Well, so much for that. Barry's on his way!

About fifteen seconds before he hit the ground Barry suddenly saw even blacker shapes emerge from the void engulfing him. Like black washing-up mops. That was what they looked like. Bloody washing-up mops. Black ones.

The shock was sudden and sharp, and just about broke his ankles and his knee. And his pelvis! Jesus H. Christ! Thank God it was a field and not a factory roof or a railway track with the fast-goods belting down the line! Sergeant Parks got out of his harness, remembered to pack up the 'chute' and bury it as best he could, and then made for what he thought looked like undergrowth. It was.

'The 'Wimpey' had caught it over Düsseldorf. Flak had been heavier than previous times, but they had gone in as briefed, Barry guiding for the last minutes over the target. They banked and made a lovely turn, and left the glow and the fireworks behind, when suddenly something went bang, the ship rocked and dropped, then wavered and steadied. Somebody was shouting over the intercom, or maybe he was screaming. It sounded like Chalky Wilkins. In the tail – where else?

Bob Semple, the skipper, had indicated the game was up and told them all to get-the-hell-out-of-it. Barry Parks was the second to drop.

Now, as he peered about him he was conscious that if the fear of the drop had left him, he was still sweating despite the cold night. He was sweating because he was scared stiff, and it was gripping him tighter every minute as he sat panting amid the hawthorn bushes. Where in Christ's name was he? Germany? Belgium? Holland? Please God don't let it be Germany! Those SS bastards do terrible bloody things to you.

After he had relieved himself, clumsily with cold fingers, and unable to stop a tardy surge from discharging upon his trouser leg, he moved off in the direction of the wind. He remembered Jack Bradford mumbling something about the wind coming from the west. That was the way home, and once having made the decision, and feeling confident about the direction, he turned into it and calmed slightly. By now he was aware that his senses were acting as if they'd been asleep all their life. Every sound and smell was magically intensified, and he felt very much alive. Scared stiff as he was, that was the way he intended to remain – alive. That meant no Jerries.

Barry was aware of the sound of the night air. A dog barked, and the sound echoed across the fields. Was it a mile away, three miles, or just five-hundred yards? He kept walking, now conscious that his footfall was waking every worm for five miles, and suddenly stopped dead in his tracks. Someone had coughed not ten paces ahead.

His eyes bored into the blackness. Slowly he edged forward, then fell head first over a moving hearth-rug. Barry sat up in a hectic movement, his heart pounding and his teeth bared, but the sheep just stared him out, champing the while.

Barry dusted himself down, cursed the unhappy animal, and set off again. Within ten minutes he had stumbled about, shocked his spine by a sudden drop in the field level, then stepped into a ditch with water up to his calf, and ripped his jacket on a branch sticking out from nowhere as a deliberate act of provocation. Within fifteen minutes he had become angry and furious, had cracked his shins on a fencing spile, and disturbed at least a dozen sheep. When the half-hour was up he had lost his fury and begun to shake with silent laughter. It just wasn't supposed to be like this! RAF blokes looked like Errol Flynn, and didn't fall about, and trip over sheep. They didn't fall in bloody ditches, and weren't scared stiff all the time. What he was up to had more in common with Stan Laurel and his fat friend.

Right now Barry decided he could use a fat friend, and he didn't mind admitting it. The one he really hoped to bump into was Bob Semple. His other oppos, Chalky and Jack, were a bit like him – gauche. But Bob knew his way about. He wasn't skipper for nothing. Half-way through a second-tour of ops and never lost a tail-end Charlie! There weren't many who could say that. Funny thing about Bob – he always came prepared for it. Shoved a battered old suitcase in the crate with him every time. He kept his civvies in there – just in case. Well, now he had a chance to wear 'em.

Bits and pieces were slowly coming back to Barry. Things heard with only half-an-ear, for obviously they didn't apply to oneself because one wasn't going to be shot down.

The evader should keep to hedges, ditches and woods, and not enter cornfields or fields of crops that would in any way show traces of having been entered.

That was all very well but the bloody hedges tore you to shreds, the ditches were everywhere you didn't expect them and made you permanently wet from the knees down, and woods had things that stuck out and bashed the living daylights out of you.

Walk by night but hide by day, if possible near to an isolated house where the number of family can be assessed by their daily outdoor activities.

Yeah! If you can get out of the bloody hedge, avoid falling into the stinking ditch, and manage to miss the sodding windmills that grow on all sides of the flaming trees in the fucking wood! Barry wondered if the blokes who wrote the guide-lines had ever been shot down outside of the officer's mess. He supposed he ought to follow the book and find an isolated house and try out his 'plume de ma tante' French. Unless, of course, this *was* Germany, and the ruddy Jerries were just waiting for him to drop in. Then it was Stalag-Luft-whatsit for Barry – or worse.

Time to make a move and, if possible, find out. That was when the second bad thought struck him. Another omission. Flying-crew were instructed never to go on ops without their 'escape-kit' issue – neatly packed plastic containers which fitted snugly into the thigh-pocket of uniform trousers. They contained small sums of various European currencies, a silk map, a compass, milk and meat tablets, a fishing-hook and line, a hacksaw blade, concentrated chocolate, and water-purifying tablets, all calculated to orient the evader and help sustain life. And he had left it behind as usual. After all, he wasn't to need it, was he? Barry mentally acknowledged that made him a bigger twit than he would have liked, but there was no getting away from it. So he had to stay lost, and hungry, and if the stink of those ditches was anything to go by, thirsty too.

He assumed that by now it was about '0-four-hundred' and it would not be too long before it was light enough to see his arm, therefore his wrist-watch, unless it was buggered-up by the landing or that thwack he had received from the sapling as he stumbled about. Time to start thinking about his whereabouts, and holing-up to take stock and sniff out the land.

2

Two miles away: Bill Semple hurriedly shed his uniform, boots, flying-gear, wrapped them in the hurried folds of his parachute and stuffed them into a shallow hole, scratched with the aid of a pen-knife and frantic fingers. The grey chalk-stripe suit in his case was crumpled and creased. Not surprising, as he hadn't bothered to remove it from the case for the last three ops, but Bill mentally lit a candle for having the bright idea of bringing his civvies with him on operations. Countless times the gibes and leg-pulling of his crew-mates had almost persuaded him to scrap the entire ploy. His foresight vindicated, he felt a glow of smug satisfaction as he struggled into the jacket from which every tell-tale label and mark had been carefully removed. Now the shoes . . . a bit tight, and the patent leather was cracking, but it was all he had to go with the suit. It was dry, so he left the raincoat in the case, snapped it shut, and set off down the sloping field towards the canal. He had noted the dull, narrow gleam as he twisted round in the last few minutes of his drop. It had to be a canal. Sooner or later it would lead him to a road . . . or perhaps he could steal a ride on a barge. The day would tell.

The old tow-path, when he stumbled across it, was muddy from the week's rain, and he trod warily to avoid messing up his shoes and trousers. It was beginning to get light when he reached the road. At least there was a general whitening of the atmosphere around him as the morning mist, spilling from the canal and banks, filtered the early sunlight. From the road, raised up some fifteen feet, he could see across the misted carpet where it lay heavy over the fields.

Bill had only a sketchy idea of what he was hoping to do. The squadron briefing stressed the business of evasion and trying to get in touch with local people who ran evasion-lines. They had a chap who had been down one line, all the way to Spain, and had got back. He gave talks, and tried to make air-crews understand and accept a few basic rules. Not many paid much attention, and most had their own ideas of how to get back and survive without any help from foreigners who might, or might not, be trustworthy. That sort of insular chauvinism was not typical thinking of Bill Semple, but he instinctively felt he could cope better on his own. Hence the case of civvy kit.

Bill checked the button-compass he had remembered to rip from his RAF issue. He was travelling south-west. That would do for now, as long as he didn't keep to it long enough to take him near the coast. Too many Jerries for comfort.

Four miles away: At Soudon, a small town on the edge of the mining area, where the grime gave way to buttercups, a small unit of Luftwaffe support-troops attached to an equally small unit of infantry seconded from one of the Radfahrer Abteilung (together with their new motor-cycles and one troop-carrier, a Krupp LH243 *boxer*), under four Volksgrenadier NCOs. They were commanded by a Luftwaffe Leutnant, grounded and seconded to the motley unit because of a stomach wound inflicted by a Hurricane in 1940. They occupied a disused printer's premises and awaited the ringing of the telephone to roust them into action. They did not have to wait long.

Leutnant Schippers listened carefully, made notes on his pad, and replied briskly and briefly. The Volksgrenadier Feldwebel was already unfolding the grubby map before him on the desk top as he replaced the handset. Schippers quickly found the map reference – just to one side of pink turnip-jam stains and almost upon the brown rivulet made by acorn 'coffee'.

Schippers gave the orders, a movement of quiet efficiency disturbed the waiting unit, and one tiny, operation-centre of the great, German war-machine shuddered into action. As the Leutnant fastened on his pistol-belt he heard the slatted clatter of broken garage doors slam against the wall, and the harsh coughing start of the Krupp *boxer*.

Six miles away: 'Chalky' Wilkins gazed about him in a sort of fearful awe. This was Europe. Probably Belgium. Bloody hell! He'd never been out of the north of England, hardly ever away from round Newcastle. He'd been to York once when his Mam broke her ankle on a church outing, and he had to go down by train and fetch her home to Ponteland. They went down to the coast at Whitley Bay and Cullercoats every summer for a week, but nowhere else. His Dad went to Blackpool now and again. On his own. His Mam didn't like that much, and was in a rotten mood until he came back. Then the war came, and Chalky joined the AFS as a messenger-boy while he finished his School Certificate exams. That wasn't too bad. He used his own bike, and turned out whenever the siren went, but nowt happened. Nowt ever did in Ponteland.

As soon as he clocked up seventeen-and-a-half he set off hot-foot for Newcastle and joined up. The RAF. He was going to be a fighter pilot like the bloke in that book he got from the library. It didn't work out quite like that. The Recruiting Office in Barras Bridge seemed anxious enough to have him, and it wasn't long before he was called to RAF Padgate, just outside Manchester. That was the farthest he had ever been – Manchester. It didn't seem much to shout about . . . bit like Gateshead, only bigger. When he was there the Selection lot confused him and shoved him about from one room to another, medicals, ENT, every damn thing, carrying a wad of papers around with him with a pencilled 'PNB' in one corner. Even that didn't work out, and Chalky ended up as a rear gunner. Still, he was seeing the world from a great height, wasn't he? And now – without even a return ticket – here he was actually IN Europe. A foreign country! A place where they didn't speak English, and he instinctively knew the French he had tried to learn at grammar school wasn't going to stand him in much stead. He was never any good at it – all them funny vowels, and masculine and feminine words. Bloody stupid! Why can't they just talk?

It didn't look much different from home. Same trees and fields and that. He'd even seen some colliery shafts on the way over. Slag heaps, too. He had to admit a slight feeling of disappointment. Still, you couldn't expect the South Seas, could you?

The main thing right now was to get lost, Chalky reflected, like they'd been told. His own nous told him that he ought to put as much mileage between him and where he came down as he could, before morning made that a bit dicey. He peered into the gloom and made off in the direction-most-likely-to-succeed.

One thing the crew of *R for Robert* had in common – none of them intended to be captured by the Germans. Where they divided was, in the first place, how they proposed to evade them, and in the second place what their object in evasion was.

For Bill Semple, the skipper, the intention was to use his own initiative and instincts, and endeavour to get back to England as quickly as possible on his own steam and with as little interference from foreigners as possible.

For Barry Parks it was no more than to hope to stumble upon resistance workers, or one of the evasion lines, and let them take him in hand, abdicating all responsibility for getting him back to Britain and RAF Framlington.

But Chalky had ideas of his own. He wanted to have a quick look at the European pastures-new, and savour the exciting tastes and sensations of everything while he was ambling his way eastwards towards Switzerland and blissful internment. Once over that border, savouring the blue skies and green mountain pastures, up to his eyes in edelweiss and cuckoo-clocks. Chalky Wilkins could relax and savour the sheer heaven of not being locked into that tail-end death-trap that was fast becoming his home and would inevitably end as his coffin. Rear-gunners did not live long. Everybody knew that. Fourteen ops and still alive – that was Chalky's unuttered boast. He intended to utter it after the war.

Switzerland must be the best part of five hundred miles as the crow flies, he thought, then added mentally: 'And I'm no bloody crow!' Had he been that crow and scanned the Belgian terrain from the vantage of flight, he might have seen one lone bomb-aimer stumbling westward towards the coast, one chalk-stripe-suited civilian walking briskly down a secondary road due south-west, and thirdly a pale-faced Northumbrian gunner heading south-east with all the stumbling guilelessness of innocence.

. . . he might also have seen a German troop-carrier disgorging its clattering load not three miles from where they had landed and buried their parachutes, for they had come down quite near to each other. The Germans in their field-grey were taking orders from an NCO who was, in turn, acting under instruction from a Junior Luftwaffe officer, who was at that moment studying a map unfolded on his knees, as he picked with his finger nail at a hard encrusted smudge of pink turnip jam.

3

Near the French border: Barry stared at the village for upwards of half an hour, waiting for the German troop-carriers to come belting down the road and disgorge their frightening hordes in front of him. It just didn't happen. He didn't even see a German boy scout on a push-bike. There wasn't any one about, except a woman who appeared in her back-yard every five minutes, and chucked a bucketful of something over half a dozen scraggy hens.

Finally, summoning up his courage and audacity, Barry stepped into the road, and marched towards the outlying houses. After all why should the Jerries, who would now be drawing a bead on him from every facing window, actually shoot him? There was no reason why he shouldn't just be taken prisoner, give his name, rank, and number, and be carted off, and stuck in the nick.

Like the long camera-track down a street in a 'Western' the houses drew closer. He could see into the village for about a hundred yards. There was a faded blue van drawn up on the right with its back doors wide open, and a pile of green vegetables and a few boxes basking in the morning sunlight. But nobody serving ... nobody buying ... whatever. The van, the peeling walls, then two doorways tracked past, and he became conscious of his footfall echoing suddenly between the clangorous walls. Then it all opened out and the village square was before him. Well, you could call it a square, though it was really just a wide area without pavements, dominated by a stumpy church with yellowish-white peeling walls and a stunted belfry, roofed on three sides. Four small trees gave shelter in the centre of the square ... if you wanted any, that is.

The whole place seemed deserted, silent, if not exactly brooding. Barry's nervousness increased and he looked about him in worried silence.

Suddenly, with a clatter, the church doors behind him burst open, and disgorged a red-faced, fat man wearing his Sunday best. It ticked over in Barry's mind that it wasn't Sunday, but by now the whole thing was unreal and not happening to him. The red-faced man wore a rosette, or something, and was fixing the doors back into place when he caught sight of Barry. He straightened up, and peered intently. His mouth dropped open, and his eyes widened ... pale-coloured, liquid eyes. He gaped, and his mouth made burping movements that reminded one of a fish in a tank. Slowly he lurched forward like a steam-roller picking up speed, till he stood ten feet from Barry, both men gaping at each other in silence. The fat man's eyes travelled from Barry's face down to his uniform, stopping at his 'wings' en route, then continued down to his boots.

A stifled sound gurgled for a moment in the fat throat, then dainty fingers clutched the air as he turned and ran back to the church, and disappeared inside the open doorway.

Barry, rooted to the dusty road, just gawped and waited ... almost too fascinated by the appearance – disappearance to move or make a run for it. Within seconds there appeared in the church entrance several figures, including that of a bride and groom, all leaning slightly forward, and peering foolishly at Barry. Then the silence was broken by sudden explosive chat, and the red-faced beaming beadle – for that is what he was – propelled himself towards Barry, arms eagerly extended, followed by equally predatory wedding guests. Barry paled visibly, and backed two paces before he was clutched, surrounded, and hauled away by eager, excited, and glowing faces babbling some appalling lingo. Women were near to fainting, old men wiped grateful tears from gnarled faces, and the bespectacled priest, wearing what looked like a black pork-pie hat with a wide brim, smiled and nodded benediction on all and sundry before Barry was raised shoulder-high, his foot twisted back-to-front, and dangerous contortion inflicted upon his limbs. Barry was now terrified out of his life. He sensed the rural populace meant him no specific harm, and the cries of 'l'Anglais' that assailed him were not demands for tearing him limb from limb, or cutting off his testicles. But the sheer friendliness was awe-inspiring. Barry had fallen amongst patriots, and there was no one to protect him.

Brussels: The tram-train shuddered to a halt, and Bill Semple stepped out behind the girl, crossed the hard, earth road, and mounted the car. So far so good.

Accepted without question, ignored almost, he had not even been asked for papers, nor – apart from the two infantrymen asking the way of an old lady – had he seen any of the enemy. Funny how one expected the place to be alive with German troops, all pounding the streets, peering and prodding for spies and escaping Allied forces. It wasn't like that at all. No Gestapo in leather coats in every doorway, no swashbuckling SS officers with searing, blue eyes, snarling and barking at terrified locals, subservient and near-slaves. Life seemed to be going on just as it always had. Bill had been in Brussels the year war broke out. It didn't seem much different now. Possibly more drab, but then Brussels wasn't exactly Rio de Janeiro.

No doubt the original occupation troops had been sent to where they were most needed – Russia – and only a sprinkling, if not a token force, policed the occupied territories. The German genius lay in organising the local police and administration into doing the job for them, and they were nothing if not efficient in that.

Bill paid his fare without incident and eyed his fellow passengers . . . mostly housewives on their way to the shops, and one business man with frayed cuffs. Soon his natural interest was distracted by the passing sights of the metropolis. Even evaders become tourists from time to time, and not even fear can totally dispel a fundamental interest and curiosity.

He reflected upon the chance meeting with the postman. The directions were clear enough, and there was no reason not to trust the man. It meant the he would be met at the tram-stop by someone either from the evasion-line, or who knew someone who knew someone . . . By now his keen eyes were assessing the area, and he realised he was nearing the centre of the city. His eyes sought out the first possible street plate – Rue de la Régence.

He was near. His intense glances found the large building that was his landmark, and he turned his head as they passed to read the notice – 'Museum of Fine Arts'. This was it. He stood up and walked to the exit, waited until the tram juddered to a halt, then descended onto the metalled road. Three men stood at the stop, and Bill's eyes searched their faces for some small sign of recognition. They ignored him, and one by one mounted the tram.

'Excuse me, please.' A female voice behind him caused him to turn quickly. It was the girl who had got on the tram at the same stop as he had. Fair-haired and rather pretty. She smiled and he stood to one side to let her pass.

'Follow me at about twenty paces. Do not speak.' She had walked away towards the pavement before Bill truly comprehended what he had heard. Then, swallowing hard, he set off after her, doing as bid, and keeping the proper distance behind. The boulevard was well populated, and keeping her in sight was not quite as simple as it sounded. Eventually she turned off into a side street, and proceeded at a brisk pace into the busy day-time of the capital. After they crossed the canal, the pedestrians thinned out, and Bill found he could examine and sum up his courier as well as keep a weather eye open for eventualities.

She was petite, blonde, and had good legs, moving with a youthful, nubile grace that was highly attractive. The raincoat she wore with a certain style, and the dull colour complemented and enhanced her very pretty hair, which she wore longer than customary, though it did not look groomed to any style. At length she stopped before a warehouse door and rang a small bell, after a surreptitious glance down the deserted street. Bill Semple followed her into the courtyard through a door cut into the double-gates of the warehouse entrance. By the side of the main building stood a medium-sized van, and general haulage debris filled the yard. The girl disappeared into a side door, and after a careful glance Bill followed.

As he stepped into the interior, unlit and dank, he was grabbed from behind – not hurtfully, but with definite firmness – and propelled through a large warehouse area towards a flight of metal steps that mounted towards a strategically placed office where foremen and managers could survey their work force and its efforts.

The office at the head of the staircase was simple and sparsely furnished with the barest necessities. As he entered the door was closed behind him, and Bill realised that he was virtually a prisoner of his supposed rescuers.

The blonde girl turned to face him, her pretty face set in a stern expression. Not unfriendly – but she would stand no nonsense, and Bill realised with a shudder that those grey-blue eyes were perfectly capable of watching him die if it was necessary.

The other occupants of the room stood around watching him intently, but Semple's eyes were drawn to the person sitting behind the small table in the centre of the office and looking directly at him. She too, was petite, young, and very attractive, and her dark eyes seemed to sum him up and extract her own answers without uttering a word. Bill was too interested in examining her to pay much attention to his surrounding captors.

'Please sit down, Flight Lieutenant. We wish to know something about you. Until we are satisfied of your identity you are our prisoner. If you attempt to escape you will have your throat cut. If you are not who you pretend to be you will have your throat cut. If you are . . . then you will be taken care of and sent back to Britain as speedily as can safely be managed.'

4

Near the French border: Barry sat replete and heavy at the end of the table facing the beadle, who favoured him with ever-reddening glances of approbation. The bride and groom sat quietly in the centre and nervously held each other's hand while looking down at their hardly-used plates. Parental speechmaking had taken up half the afternoon, between gorged mouthfuls of long-saved food and gallons of raw red wine, punctuated by the most appalling belching that Barry had ever experienced. Initially shocked, then falling to schoolboy giggling, he eventually joined in wholeheartedly, shaking the rafters with his full-throated explosions. Each and every grumble or bark brought forth heartfelt cries of *'Liberté', 'Vive l'Angleterre', 'A bas les Boches'*, and suchlike sentiments.

The schoolmaster had a smattering of English, and entered into slow conversation with Barry. From him he gleaned that in two-and-a-half years of war the village had only seen four German soldiers, and they had arrived after having mistaken their road. For the rest the war almost did not exist. To be sure there were a few shortages, but the village was virtually self-supporting, and the stocks of French wine were still adequate to see the year out. Hitler was another name for the bogey-man, and Russia merely a place over the rainbow where it snowed and Napoleon didn't stay long.

Resistance was unknown. Well, dammit, you can't have resistance if there is nothing to resist! The war was little more than a subject of conversation. Every ancient receiver in the area was tuned to the BBC as a matter of course, and the populace kept an interested patriotic focus on matters of great moment, but in a detached way. The war happened 'over there somewhere', and patriotism was a colour one wore like a gage or a feather in a cap . . . fluttering and highly-coloured, and totally unserious. Barry felt in a seventh heaven, and blissfully beamed at his hosts. RAF Framlington wasn't like this. Barry stood up unsteadily, and belched once again. His full-throated cry brought further tears to the pale, liquid eyes of the beadle, and a nodding smile of approval. The Prodigal had returned to the fold, the fatted calf was before them, and bringing forth glorious flatulence. God was in His Heaven – all was right with the world. As long as you didn't look too closely and become serious about it.

The party broke up around late afternoon. It seemed to Barry it was the same day . . . at least there was no evidence of overnight sojourn, though the middle hours had not been uneventful, or without certain recompense. Some time around three-thirty Barry noted that he seemed to be holding his liquor better than the local populace, who were now either prostrate across the folding-tables, or sprawled indiscriminately in their respective chairs. Barry's beadle no longer eyed him with bleary and fast-fading eyes, but snored in his place, still upright and unbowed, his mouth open, and nether lip trembling with each noisy exhalation. Morpheus had descended and touched the lusty, innocent hearts of the villagers. All except the patient bride, who sat mutely in her finery, and pouted her displeasure by the side of the recumbent groom.

Clearly the new husband was found wanting, at least for the moment. The flushed face of the girl turned to Barry, and her eyes spoke volumes. Quite a pretty, little thing Barry noted, and unforgivably, inappropriately deflated. Barry grinned and shrugged, but a quiet smile was already playing round the pouting mouth of the expectant mademoiselle . . . or rather 'madame', if not yet in toto. After several moments' ocular converse she got up from the table, and made for the rear door of the establishment. Barry sucked his teeth for a moment's consideration, cast a weather eye round the guests, then followed. Hymen should not be deprived of traditional ritual. Barry would see to it that the proprieties were duly observed.

When, at long last, the assembly revived, and proposed to send their uninvited guest on his way, Barry was back in his place, and the demure bride patiently waiting the awakening of her spouse. Only the relaxed expression on her face, and two or three pieces of straw about her reassembled coiffure would have hinted to any observant relative that she was in any way changed.

The Beadle awoke with a start, and promptly belched to denote that revival. Barry's fears of a second barking contest proved groundless as, with enormous gravity, that great red face rose from the sluggish throng, and loudly pronounced some scheme which was received with riotous applause, every face turning in benign approbation towards Barry. Within seconds they had descended upon him, and hoisted him shoulder-high, while a half-dozen, including the beadle, hastily disappeared.

Minutes later, emerging into the cold air of the late afternoon atop several well-padded shoulders, Barry found himself face to face with the six who had left, now bearing huge, burnished, olden instruments about their persons. Their suits were now bedecked with tricolour ribbons and sashes, and all stood expectantly behind the portly form of the red-faced beadle, a superb, plumed creation upon his perspiring pate.

The village band turned about and burst into a joyous cacophony, whereupon the cortège set off down the village street, followed by the twenty-odd local inhabitants and four excited dogs, who lent their own howls to the general mêlée. Barry, by this time perfectly sober, stared about him in nervous disbelief, still wary and concerned lest some stray German patrol should hear the bucolic paean, and rush to investigate. But nothing untoward occurred. The procession left the village and marched vigorously down the road, singing and laughing in rhythmic counterpoint to the martial selections rendered by the preceding band.

At long last the purpose of the progress became evident. Ahead Barry could see the bare and simple structure of a local railway station, with overhead cables and pylons stretching in either direction along a single track. The music had drawn the station staff to the entrance and that worthy, elderly and unkempt, stood in his uniform trousers, flannel shirt and braces, staring unbelieving at the approaching crocodile, which bore a young person in what appeared to be RAF uniform.

The old eyes watered, and the white bristles of the unshaven chin trembled as Barry was lowered to the ground, and stood uncertain of the next move, while the Beadle argued with the station-master for a free ticket to *'Angleterre'* – one way, and first class.

Speeches followed with many a *'Vive l'Angleterre'*, *'Vive la Belgique'*, *'Vive le R A F'*, and what seemed like a toast to Charlemagne, during which Barry maintained a steadfast smile of gratitude and benediction. A toot from down the line indicated that a train approached. Immediately Barry was man-handled, willy-nilly, towards the flat, ground-level platform where the single coach trundled to a stop. Hoisted upwards and propelled into the central entrance Barry could only turn and wave his thanks and good wishes. Old folks wept, younger ones cheered, the beadle clasped his hand, and wrung it with a pumping motion, his pale eyes releasing their lachrymose torrents in an expression of benign patrimony; the young bride lowered her eyes over a suppressed smile; the train tooted and pulled away from the halt, and Barry waved. It was all over. Barry was on his way.

5

The edge of the Ardennes: Chalky Wilkins didn't much like the sausage. It tasted of acetylene, with a bitter, smoked tinge to it. If this was what they ate in Europe you could bloody well keep it! The bread was good, mind you . . . the best he'd had for a long time. Even better than his Mam's stotty-cake, which you could chew like meat and feel there was something in your gob. Not like that sorbo they dished up in the canteen back at squadron . . . or that artificial stuff they made into sandwiches in the NAAFI. The stew he was given was a bit queer, too. It didn't half stink of garlic! Hoots – something, they called it. Bits of meat and stuff in it, filled up with red beans. He wondered if that was what they called 'cordon bleu' cooking, and mentally decided a plate of Leek-and-bacon pudding put the lot of them in the shade.

Still, they were being kind, and probably were giving up quite a bit of their rations for him, and he was grateful. No one spoke any English, so they didn't bother to communicate apart from smiling encouragingly.

As he was leaving the woman pressed fifty francs into his hand, and closed his fingers over the coin to imply the incident was closed. Chalky didn't like taking it, but didn't wish to give offence either. He summoned up his courage, and kissed the woman on the cheek, which seemed to satisfy everyone. The husband, or uncle, or whatever he was, pointed out the direction, and Chalky shook hands, and left.

The mining villages now behind him, the landscape softened, and the distance implied both hills and forest. He tried very hard to imagine the relief map at school made out of layers of plywood they had painfully knocked together in Geography with old 'Fungo' Hunter, and a bit of assistance from Mister Strother, the woodwork teacher, in the huts at the back of the school. He should know what those hills were, but his mind was a blank. They couldn't be the Alps. That was certain. It was hours later when the remembered word 'Ardennes' flashed into his mind, and he smiled to himself with belated satisfaction, but it was not until the following day that he reached the first slopes leading to the higher ground and the forest areas beyond.

Instinct told him that from now on he'd better be more wary. He found himself amid a barren, heath-like area which afforded quite a bit of cover in the numerous potholes and craters that dotted the landscape, amid sparse and puny conifers, and clutches of couch grass. Most of the holes had four inches of muddy water in the bottom, but he found one that was dry, and decided to take a kip until nightfall, when he could proceed cautiously again. Sleep came quickly and soundly.

He awoke in the middle of a nightmare, in which he was being shelled and shot at by every conceivable weapon in the manuals. The noise was horrendous, with mud and earth flying from all around – no doubt with lethal bits of shrapnel screaming to tear holes into the frightened body. Chalky's awakening was worse than his nightmare. Explosions deafened him, and spurts of earth rose into the air, as stones and metal pieces whizzed past his head. It wasn't a nightmare at all! This was the real thing! Chalky was being shelled to pieces, and he was terrified as he had never been in his life.

It was about then that the hair-lines on the Zeiss field-glasses crossed the grey-blue figure making a dash for it towards a bigger hole. The glasses stopped in their sweep and returned to scan the area. Hauptman Hinrichsen turned to Leutnant Luschke and barked an order to cease fire. Within three minutes the word had got round the practice range, and the 21cm Nebelwerfer 42 multiple barrels began to cool. The men sitting behind the Raketenwerfer 43 anti-tank projectors removed their tired and aching hands from the ridged, rubber grips, and stretched their bent knees, while their officers looked enquiringly from one to the other, and shrugged.

Leutnant Luschke and eight men armed with carbines ran into the pock-marked area, and made for the position where Chalky Wilkins had last been seen to the amazement of the Hauptman in charge of the practice, who now stood, lips pursed beneath the sweeping searching gaze of the Zeiss field-glasses.

No time was wasted. Chalky, in a state of considerable shock, walked tremblingly from the area, his hands on his head, prodded by the carbine of Trooper Geyer, and escorted by the cocked Luger of Leutnant Walter Luschke, whose mild, and blond-eyelashed gaze seemed stunned into disbelief by the sight of an RAF uniform in the centre of the practice mortar-range . . . as well, indeed, he might be. Luschke had never seen the enemy at close range, or even in the flesh at all, and, frankly, he was not impressed by Chalky, whose appearance was unprepossessing at the best of times, and right now was positively dishevelled. The much vaunted, British stiff-upper-lip was conspicuous by its absence and, really, Chalky Wilkins' somewhat stunted physique was not calculated to impress a Master Race stuffed to the gills with sauerkraut and bierwurst. Luschke did have the honesty to admit to himself that even he might not look his pristine best if he'd been subjected to the pounding the little British shrimp must have received in the last five minutes. The Nebelwerfen put the fear of God into him, even at the delivering end.

Within a quarter-of-an-hour Chalky was sitting shivering on the back of a truck on his way towards Namur, escorted by three huge, po-faced troopers armed to the teeth, evincing every intention of using whatever they had if Chalky as much as moved a muscle. He had been given a mug of acorn coffee, and a foul-tasting cigarette, and was now swathed in a grey blanket to stop any after-chill from his experience. They didn't seem that bad . . . for Jerries.

6

Brussels: The 'Restaurant Candide' stood towards one end of the Rue Deschanel. In warm weather its frontage sported four, small, round tables with red-and-white gingham cloths, but the convenience was seldom taken advantage of by local customers. They knew about the cold wind that blew down Rue Deschanel, whatever the weather, and went indoors. The odd German soldier would brave it out . . . once. Old hands would sit inside, and time him against the wall-clock behind the bar. They would even lay minuscule bets as to how long the unsuspecting conqueror would stick it out.

Albert Foiret, the proprietor, watched his regular customers about their little game, slightly irritated that their harmless joking could alienate his German clientele – from whom he derived a considerable part of his profit, and who inadvertently lent him protection by their very presence.

Albert, though liked by the local people, and loyally supported by his regular customers, was sometimes considered as hovering dangerously close to the position of *collaborateur* – a label he wished to avoid, despite the temporary protection it gave to his clandestine visitors and the members of the evasion organisation of which he was part.

He looked up briefly as Natalie Chantrens came from the back room and crossed the restaurant-bar, smiling and joking with the men. They knew her as Monique's friend, who helped out with the housework and did things for Albert's invalid wife. Natalie's slightly exotic appearance did her no harm . . . at least not in any man's eyes, even those of Albert himself. Only eighteen, and with a certain sense of the world being her oyster – despite the restriction of the war – Natalie possessed a carefree charm of manner which, together with her touch of Central Asian physiognomy, was highly attractive. Not that her look was in any way oriental. It wasn't. Just a certain something about the shape of the face, and above all the eyes, hinted at the fabled Circassian. Many a young man had bit the dust thanks to those eyes, and many an older one had prayed for rejuvenation when held momentarily in their steady gaze . . . neither arch nor impertinent but promising, with a touch of mockery.

Albert picked up another glass from the tin sink of yellow water. Funny how the tap-water had turned yellow in the last six months . . . almost as if the German controller had decreed a tint to be added. It had happened when they first took control, but only for a few days. Now it was all the time. Albert sighed and allowed his eyes to scan the restaurant . . . the drinkers . . . the diners – and the near-empty-glass sitters. The last were the bane of his life. With a small place like the 'Candide' one couldn't afford sitters or sleepers. Not with regular customers coming in looking for a seat or a chat. Not with Wehrmacht troopers trying to knock back as much as they could in two hours.

One thing bothered Albert, and he was sitting at the second table from the door, quite alone, apparently in a world of his own, but surveying the room and its occupants with more than casual interest. Who in hell was he? What was he doing, and why? Albert sensed he was not just a casual drinker seeking peace and quiet. There was no reason to think otherwise, but two years of occupation had sharpened his instincts, and lent him a new awareness.

Monique came in from the back room. Albert responded to her presence with a quickening of his pulse as he became aware of the perfume she wore. Cheap and unsubtle as it was, association had given it the power to awaken him as nothing else could. He turned and smiled quickly, let his eyes rest for a brief moment on her decolletage, where the creamy texture of her splendid bosom made him wish that closing time was nearer. Her eyes indicated she knew what he was thinking, and she suppressed a tiny smile, both acquiescent and complaisant. 'Table four – any idea who he is?'

Monique glanced across quickly, then laughed easily as old Emile gave her a broad wink. She bent to assist with the glass washing.

'I don't know. But he was in yesterday, too. D'you

think there's something wrong with him?'

Albert shrugged, and fingered the edge of his shirt-collar.

'My neck itches. Every time it itches there's trouble. I don't like the look of him. I don't like what he spends . . . and I don't like the colour of his shirt.' It was yellow . . . butter yellow.

Monique's eyes, though casual and roving, had never really lost sight of the object of their interest. She turned, picked up a tray of knives and forks, and went through the door into the back room. No sooner had she left than the man with the yellow shirt stood up, and walked towards the door. Almost as he left Monique returned, already with her headscarf on her head, and slipping into the raincoat she permanently carried with her. Albert raised his eyebrows, and stared at her.

'How did you know he was leaving?'

'If you can't tell by now you never will, chéri. I'll just see where he goes.'

Before he could reply Monique had gone, skilfully evading the lascivious hands anxious to slap playfully or rest momentarily upon her delightful rump. Albert sighed, then returned to the gruff demands for Stella Artois, and *kriek*.

In the street it was beginning to rain slightly with that dank drizzle blanket that pervades Brussels all too frequently. Monique pulled her thin raincoat round her, and tightened the tie-belt. Her face was directed at the ground before her black shoes, but her eyes kept the back of the man steadily in focus.

He skirted the edge of the fish market and worked his way through to the Place Ste Catherine. Monique held back slightly as she turned the corner of the old church. Too many people were idly clearing up the stalls of the market. They knew her, and she knew them. She would not get past without some remark, and that could be her undoing. She would have to circle round by the alley and the side street, and come out at the far end, hoping to catch sight of her quarry as he crossed the main street.

The street was almost empty. Monique mentally cursed, and hurried forward to see if the man was delayed by anything, when a rough grip on her arm, and a sudden, strong twist brought her face to face with the man she had been tailing. Monique whimpered slightly at the pain of that twist, and her heart pounded suddenly against her bra cup.

'Now, Monique, just step through here, nice and quietly, or I'll break your bloody arm.'

The sharp extra twist confirmed both the intention and the likelihood, and Monique obeyed instantly. She was guided into a narrow entrance, arched with peeling plaster over cheap brick that showed through in patches. Her captor indicated the small yard to the left which had a heavy colonnade on two sides, and a tall, blank, brick wall at the far end.

She was very frightened. The quick glimpse of the man's face and the hard cruel eyes gave her little doubt that whatever fate had in store for her would be unpleasant. She was, in fact, terrified. Everything she'd had drilled into her was gone from her mind. All she seemed aware of was the trembling right down her body and legs, and a sudden cold dampness under her dress. The stench in the yard was strong, and it flashed through her mind that she was behind the old dyeworks.

The man shoved her brutally against the end wall, and then shook her, banging her head in the process.

'Now, you stupid bitch, what're you playing at? Why you tailing me, eh? What've I done to you?'

Monique remained silent, staring at his unshaven cheeks, and conscious of his tobacco-laden breath as he slowly applied more pressure to the arm behind her back, and raised it towards her neck with excruciating effect. She bit her teeth to stop a cry.

'Maybe you fancy me . . . that it? Big fella like me . . . do you a bit of good, eh?'

With forthright crudity he stabbed the two main fingers of his free hand between her legs, and commenced to explore roughly what her dress would permit. Monique could retract no more, pressed as she was against the dirty bricks of the wall. Her thoughts momentarily centred on a fate worse than death, which, despite the utter revulsion, did not perhaps deserve its pride of place. All she could think of doing she did. She spat into his face. It had the desired effect. He withdrew his hand, and slowly wiped the spittle from his face with his sleeve. The eyes glinted nastily.

'Only for Albert, is it? We'll see about that. It can wait for now. What's he up to at that café? Come on, girlie, don't be shy . . .'

Monique cried out with a long moan as her arm almost broke behind her back. In a last desperate thought she tried to knee her assailant where it would hurt most, but he was nobody's fool, and stood in such a way as to prevent her doing anything.

'You can forget that, sweetheart. Ladies don't do such things.'

He said the word 'sweetheart' in English. Straight out of a Humphrey Bogart film, though the borrowing did nothing to comfort Monique. Even the slightest movement from her brought an increase in arm pressure which was now almost excruciating enough to make her lose consciousness.

Suddenly the man's face changed expression, and he made a noise half-way between a gasp and a belch. The pressure on her arm relaxed, and she shuddered backwards, only held by the clammy, stiff fingers of the man whose expression was questioning and surprised. He seemed about to say something before he slid slowly to the ground down her body.

Monique shuddered, and a trembling moan left her lips. Albert withdrew the long-bladed knife as the man fell, and regarded her ruefully.

'All right?'

She flung herself at him, and sobbed her heart out. He didn't move, just quietly put one arm round her, and held her firmly until she recovered her composure. It was only then that she realised they were not alone. Someone was bending down over the dead man, and going systematically through his pockets. It was 'Yvette'. Calmly, coldly examining every single possession about his person. Monique gulped thankfully, then turned back to Albert.

'Who's looking after the café?'

Albert chuckled. 'Just like a woman. The moment the immediate danger is over . . . back to business. Natalie is looking after things. It's all right, my love . . . all over now.'

The last was in response to a single tear running down Monique's cheek. Albert rubbed it away with his finger, and put the hand gently behind her neck, and kissed her. She hugged him with a sense of gratitude and desperation, as well as love. She was still trembling uncontrollably when Lisa spoke coldly and calmly.

'We were right. Look . . .'

She handed up a crumpled piece of paper. It was a simple pay-slip, and bore the stamp of the Geheimestaatspolizei.

'Careless of him,' was all Lisa commented as she stood up. 'What shall we do with the body, Albert? We can't just leave it. There would be reprisals.'

'Bring him in here. You take the feet . . .' Albert picked up the man under the arms, and started dragging as Lisa assisted by lifting the feet. They took him to the wooden door of the dyeworks. One quick examination from Albert, and a sharp thrust of the boot burst the old and inadequate lock on the door. They dragged him into the black interior. Albert produced a pocket-torch, and swung it round the large area revealing the huge dye-tubs set into the concrete floor.

'Get him on my back . . . I'll stuff him in one of the tubs.'

Three minutes later the man, whoever he was, was changing to a lurid green, probably 'fast'. Albert climbed down from the wooden stir-step, and rubbed his hands on his trousers.

'What about a decent drink?'

Albert took both women by the arm, and led them across the yard out into the street, and thence to the main thoroughfare.

'How long have we got?'

'An hour-and-a-quarter to curfew. Back to the "Candide"?'

'Certainly not! I want a decent drink.'

The three made for a small café at the end of the fish-market in a forced jocular mood, mainly for Monique's benefit, and slowly relaxed over smuggled Dutch Geneva that the patron produced for his colleague.

'The dyer will get into trouble, Albert. We should warn them so they can make the report.'

'Dercksz is the worst kind of collaborator. The Germans will know he wasn't responsible, and take it as a sign that people object to collaboration. What concerns me is how and why he got onto us. What was he doing at the "Candide", and how many people know that he was onto something?' Lisa turned to Albert. 'We must look into it tomorrow. Gaston's cousin works for them from time to time. He will keep us informed.'

'Meanwhile we just continue?' Monique's query showed that she had calmed down. Both women looked at the pensive Albert.

'What's the matter, Albert?'

'I was just thinking . . . that pay-slip. Did you realise there were no tax deductions? They get away with murder, those people!'

Lisa and Monique stared at him unbelieving, then collapsed into laughter.

7

The Ardennes: The battered truck pulled out of the yard almost before the tail-board had been slammed into position and bolted. Only one guard was with them this time. That could be interpreted as a sign of contempt, or a realisation of the weakness and lack of morale that had become part of their person now. The guard sat opposite a small, thin, pale Geordie whose dejection was only partially due to his captivity. 'Chalky' Wilkins knew he had come to the end of the line. He was not going to Switzerland. He was not even going to experience Europe in the way he intended. He was going to Stalag-Luft-something-or-other, and was going to be incarcerated for the rest of the war unless he got the hell out of it somehow. He didn't feel too good. He had been on very short rations ever since his capture, and, never a robust person, seemed to shrink under the deprivation more than others.

Some of the blokes didn't show too much. They had quite a bit of stamina. A camel's hump to draw upon and sustain them over the long internment, and keep them fit enough to stand up to the regimen of deprivation that was their lot now. Chalky had no such stock of 'money in the bank'. He was tough and wiry, certainly. That helped him sometimes, especially in short bursts of activity without rations. He almost didn't notice it. But when it became prolonged his years of sparse feeding, lean sustenance, revealed their deficit in terms of body stamina. Chalky was a miner's lad. His narrow chest and thin blood spoke of generations of poverty and disinherited stock. But he was mentally and philosophically resilient. Show me a miner who isn't!

The truck rocked and bounded as it negotiated the rutted road, and splashed filthy water to either side as it sped towards the German border.

The grey misted day told them little of the terrain but from time to time the wooded heights of the Ardennes peered cautiously through the banks of low cloud.

They left Bullange, then turned off onto a minor road signposted to Hollerath. Some wit had scratched out the arrow pointing Eastward over the sign marked 'Allemagne – Douanes' and painted a new one with a long Westward indication. The Boche were confident. They had every right to be. The frontier of Germany was now the English Channel and the North Sea. The barrier was tied back in the vertical position, and the Customs Post unmanned as they slowly moved through behind a convoy of trucks.

Schleiden was the first German town Chalky had seen. There was still a flicker of interest in him, and he was observant enough to appreciate the differences in appearance, but they did not stop, and no one showed any curiosity about *him*. Then, why should they? Allied prisoners could be no novelty in this area.

The truck turned northward once through the town, and Chalky fell into a troubled sleep until the sounds of Bonn woke him, and a nudge from his neighbour caused him to regard the Rhine over which they were now passing.

'That's the Rhine, mate.'

Chalky gazed in wonder. 'The Rhine! Imagine that!'

'What's this place, then, Alec?'

'Bonn I think. Hey, Fritz . . . this Bonn?'

The soldier glowered momentarily then shrugged.

'That is Bonn . . . back there . . . We enter Beuel, now. Nice place.'

'Where are we going, Fritz? D'you know?'

'Ja. I know. We go to Eibelsberg, in the Westerwald. Good prison-camp there. I am prison guard there three months before they send me to Belgium. Is good Kommandant. Not too strict . . . you are liking this, I think.'

'Oh yes . . . love it, old man. Always wanted to be behind barbed-wire.' The well-built young navigator turned to Chalky as if to say 'He's got to be joking', but stopped in mid-flight when he saw Chalky's face.

'You all right, Chalky? Hey! Chalky! Wake up, you stupid Geordie!'

He shook Chalky, but the little miner's son who had just entered Germany slid to the floor in a little, bony heap. The German guard stared down at him, not knowing whether it was an escape ploy or not, then quickly realised it was not, and thumped the back of the cabin with the butt of his carbine, shouting to the driver to stop.

Once halted the flap was hung down, and Chalky carried out into the air, and laid on the ground. An officer from somewhere hurried up, and bent over him. But

Chalky was quite dead. His constricted heart had given out without warning.

8

Over Occupied Europe: The throb of the Wellington's engines merely formed a background noise. Curtis had noticed during his many ops that initial awareness of the engine noise soon faded into the background. It seemed to happen more or less over the Dutch coast, and by the time the German border was crossed it hardly existed. He supposed the effect was a blend of heightened awareness of other, extraneous sounds, the repeated if not continuous use of the intercom, and, most of all, the slowly emerging vibration that developed into a rattle on the return trip.

Curtis heard the slight click in his headphones.

'Navigator to skipper. Alter course to one-three-seven.'

'Steering one-three-seven, Tommy.'

Curtis eased the aircraft onto the new course, and his eyes searched the interminable blackness. Somewhere out there, not too far away, were the other seventeen aircraft from the squadron, all moving towards their target, all wondering if they would be returning to base in the early light. Soon there would be night-fighters, searchlights, flak, and all hell rocking the boat in that empty blackness.

'Skipper to rear gunner. We're approaching the night-fighter belt, Mike. Anything out there?'

'Not a damn thing, skipper. I'll let you know.' Curtis

smiled to himself at the urbane reply. Always the same from Mike. Slightly bored, and a flat expressionless voice. Nothing could be further from the truth, Curtis knew. Mike would be beginning to sweat, and feel loose-bowelled. He was the exposed member of the crew. The one least likely to survive. They knew it. He knew it. And it was never mentioned except to joke about when the mood permitted . . . and Mike always started it.

The starboard engine suddenly misfired, missed again, coughed twice, then settled down. All the crew, except perhaps Mike, had turned their heads momentarily to listen to the engine's response before resuming their respective tasks. Curtis glanced out of the side panel. Nothing to see—it was instinctive. It didn't heighten their apprehension. It would take flak or the Luftwaffe to do that, which would be soon enough. Curtis stared at his instrument panel. After a moment it went out of focus and he turned his head slightly, his eyes drifting once again over the cabin structure. He noted again the slight movement between metal plates, the places where constant rubbing had worn the sprayed paint and revealed the shiny metal, the inevitable tattiness and lack of 'finish' possessed by all operational aircraft, the patching, the replacements, the two cracked glasses in the panel.

'Navigator to skipper. E.T.A. twelve minutes unless the headwind increases.'

'Thanks, Tommy.'

Essen and the greater part of the Ruhr was already on alert. The night-fighters of the Luftwaffe were airborne. Batteries of Flugzeugabwehrkanonen – 'Flak' to the RAF crews – were standing-by for range readings. The light 2cm Flak 38s stood down for the moment. Their range was effective only to 6000ft. The big 8.8cm Flak 37s and 41s were ready to begin their pounding, standing tensely for the word of command . . . maximum effective range 20,000ft.

Fingers of light suddenly blinked, and shot up into the black night – fingers that glowed almost pink for one brief second before settling to the blue-white of the full arc. Immediately they searched and probed, fanning and boxing to seek out the invader.

'Rear-gunner, Skip . . . searchlights to port . . .'

Curtis did not acknowledge. They had all become aware of the light beams that crossed, parted and swung, apparently haphazard. But they all knew the searchlight-crews knew their job, performed quickly and efficiently, systematically sought them out, and once found, held on to them like grim death.

German dolts and dummkopfs existed only for the folks back home, who made their contact with the enemy through the cinema. The Allied military knew the German for what he was, a damn good fighting man, courageous and determined, and – what was perhaps more dangerous – still flushed with a succession of victories. He still knew in his heart the Third Reich was going to win . . . and that internal strength almost made it a fact.

'Eyes peeled everybody . . . we're going in.'

Brussels: Albert peeped through the curtains for one brief moment as he locked up the café. The night was dry, crisp but not too cold, and the sound of passing bombers was long over. They were probably on their way to the Ruhr, but you couldn't tell for sure. Albert shot the bolt on the door, and then drew it back again. He remembered that Monique was still in the back room making egg custards for Andrée with eggs bartered for a bottle of Moselle. He had found a case of sixteen bottles tucked away among cardboard boxes at the back of the cellar when he bought the place. Good wine, too.

That left three. One bottle for two dozen eggs, mainly for Andrée . . . but what could one do? She was an invalid, and needed little things to boost her wretched existence.

He padded back to the counter, switched off the dull light he had fitted over the bar sink, and plunged the café into darkness.

In the back room Monique was quietly beating eggs in a basin. She glanced up at him. Albert smiled feebly, almost regretfully, and Monique knew he was apologising for her having to go home to her poky little flat seven minutes away from the 'Candide'.

She almost hated him for it. Partially for being in the stupid situation he was in, which she knew he couldn't really help, and which was just part of 'Albert', but mostly for being weak and apologetic about it. If he just told her he was stuck with an invalid, but he wanted her, and was going to make his play whenever he got the chance, it was at least positive, manly, and a statement of plain fact that one could take or leave. She didn't want his constant sense of guilt, his apology for being alive.

Monique knew Albert well . . . better than she had known anyone . . . and she loved him deeply. She knew him for the kind, gentle, courageous man that he was. She loved him for the responsibility he assumed, for the ability to take life in an act that was abhorrent to him. She loved him for his concern for others, and his selflessness, and she loved him as a man who is good for his woman. But she detested his guilt, and his sense of burden, that could from time to time unman him properly. When she thought about his wife, Andrée, which was not often, for she deliberately strove to erase her existence from her mind, it was not with hatred, nor was it pity. It was a blank, almost unemotional response to a situation that she just wanted to go away . . . to disappear from her life.

'You can use this for your breakfast. The custards are in the cellar . . . on the shelf. And we need some more nutmeg . . .'

Monique almost bit her lip. It had slipped out again. 'We' need some more of this . . . more that. Who was this 'we'? Albert and Andrée were 'we'. She was just the mistress . . . the husband's whore . . . the convenience and the slave. There was no 'we' for Albert and her, and the thought made her wince inside. She turned almost angrily from the table, and took up her coat lying ready on the chair. Albert came to her, and tried to touch her, but she moved away and donned the coat, her face a blank, unemotional mask concealing her unhappiness and her momentary anger. Albert sensed it, of course. It had been going on too long for him to do otherwise.

He held back as Monique walked out mumbling an estranged 'Good night'.

'I'll come and lock up . . .'

Again the hesitant, embarrassed, apologetic words and inflection. Monique walked quickly through the café and into the street. Albert closed the door unhappily, and shot the bolt. The telephone rang in the rear room almost as he touched the bolt. He sighed and hurried through to the summons.

'Candide . . . oui, c'est Albert . . .' Albert commenced making notes on a small pad . . . notes that no one else could understand let alone read. Over the last two years Albert had evolved his own form of shorthand, cryptograms, and encoding that would have amazed the Allied experts. The German 'Enigma' machine was complex; Albert's mental process was devious. One could be forgiven for imagining that remembering a message verbatim was infinitely easier than remembering the method

Albert used. But it hadn't let him down yet.

'... between Sadaert and Sainte Eglise? Mmh ... mmh ... I hear you have foxes in the area ... should make the hunting more interesting. Yes, Claude, I will tell her ... au'voir.'

Albert tore off the note from the pad, and stuck it at the rear of a clip of shop-reminders on the board of the dresser by the wall-phone. He checked his watch and drummed his fingers on the board for some moments while he reviewed the manpower situation. After a considered elimination of possibilities he picked up the phone again, and waited.

Over Essen: Alec Davies had his eyes glued to the bomb-sights. A long way below, the almost-focused ground moved slowly past towards his chest. the black-and-white tartan pattern seemed to shudder from time to time as another yellow-pink burst lit up an area, and left a puff of smoke and dust hovering, only to be illumined once more by a neighbouring burst.

'Steady, skipper ... left ... left ... Hold her steady ...'
The ship shuddered and rocked from Flak blast.
'Damn! ... left again ... left ... steady ... steadyyyyyy. Bombs gone! ... Camera running ...'

Curtis held the Wimpey as tight as he could. There was a veritable holocaust of Flak burst, but he needed to keep her steady ... just another few minutes, then, quick as maiden's blush, get the hell out of it.

'Picture taken, skip ... bomb-doors shut.'

9

Liège: Louis and Maurice Anderlecht sat on the big, warped hatch of their barge, and silently stared up into the night sky. It was almost impossible to count aircraft passing over merely from the sound of their engines, but both men reckoned the number to be in excess of thirty, and from the look of the distant skylines where thin bright fingers fitfully pierced and probed the cloud, or where dull reddish glows could just be discerned tinging the night horizons, it was not the only force carrying death and destruction to Nazi Germany. One could almost hear the joyful intake of cold air as both men laughed silently, and mentally lit candles in their hearts for the British and American flyers.

The Boche were getting a taste of it at last.

When the sounds had died away Louis went below, and returned with his fishing tackle. The Anderlecht brothers had, over the years, developed a highly efficient technique for night fishing. It was no more than using a phosphorescent floater with a very short double-baited line below it. Every day the phosphorescence was recharged on deck in the sunlight, and every night it was dropped into the murky waters of the Meuse.

Maurice sat with his back against the deck-housing, and smoked an old, stumpy, meerschaum pipe with a nibbled and cracked stem. Louis sat hunched over his line, and silently waited for the fish to bite. Perch mostly.

It was about one-thirty when Maurice took the pipe from between his teeth, and lifted his head to listen. Louis had heard it too. A curious sound . . . rushing and flapping. The sound of wind through telegraph wires mingled with the flapping and rustling of a torn blind in a disused house. It wasn't a sound you heard . . . it wasn't loud enough, really. You felt it down the back of your spine, and it raised the hairs on your neck. It was above one's head . . . like the wings of the Angel of Death. The two brothers looked at each other. Maurice laid down his pipe. Louis stuck the end of his short rod into the damp sand in the old sack that stood against the rail. In case of incendiaries: it was regulations. They stood up as silently as possible, and strained every muscle controlling the ear to search out and catch the indescribable sound, and decipher it.

Without much increase in volume it was nevertheless nearing . . . a descending sound. Suddenly Maurice turned his head half-upwards and to the left. Something white had caught his eye for a moment. Louis followed his look, and tried to pierce the night. It wasn't true what they said about carrots. Did you ever see a cat eating carrots?

'It's stopped. Over there . . . on the embankment. There's summat.'

Louis was already lowering the dinghy. Maurice dropped into it after him and shoved off. Louis sculled across the river swiftly and expertly, hardly making a sound. Liège was very quiet. There was no traffic, even in the town, and police patrols were infrequent. The dinghy bumped against the stone steps. Maurice tied off on the bottom iron cleat, and both men silently mounted the stone steps towards the embankment chaussée. As their heads approached the massive parapet something white and floppy was seen suspended in the night air. It was only when they reached the street level that they could see it was a parachute, caught in the overhead tram-wires.

The brothers approached slowly. No one was about. No one else had heard anything. But then no one else was stupid enough to fish in the river at two o'clock in the morning. Their heads craned up at the dark bundle suspended below the torn white awning. It was a man in RAF flying-gear, and he was dead. The dangling legs terminated just about the knee-joint leaving bloody stumps and shredded uniform trousers where something had severed the limbs: tracer-bullets, shrapnel, prop-blades – it didn't matter what. He was dead anyway.

10

Limbourg: Mike Lambert actually landed on his feet. He'd never done that before. There wasn't a breath of wind, and the parachute silk umbrella slowly deflated about his ears, and sank silently to the ground. Just imagine! If the ruddy instructor could have seen that! He didn't even stagger. Just a lovely landing on both feet. Not bad for a rear-gunner!

The parachute was quickly wrapped and bundled into a hastily-made hole in the soft ground. Despite the elation of his superb landing Mike was feeling, very, very scared. He knew his chances of not being picked up by the Germans was about twenty-to-one. None too decent odds. He recognised that he was nervous, and trembling slightly. Being alone there was no need to pretend it was the exhilaration of the fall and landing. No, he was trembling because he was apprehensive, scared stiff – not to put too fine a point upon it. The stories and propaganda leave a certain mark on anyone. Mike was no student of contemporary history nor an avid reader of newspaper leaders, but it had filtered down to him that these Nazi boys were not very nice, nor very considerate to prisoners if they wanted information. He, too, had heard tales of concentration-camps in Eastern Europe, some even nearer than that, and those recollected snippets suddenly assumed importance in his memory, and rushed to the forefront.

He decided that it was better to move than stand still. He had remembered his escape-kit, and remembered that half his buttons were small compasses. Quickly he ripped one off, and consulted it. South-south-west seemed to be the general direction he wanted to follow. He was going to be hard put to it, he reflected. He had looked at a map of Belgium only the day before yesterday. Something had made him do it. That last operation had given him the 'willies'. He looked down once at the cold landscape, clear in the bright moonlight, and it struck him then: 'What if I *am* shot down and I have to get out across that lot down there?' He knew nothing of Belgium, nor had he bothered to find out... until yesterday and the day before. Something had made him take a slow, careful look.

He wasn't sure where he was. The plane had copped it over the Ruhr, but they had flown quite a distance since then. The instrument-panel had shattered to hell, and they had little control over the aircraft. The Skipper, John Curtis, had done his damnedest, and willed the lousy Wimpey to maintain some sort of westerly course, but he knew they had drifted and turned, right round on one occasion that made them head straight for Germany. But it had been countered, and the descent had sped towards the Franco-Belgian border. Most of them agreed on that. He and the others had jumped when the skipper said so, but Curtis had stayed in the aircraft to keep some control and stop the crate from crashing in the centre of a town, if he could. He was a good skipper,

Curtis. Poor devil! He'd probably left it too late to bale out. He was a good man as well as a good skipper.

But where was Mike Lambert? That was more to the point at the moment. Somewhere round about Liège, he fancied. He had seen a big town for a moment before he jumped, then it was gone as he had fallen through some low-lying cloud. He had a sense of industry, and there was the smell of iron, or coal, or gas, or something in the air. Mike recognised it. He had grown up with it. A miner's son, saved from toiling underground by a selfless and determined father, and a sensitive, equally-determined mother. Both determined he was not going down the pit. Here he was, feet on the ground in Belgium, and it was the same grime and coal dust he had left behind in Nottingham. Within five minutes a huge slag-heap was silhouetted against the night sky, followed a moment later by the skeletal uprights of the winding-gear. It was just the same as home. After some exploration he realised that he had fallen onto waste ground, black scrub, on the edge of a mining area – perhaps even *inside* the area. The rolling clatter of steel wheels over rails and points could be heard, followed by the clunk of buffers meeting. Just the same as home.

God! Could you never get away from blasted mines? Mike was no snob, he had no pretensions. He just wanted to be away from coal and pits and slag, with all the sense of importance that his parents had given to that escape.

He tried walking across the country, but came up against high wire, perimeter fencing. Without cutters there was no way but round. He set off, only to encounter another wall of the same fencing. There was only one thing for it. Follow the wire until a gate or opening or – better still – a break presented itself, then get the hell out of it, and make away from towns and industry.

Where there were factories or industry there would be Germans guarding their new possessions, newly tuned to their own war effort. The new moon gave a bleak, cold, blue light over everything. It wasn't too bright to be dangerous, but gave enough for him to see by . . . so he could, in turn, be seen.

Sheds loomed up ahead; large, old, and falling to pieces . . . just like home. The ground under his feet was little more than coal dust and pools of black water, ringed with multicoloured skins of oil or petroleum, were visible as such even in the dark. The metallic clunks sounded near-by, then the rumble of wagons and hoppers approached as a 'tram' set off down the incline towards the railway-sheds, and the steaming, black, tank-loco that hissed a quarter of a mile away.

Then there was an opening. It was the wide gate which led onto the cobbled street outside, and through which the metal rails ran. These crossed the thoroughfare onto another area of pit property running between workers' houses and a peeling, empty-windowed shop that seemed only to offer faded adverts and yellowed doilies to its customers. Down the line one yellow light, and one red one, blinked like infernal eyes, and drew him as a moth to the flame. A second tram of hoppers trundled past across the cobbles and down the incline. Perhaps he ought to make a dash for it now. Mike hurried forward, and was about to turn into the street when he heard a voice some distance behind. Startled, he made a headlong dart for the gateway, and bumped into two German soldiers standing silently smoking, apparently guarding the crossing.

Who was the more startled was anybody's guess, but Mike turned back and dashed into the pit yard, running hell-for-leather across the coal and asphalt towards the piles and slag-heaps.

The two Germans, suddenly aroused from their stupor, unshouldered their carbines and ran after him into the enclosure, one calling out some thick, Swabian commands. Two shots rang out. More barked commands in German. Mike dashed forward, anywhere, just away from the Jerries. He felt his feet sink into the soft coal dust and rubble as he ascended. It was a foolish thing to do, but Mike wasn't thinking. Every desperate step he climbed pushed more coal dust behind him, and his ascent was minimal. Suddenly the whole area was bathed in yellow light as the floodlighting was switched on. Mike felt himself centred in a blaze of light, and struggled to escape even more, with even less advancement. He didn't really hear the barked commands to stop, put up his hands and surrender. But he heard the shot about the same time as he felt the bullet hit him and knock him forward onto the slag.

There was just a bright flash in his mind, then nothing. The bullet had hit him squarely in the centre of the back, breaking the spinal cord. Mike was dead almost as he hit the dirt. A young man who had dedicated his life to escaping from the mines lay spreadeagled and lifeless upon the black dust of a coal mountain somewhere in a foreign land.

11

Somewhere in Belgium: The parachute descent seemed like half-an-hour, but it could only have been seconds. Curtis had left it rather late before jumping himself. Almost too late. He had ordered his crew to bale out at least six minutes before he realised the Wellington was losing height too rapidly to make delay anything but foolhardy. It meant, of course, that he would land a considerable distance from the rest of his crew. The likelihood of meeting up with them was slim, and there was little point in trying to do so. As skipper he had a certain responsibility to his crew, but Curtis was a realist, and understood sentimental gestures were empty and wasteful. They were grown men. They would cope, and take their chances as he would. Now he was once again on terra firma.

For some stupid reason the harness-buckle wouldn't part. He mentally called himself butter-fingers, and even blamed the inability on his nerves, but the wretched thing had fouled somehow, and it took him what seemed ten minutes to separate the pieces. Burying the chute was no trouble – the ground was reasonably soft. Curtis checked his escape-kit, and sought the advice of one of his compasses before proceeding in a west-south-westerly direction. He had advised his men to stay clear of Brussels and the big towns, yet here he was making directly for the metropolis himself, against his own advice. In his own case it was not so foolish as might be imagined. John Curtis had spent quite a lot of time both in Belgium and France before the war – initially with school friends – subsequently on a study course and in his first job. He spoke the language very well. As with the majority of Englishmen born in the north, his flat accent made the pronunciation of most other languages easier. That, together with a natural ability to assimilate a language and its idioms, gave him a head-start over his colleagues. He was unlikely to be faulted simply by opening his mouth.

He crossed the dark fields without mishap, and warily approached the road. Within ten minutes of following the road, so far without encountering or even seeing a vehicle or human being, he came to the river. It was big enough and deep enough to provide an obstacle which he either had to cross by some means or swim, and the latter was just not on as far as he was concerned. Wet uniform, soaked shoes, general messy appearance – it was all asking for trouble. He decided to chance it, and stepped out into the main road to walk towards the bridge. A brief reconnoitre showed that it was not guarded, and he set off smartly, having first picked up some of the switches and cuttings lying around the river willows that had been recently pollarded. He made a bundle, and tied his shoe-laces together to make a longer binding for the bundle, and shouldered it. He figured that anyone in the early morning in the country was out doing something, not just ambling about. Country people didn't amble – they either worked, or did nothing at home.

It turned out to be a sound inspiration. He had not gone ten yards onto the bridge before the sound of a truck was heard approaching from behind. Curtis tensed. He just knew it was going to stop, and someone would ask him something. He was not wrong. The vehicle turned out to be a battered $4\frac{1}{2}$ ton Bussing-Nag lorry, laden with half-asleep infantrymen belonging to a divisional service unit. The driver leant out of the wood-and-cardboard cab, and questioned him in a strong Hamburg accent.

'Which way to Diest?'

'Down the road . . . first on the left.' Curtis' reply was quick, and from behind the bundle of willow switches. Could they see he was in RAF uniform, or was it too dark to really make out? Apparently the latter, as the driver grunted, and pulled away with a stiff motion of the hand indicating some form of salutation best known to himself. Curtis' heart was pounding, and beads of sweat dampened his forehead. So far so good, but that was too close for comfort. Thereafter he kept to woods and ditches where possible. There were times when he wished the English hedgerow was as much a feature of continental husbandry as it was of the shires. There is something about a Belgian or Dutch landscape that makes one feel exposed, and at this moment it was a feeling Curtis could do without.

The remainder of the day was uneventful. Curtis tried to keep it that way. He avoided every possible contact, rested up whenever a suitable covert presented itself, and was generally wary of being glimpsed, however casually. When it became dark he made for a small Dutch barn and sought refuge among the remnants of last year's hay, dank and ripe, and not conducive to comfort. It would have helped him sleep, there was no doubt of that. Damp hay, rejoicing in its own combustion, exudes a scent that is highly soporific. His young days around the dales' farms had taught him that. Had he spent ten hours asleep on it he would have been well on the way to rheumatic fever. He had learnt that too – the hard way – and he wasn't about to repeat the experience.

He found a corner out of the wind and huddled himself into a self-warming bundle. He finished off the chocolate and malted-milk tablets, and slaked his thirst at a stand-pipe by a concrete trough. Sleep was slow in coming, and when it did he dozed fitfully. Some wretched dog half-a-mile away kept barking, and waking him up.

Dawn found him very cold, stiff, and aching. There was no one about. He turned, and settled himself against the dry, cobwebbed boarding, pattined with oats and dead flies, and went to sleep again. This time it was deep and undisturbed. It lasted for almost two hours.

When he woke it was with a sense of sudden panic that he had permitted the day to advance so far without moving off. Then he noticed it. At his feet was an old haversack, greasy, and shapeless with age. It had been a gas-mask case from the First World War, long used for ploughman's lunches, fishing-bait, and God knows what else. In it was a bottle of rough red wine, and a piece of bread with boudin sausage and some cheese wrapped in greaseproof paper. Tucked underneath the packet was a small packet of French cigarettes, and a box of matches. A folded scrap of paper, torn from a child's exercise-book bore a few words written in pencil, in the almost indecipherable, clumsy hand of semi-literacy. It said 'Bonne chance, Tommy'.

Curtis looked about him quickly and keenly, but there was no one. No one to be thanked, and no one to be involved. Santa Claus had been during the night.

The stiffness was with him for most of the morning. It reflected how he felt mentally. He had been stupid and unrealistic enough to drop into a sound sleep. Someone had come, and, luckily for him, gone without malice. It might have been otherwise.

He made the bread last all day, and drank the harsh wine sparingly. It was new and fruity, but he knew from experience that if he drank it in any quantity it would give him the squirts . . . pink squirts . . . and that he could do without right now. He kept away from habitation, not always easy in that part of the world. He followed lines of poplars, still without their foliage, in the fond hope that they afforded some sort of protection by simply being there.

That night he slept in a ditch. It was dry, and filled with old bracken and long dry grass. The fresh green of the new year's growth had not yet fought its way through the dry tares of the old months. It sufficed. It was even quite comfortable once you got settled and wriggled the hip into a depression.

It was on the third day that Curtis ran into the deserter. He had been holing-up round a farm until driven off by a barking dog who was beginning to rouse the entire neighbourhood, and was making his way through the dull, raining, grey, miserable day towards a wooded area. Long lines of the omnipresent poplars gave onto a wood of considerable area, made up largely of beech and silver birch, with a certain amount of coarse undergrowth. He had been travelling for ten minutes through the wood when he sensed he was being followed, and dropped into the shrub and gorse, tensed and apprehensive. He waited in total silence for almost twenty minutes before he heard the rustle of cloth against undergrowth, and the soft, crisp sound of breaking twigs and dried ground-fall, which even the rain and general damp had not deadened.

The man saw him about the same second as he regarded his pursuer. Both men, now still and hardly breathing, stared at each other. The other man was lean, and hollow-cheeked, tall, and dishevelled. Immediately he did a slight, almost humorous 'hands-up' gesture, and stepped forward towards Curtis. Curtis rose to his feet as if to confront him.

'Who are you?'

The French was thick and richly accented. The tongue of the true Frenchman, not the rather lazy, debased speech of the Belgian French-speaker. Curtis replied in English, thinking it wisest not to give away too much too soon.

'RAF. You?'

'French army deserter. I've been on the run for ten weeks.'

'Why are you here... in Belgium?'

'I was captured in 1940 during the offensive. I have been working in Germany since the Armistice, but three months ago I escaped and got out of Germany . . . I couldn't go south through the Ruhr . . . too dangerous . . . so I crossed into Belgium, and I'm making for the French border now.' He eyed Curtis cautiously.

'When were you shot down?'

'About three days ago. I'm making for France, too.'

Curtis eyed his companion as they walked and talked. Something about the man's expression – the hunted, 'lean and hungry' look – did not encourage confidence. So far he had not attempted to speak French, but let the deserter stumble along in halting English. Language ignorance might prove a useful ploy, and let the man make his own mistake in his own time by assuming that Curtis did not understand what he was saying.

The landscape was bleak, and night drawing in fast with further rain, probably, throughout the night and early morning. Curtis nudged his fellow-traveller.

'It's going to rain again . . . we should find some shelter for the night.'

'Soon.'

His companion was curt, and seemed preoccupied. Constantly his eyes searched the fields and the lanes ahead. On two occasions they had to dive for the ditch when a vehicle was heard approaching. The first one turned out to be a farm-truck with an old man at the wheel; the second was a more cared-for vehicle, judging by the purr of the engine as it approached. As it passed Curtis saw it was an elderly Citroen, and carried two, uniformed, Belgian police. The small, dark eyes of the deserter followed its progress before he spat onto the grass in a gesture of disgust.

'I gather you don't like the police.' Curtis attempted a smile of complicity.

'Pigs! All of them! The Germans let the young ones stay at home if they are police, then they use them to do their work, and have always the threat of sending them as forced-labour if they do not do as they say. They are the keenest police-force in Europe!'

He scampered across the road, and made for the bushes on the far side. Curtis followed a moment later.

'There's a farm building over there . . . it looks unoccupied.'

The flaking paint on the faded blue door showered onto the ground as they kicked it in. Inside the rooms were, indeed, unoccupied, and falling into disrepair that would soon be beyond rescue. The roof was open to the evening sky in two places, but one chimney and fireplace seemed intact. It was shelter . . . in part it would keep out the rain and wind . . . and with any luck would provide enough old wood to make a fire possible.

'I doubt if anyone would be able to see the glow if we lit a fire. It could be a cold night.'

The Frenchman nodded absently as he wandered about examining the interior.

'They won't notice smoke once it's dark. We passed a field of turnips. We could make soup.'

He nodded again, and peered about through half-closed eyes, then crossed to the boards that had been nailed over the broken window, and looked out onto the field and footpath.

'You think anyone followed us?' The man was nervous, and his throat sounded dry. Curtis joined him by the slats, and peered through a chink in the boards.

'We'll know soon enough if they did. It would take them half-an-hour to get back into town, or find a phone. Assuming anybody cared it would take them at least another half-hour to get out here . . . if they had transport available. That gives us an hour of peace. You can sweat it out then if you want to. If they haven't come by eight-thirty no one is coming, and we can sleep. It seems fair enough.'

The Frenchman turned to him and glowered.

'You have it all worked out, don't you? The calm, cold, Englishman. Fatalist to the end.'

'If you don't like it, you know what to do, don't you? D'you want to bust up some wood for a fire, or go and get the snadgers . . . turnips to you? I'm easy.'

'I'll attend to the fire.'

'Okay. But don't light it until it's dark.'

Curtis slipped out of the door they had entered, and made his way across the hard, broken earth towards the cover of pollarded willows, presumably running along the side of a ditch or small stream. It turned out to be a ditch, and it was bone dry, filled with old leaves and brambles. It served as cover for the first part of the walk, even if the brambles tore at his hands and trouser-legs. By the time he reached the open fields Curtis was wondering which was the lesser of the two evils – being in the open and observable, or being torn to shreds by the clinging thorns of the bramble creepers. The last bit he performed bent double and close to the ground. Perhaps it was pointless and stupid. They didn't know anyone was about. Apart from the two workers clearing the undergrowth in the plantation they had seen no one all day. Why was the Frenchman bothered about those two? They hardly noticed the two evaders who grunted a greeting in the cold, late afternoon as they hurried past.

By now his fingers and heels were digging into the hard earth, and revealing the greenish-purple tap-roots of the turnips. He quickly stuffed eight or nine inside his jacket and pockets.

When he got back to the ruined house the Frenchman was waiting, sitting back to the wall of the fireplace, breaking old, whitened laths into smaller strips for kindling. His eyes asked the question.

'No one about,' Curtis grunted as he unburdened himself of the freezing cold turnips. 'You got a knife?'

The Frenchman fished inside his trouser pocket, and brought out a long-bladed, folding knife, ideally suited to cutting up things like turnips, or sliding between the ribs of offending Germans (or British, if it came to that). There was an old, battered, galvanised bucket in one corner of the room, the inside covered in long-hardened cement. Curtis swilled it round in the iron bath at the back of the house, fed from some spring which kept the water moving and sweet. The cement didn't budge, but it wouldn't during the cooking either. He filled it with about two quarts of water, then cut up the turnips into cubes and dropped them in.

'I think we can light the fire now. You got your lighter?'

By eight o'clock the Frenchman's nervousness had increased, and the turnips were soft. They ate the tasteless lumps in silence and listened to a dog barking across the fields outside. He was on his last piece of turnip, eaten with pink fingers that were par-boiled at each dip, when Curtis heard the slightest of sounds from outside. A sound suggestive of metal on stone, small and dull, like a boot toe-cap catching a flint. He tensed, as did his companion. A second later the door was sent flying into the room with a hefty kick. In the doorway stood a burly man with unshaven chin, a red sweat-rag about his neck. He was one of the labourers in the plantation. In his great hands he held a shotgun, both barrels loaded and cocked. He stepped to one side immediately, and allowed three gendarmes to enter, one with a service pistol in his hand.

The French deserter, his mouth open and his sullen eyes glinting under the dark brows, slowly stood up. Curtis continued eating his turnip lump.

They were taken to the small town of Maulesuyt, and pushed into the single cell of the police station. Curtis' request for tea or coffee was rewarded with a sharp jab in the groin which he managed to deflect partially.

The Frenchman was clearly nervous. Curtis took it philosophically, and kept his own council. He had noted the station set-up as primitive and understaffed, and mentally weighed up the chances of getting out. Not impossible if the right moment came along. They sat for twenty minutes before the Frenchman suddenly got up, and banged on the door, shouting through the Judas-hole that he wanted to talk to the officer-in-charge. He was taken out into the corridor and the door re-locked. Curtis hastily put his ear to the Judas-hole, and strained to hear what was said. The Frenchman was explaining that he was a deserter, had been on the run for over a year, and only wanted to get back to his mother in Rheims. If they would close their eyes, and let him go, he would tell them about his fellow prisoner. Curtis realised he was about to be sold down the river, but didn't really blame the man for trying. Survival is all.

What was one deserter more or less? If he was handed over the French would shoot him . . . or the Germans . . . or someone. He wasn't a criminal. Just trying to stay alive, like hundreds of others in a similar position all over Occupied Europe, Germans as well as the unfortunate occupied. The voices withdrew, and Curtis went back to his place. He remembered he had the Frenchman's knife in his pocket . . . they hadn't bothered to search him thoroughly, and so far he had not been questioned. Nothing happened. He sat there for two, three hours, and the Frenchman did not return. About three in the morning he was roused by a gendarme entering with an enamel mug of coffee and a great wad of a sandwich with bacon fat between the bread slices.

The policeman eyed him with something like respect. 'You are British?'

Curtis nodded, and sipped his coffee apparently unconcerned.

'You are bomber pilot?' He pronounced both b's, and spoke hesitantly, not used to English. Curtis nodded again.

'Did that Frenchman tell you?'

The policeman nodded, then left. Curtis quickly tried the door, but the man had locked it. So much for natural sympathy.

An hour later Curtis was taken from the cell, down the corridor into the station desk-room, and informed in halting English that he was to be interrogated by the area inspector before being handed over to the German authorities.

Curtis nodded, then requested to go to the lavatory. He was escorted to an outbuilding – there was apparently no inside toilet for the use of prisoners. It was little more than a foul-smelling out-house with a buff-coloured sink, which Curtis suspected had once graced a country kitchen, strategically placed to function as a pissoire. Ventilation was provided by a hinged window above the sink, rusted and jammed.

Quickly Curtis applied the Frenchman's knife to unscrewing the hinges. The blade snapped almost immediately, but the broken blade, if anything, performed the service of a screw driver better. He had just got all the screws removed when thumping on the door denoted impatience and concern from his captors, and he decided it prudent to emerge there and then.

The Area Inspector turned out to be a self-important official with little idea of how to set about an interrogation. His technique was non-existent, and he became angry at Curtis' refusal to divulge anything other than his name, rank and number, but resumed a certain dignity when Curtis invoked the name of the Geneva Convention. No doubt the little man had been dragged out of bed, possibly not even his own. He was understandably irritable, and decided that the whole matter ought to be referred elsewhere. The 'elsewhere' obviously meant German Military Authority; probably the Luftwaffe Police, possibly the Gestapo.

Curtis was returned to his cell, where he managed to kip until first light. Then he was rudely awakened, and told to get ready for removal to Brussels. He managed to convince his captors – also feeling tired and early-morningish – that he needed to relieve himself once again, and was escorted to the lavatory. Immediately he used the broken blade of the knife to lever the now unscrewed window-frame out of its housing. It moved hardly at all until the blade slipped behind the wooden frame, and then it was easy. Curtis was halfway through the opening when the door was thumped, and his escort demanded that he hurry. Curtis grunted a reply as convincingly as he could, and wriggled through the window to drop onto the asphalt outside. Without looking back he bolted across the clearance site that backed the police-station, and was away into the town before the policeman broke the door down, and found his bird had flown.

12

Northern France: Barry slid off his stool, and nodded to the proprietor who preceded him to the door, and peered out before indicating the way was clear. The gentle squeeze on the arm was encouraging, and, fortified by the coffee and plate of brawn and bread, Barry felt in reasonably good spirits. It was still early – between six-thirty and seven – and not a bad time to put a few miles behind you, before the world started operating at full steam. Trouble with Europe was people seemed to get cracking earlier than at home, and pack up later. Christ! If you stuck to the drill, and travelled only at night, you'd never get anywhere. And where were these ruddy evasion-line blokes anyway? Here he was barging around in broad daylight, RAF uniform for anyone to see. He'd been on the go for ten days now, and not a bloody sausage! They couldn't be much good. Barry reasoned there was a hell of a lot of Europe anyway, and no bunch of amateurs could hope to cover the lot. Still, he'd managed on his own so far . . . Why not keep at it on his tod? He turned into the street, and set off down the incline towards the factory area. They said that was the way out of the wretched town. They should know! They lived here.

There were several early movers about . . . two or three men on the way to work who didn't give him a second glance. A couple of women about their business, who glanced at him curiously, and then muttered to each other. Lastly a cheeky-faced boy on a bike with a panier full of long bread loaves who stared at him as he stood on his pedals, and then shouted some encouraging obscenity in the local patois. That was enough for Barry. Time to get off that ruddy street, and out of the way a bit. He turned right into a grimy side alley that led down between two factory walls, behind which rose chimneys, and curious tower-shapes with wooden louvre-vents that emitted steam in never-ending puffs. The factory-gates were arched by a great, metal construction, both triumphal and self-laudatory, as it disclosed the intricate name *Jaavard et fils* in heavy cast-iron letters above the cobbled entrance.

Barry passed on, hands stuffed deep into his trouser pockets. The road was wide enough to permit two steam-trucks to pass each other without concern, but the walls rose up twenty feet in dirt-encrusted brick on both sides, unrelieved by window or advertisements. Someone had made an effort to scrawl some inflammatory message, and rounded it off with a hammer and sickle, all of which the local city-fathers had obviously attempted to erase unsuccessfully. Barry glanced at it glumly, and continued down the never-ending canyon of blackened, red brick towards the corner, when suddenly a sound came to him that made his blood freeze in his issue boots. It was the solid, scrunching tramp of many pairs of boots . . . military boots, marching in step, and closer with each footfall. A quick desperate glance disclosed that he had no ready escape. The walls were too high to mount; the street was too long to run back along. There was nothing for it but to face it out. One solitary figure in RAF uniform could hardly be lost in the crowd in an empty street. This, thought Barry to himself, was it.

With one of these flashes of inspiration which sometimes come to the desperate or the fortunate Barry stuck his cap in his pocket, and turned to face the wall to pee against it, just at the very moment the Wehrmacht rounded the corner. A squad of thirty-odd infantrymen under the charge of a spit-and-polish Feldwebel. No one turned a head to regard the pissing flyer. If anyone recognised, or even saw the grey-blue uniformed man without any headgear it was never mentioned, and every head remained steadfastly staring forward at the neck in front. The helmets, Barry reasoned, performed the function of horse-blinkers, and the pompous strutting of the Feldwebel seemed to preclude any extraneous thought or vision. The upshot was that the contingent passed without incident, the last four men stepping over the trickle of steaming urine, which ran in a swift rivulet towards the centre of the road from between the nervous feet of a British flyer who just couldn't believe his luck as he gulped, and silently and swiftly buttoned his trouser flies before hurrying on his way.

13

Brussels: Monique answered the phone on the wall.

'Restaurant Candide . . . oui. Ah, c'est vous, Grandpère... qui? ...'

Albert looked up at the mention of 'grandpère' – their code-word for Maurice, who covered the area to the east, and was the collector of all information for the area. Albert crossed quickly, and took the ear piece unceremoniously from Monique.

'What is it? I see. No . . . if it is an orphan all the more reason to try and find him. Children must be looked after, Grandpère . . . Ah . . . I see . . . Yes. Just let us know when you are ready. He may have cold . . . what with this weather and being lost . . . yes, I will. *Au'voir.*'

Albert turned round, and sighed. 'Maurice has heard that an RAF evader escaped from the police station at Meulesuyt. They haven't caught up with him yet.'

'Who tipped him off?'

'One of the gendarme's brothers works with the resistance in Antwerp. It came round to Maurice in the end. They'll keep their eyes open.'

The sound of a pan boiling over came from the small

kitchen, and Monique went to attend to it. Albert followed her, and cupped his hands under her breasts and pressed her to him while she stirred the stew in the pan. Monique held her head back against his, and tightened her arms over his wrists. She held the moment for several seconds before replacing the pan lid, and turning to kiss him, and press herself against him. It seldom happened that both felt the same inclination at the same time. There was the café, the phone, Andrée, and the almost constant attendance of someone from 'Lifeline'. It was not easy to get away and spend some time together, and making love in Albert's own room, just across the landing from Andrée's, was pushing it a bit, and inhibited them both. Only in the somewhat constricted comfort of Monique's own flat could they be truly together, and such assignations were of necessity few and far between.

'Will you come home with me this afternoon? It's over a week since you were there...'

Albert kissed her again, and nodded, then released her as a noise came from the restaurant, and he went to investigate. Monique continued her culinary supervision with pleasurable anticipation until she saw the eight soufflé dishes set out on the shelf, each containing an egg custard for Andrée. Eggs were difficult enough to come by in Brussels, and cost the earth, without using the whole damn lot for that wretched invalid, who picked at them anyway, and had nothing else to do but find fault with everything that was done for her.

Thus soured she strained the vegetable collander standing in salted water, and set about preparing hutzepot for the following day's luncheon. Albert returned similarly disgruntled.

'I must get over to the Rue Malibran. The police have been searching the next two houses. Someone must have shopped us, but didn't know the number of the house. Keep your eye on things here . . . and don't forget to take Andrée her lunch.'

'And this afternoon?' Monique's voice had a slight edge to it that Albert was not slow to appreciate. He sighed and shrugged. 'I'll come straight to your place as soon as I can get away.'

Monique sighed, and slowly sat down on the single kitchen chair. She was frustrated, unhappy, and the whole wretched situation was beginning to tell on her. Six years ago, before the war was even thought about as a possibility, she had become barmaid at Albert's previous establishment – the tiny 'Chanterelle' in the tatty Boulevard Maeterlinck – and had slowly become his reluctant mistress. Albert's wife, Andrée, was even then an invalid. After the initial intimacy Monique had assumed Albert would 'forget' her, but he hadn't. The relationship remained – clandestine and unlovely – until Monique packed her bags one Saturday and simply left.

Then came the war, and Albert bought the 'Candide'. Soon after the Germans occupied Belgium and France, Albert sought out Monique, and asked her to come back to him. He was involved with an evasion line, and needed a barmaid whom he could trust totally. There was no one else. She moved back, but this time only as a dayworker, returning to her small flat each evening after the café closed.

The relationship had resumed as a matter of course. Both had missed what each had to offer. There was no real change in anything but, then, what had they found elsewhere? Albert was nobody's idea of Adonis, but Monique liked him. She slowly realised that the resistance work had wrought something of a change in him . . . brought out and developed one side of his character which could easily have remained unknown, even to himself, had it not been for the war and his evasion-line work. Albert showed command, strength, courage, and sheer manliness that awoke the remainder of Monique to his sexual advances, and they became lovers in a way they had not hitherto. She gave herself to him without stint, and he, in turn, showed her consideration, kindness, and love.

But there was still Andrée.

14

Brabant: The town Curtis was approaching was Oarschot. That much he remembered from the quick glance at the handkerchief map.

It was foolish to attempt a town of any size until he at least acquired some papers. He took to the fields again, and skirted the main built-up area of the town.

It was when passing round a small 'street' of four 'once-rural' cottages that he was accosted. A man stepped out of the shadows, and confronted him.

'Is the Aalter farm back that way?'

The accent was thick, and Flemish. Curtis eyed him warily, and tried to swing the bundle of switches from his aching shoulder across his front to hide whatever he could. He replied that he didn't know the Aalter farm, but the questioner might try someone else further down the road. By this time the man had come close enough to be able to see every detail of the RAF uniform, and his eyes clicked upwards to stare into Curtis' face. At the same time Curtis felt a slight pressure against his lower ribs, and he realised it was the muzzle of a gun. The man then spoke in English with a strong accent.

'Just drop the bundle and walk ahead.' Curtis did as he was told. There wasn't a lot of alternative.

He was taken to the milking-yard of a near-by farm, where he was required to edge his way through the first milking. Cows lowed, and turned their heads to regard him as he pushed between their flanks in the dim, early light. His captor dug him in the back once to urge greater progress, and he stepped into a newly dropped and steaming cow-pat. The two farm hands shepherding the animals from the byre into the yard affected not to notice either of them as they entered the small dairy which leant to one side of the byre. The latter had standing for about twenty beasts, mostly Friesians, and gave a clue to the size of the holding. Inside the dairy another man waited, and eyed the two solemnly after they entered and closed the door.

'Name, rank, number?'

The question was cold, matter-of-fact, and efficient. It was not the first time they had asked the question.

'Curtis, John – Flight Lieutenant – 012578.

'Squadron?'

'That's all you're getting. Now, what about giving *me* a few answers?'

'Why should we? You are the one who needs help.'

'And how do I know I'm getting help. You could be Jerries for all I know.'

'We could. You'll find out eventually, won't you?' Then he relented a little, and grinned, offering a cigarette, which Curtis took gratefully.

'You tell us who you are. We check with London. They give us some questions to check you out properly, and if you are okay everything is fine. We can get you out of Europe quickly. You will see.'

Curtis eyed both of them through the new smoke.

'What happens now, then?'

The first man – who still held the pistol pointed at him – grinned a slightly crooked grin, more a grimace in fact, though it was not unfriendly nor without a basic humour.

'You stay here in this dairy. They don't use it any more. It's not too bad. The heat from the animals will keep you warm. Someone will bring you food. You can sleep on the straw at the back. There is water in the tap, but they will bring you a jugful from the well. It is better. Just rest. Take it easy. We will be back with someone to interrogate you in a day or so. Don't wander. You will be watched, but we won't shut you in unless you show signs of trying to get out. It is for your own safety.'

Two minutes later they were gone and the door shut. Curtis sighed, found himself a firm area of the straw where it was not too deep, nor building up internal combustion from the damp on the floor, slung a pair of sacks over the top, and settled down to sleep the sleep of the just.

It was on the fourth day of his dairy confinement that Curtis again saw the men who had brought him to the farm. This time they were accompanied by another man, obviously not a farm worker, or even a countryman, wearing a moustache, and with a broken nose. With him was a very pretty young girl of possibly nineteen years, who answered to the name 'Natalie'.

The questions were simple to answer, but he was bright enough to realise that an impostor would have had to have been impossibly thorough to have done so.

'Which school did you attend after you left the South Leeds Primary School?'

'If there is such a school as the South Leeds Primary I'll be very surprised. I've never heard of it. I went to a Church of England Primary school – St Mary the Martyr's, in Farrow Street. When I left there I went to

Ancaster Road Elementary school, and then to Leeds Grammar after the Scholarship.'

'And whose wedding did you attend the day before your thirteenth birthday?'

Curtis swallowed hard. He knew he was both angry and reddening slightly, and deeply reluctant to answer the question.

'Please answer, Flight Lieutenant.'

'My mother's.'

One of the two men who stood by the door chuckled, and Curtis shot him a glance that would have killed had it made contact. The interrogator ignored the chuckle and the reaction, and consulted his small notes once more.

'What was the name of the pilot you replaced in your present aircraft . . . the one that was shot down; and how many persons were aboard the aircraft on that last flight?'

'I replaced Squadron-Leader Horton. He died of shrapnel wounds about three months ago. There were actually six men aboard the Wellington, not five as is customary. We had a special observer with us.'

The man stood up and beamed at him.

'Thank you, Lieutenant. We will be moving you from here the day after tomorrow. We can't do it before then as we simply do not have enough room in our safe-houses. But we are expanding. We expect – and hope for – much more business in the future. The less you know about us the better, so I will make no introductions, and offer no information. I trust you understand.'

Curtis nodded. A great sense of relief had gone through his whole body. No one had said anything about him being accepted as bona fide, nor had anyone made comment upon his answers, but he sensed that he had cleared himself. The moustached man shook hands, and the girl smiled briefly. The man by the door, who had chuckled at Curtis' answer, came to him and offered his hand with a yokel's big innocent grin, as if to apologise for his behaviour. Curtis grinned back, and accepted the firm, rough handshake. Then they were gone.

The day after the morrow, as they had stated, a man came for him, a different man, who said his name was Claude, and did not bother to converse in English once he heard Curtis speak French. They left the farm quietly. There was no one to thank . . . no one wishing to know the cuckoo was no longer in the nest. Curtis and his lean companion made for the town he had passed round almost a week ago. He had been given a suit of civilian clothes, but his own shoes would have to suffice until he reached Brussels, where, he was told, he would be properly kitted out. He had an identity card, much thumbed, and really only to be used in emergency. Again he would receive proper papers in a few days.

They boarded a bus to take them into Brussels, and the journey passed uneventfully. Thanks to his language efficiency Curtis kept up a conversation without any sense of strain. The inflections, the vocabulary, even the attitudes came back to him with great rapidity, almost as if he had never been away from Europe.

15

Brussels: Curtis followed the man called Claude up the narrow staircase, across a carpeted landing, down another narrow passage, past several doors. It terminated in an elderly bathroom, which sported a huge, copper heater over one end of the ancient bath. Quickly turning a brass tap-handle on the wall behind the boiler Claude heaved, and a section of the lap-boarding hinged back revealing an opening beyond. By stepping into the bath it was possible to slip behind the copper boiler and into the opening. A steep set of steps led up into the loft and the eaves of the house. As Curtis' head emerged over the floor level he was aware of two anxious faces staring at him ... other evaders, he assumed.

Claude handed him over.

'Introduce yourselves when I've gone. Any problems?'

The tall one spoke. 'Nothing so far. It's a bit cold sometimes when the wind gets up ... under the eaves, you know. Any chance of a blanket or some sacking ... anything? Perhaps even newspaper to stuff up the holes ...'

'I will see what I can find.'

'And ... er ... the can?'

Claude nodded, and took the old bucket from the tall man's hands. No examination was necessary. The odour signified the contents. Claude returned a moment later to the sound of a flushing cistern, and handed the empty bucket back, this time containing a strong smell of carbolic.

'I return tonight.'

With that he was gone. The two men stared at Curtis before the tall one extended his hand.

'Bill Semple ... this is Joe Harris ...'

'John Curtis. Been here long?'

'Six weeks for me ... two-and-half for Joe. Seems like half-a-century. I take it the war is still on?'

'Neither of us speak much French ... Now there's three of us they might take us down the line.'

Little Joe's anxiety was evident and asking for confirmation.

'I expect you're right. I speak fluent French as a matter of fact. That could be useful.'

'You been going long?'

'Not so long. Two weeks-three days. I was picked up by "Lifeline" four days ago, but I wasn't cleared until this afternoon . . . They're thorough. I like that. It makes me feel safe. I think they are ruthless, too, if the need arose. That makes me feel even safer.'

'That's about how I see it. Have you met Yvette, yet?'

'I don't think so. Someone called Dirk found me, and I was interrogated by a man with a broken nose . . . Albert, I think they called him. There was a girl present, but I didn't hear her name.'

Joe beamed, and looked up at him with fervour.

'Wait till you meet Yvette! Brother! She's a honey! She runs the whole shebang, I think. She can't be very old, but she's beautiful. I think I'm in love.'

Curtis could not help smiling at Joe's ingenuousness and his obvious enthusiasm. Bill grinned.

'He's been like this for over a week. Better find yourself a corner . . . and watch out for draughts.'

Two days passed uneventfully. Curtis went through the process of becoming stiff in certain joints, and then loosening up again. The loft became smaller, draughtier, smellier. Neither of his companions were talkative, so they did not get on each other's nerves. Late in the third day they heard a scuffling, the sound of the door opening, and feet on the ladder. One second later a very pretty female head wearing a headscarf appeared through the opening between the floorboards. The dark eyes glanced from one to the other, and settled on Curtis before the face broke into a radiant smile. It was Yvette.

'Is everyone all right?'

Bill and Joe crossed to her with eagerness. Curtis joined them, and all three attempted to assist her onto the rafters then across to where the sides of tea-chests had made a floored-area that was 'home'. As they talked Curtis studied her. His companions had not exaggerated. She was indeed very attractive, and the face was both delightful, and reassuring. She had an air of confidence and competence that was disarming to anyone disposed to question her authority. Indeed that very authority sat well upon her. At length she turned to him.

'So. You are John Curtis, I understand. I am also told that you speak almost perfect French.'

Without more ado she launched into a long, fast-speaking statement of their position, what was expected of them, and proposals for moving. Curtis replied in like fashion. At last she smiled.

'They were right. You speak excellent French, and very idiomatic. Tomorrow I want you to take these two out into the streets, and just walk about, behaving naturally. You must get used to rubbing shoulders with French and Belgian people, and not take panic at the sight of a German uniform. It is very important. When you leave here you will probably be travelling with German officers. It is essential that you behave naturally, and you will only do that if you become accustomed to it. Someone will take you out quite early. He will have all your relevant papers, properly stamped. You must understand that these are perfectly good documents. There is no need to be nervous of them. Both the document itself and the stamp are genuine. They are NOT forgeries. Only your names and particulars are fictitious. You will spend one half-hour learning every detail before you go out.' Then a warm smile. 'Okay?'

Forty seconds later she was gone.

16

'This is the Avenue Louise. Up at that end is the park ... and the Gestapo headquarters.'

The man who was escorting them was dark, probably mid-thirties, and walked with a limp. They knew him as 'Jacques'. He walked with Joe, slightly ahead, apparently deep in conversation. Curtis and Bill Semple followed some fifteen yards behind. That way there was someone who spoke French with either pair, though they had been warned that at the first hint of trouble Jacques would melt into the landscape, and they would be left to their own devices.

They crossed the main Boulevard watching the two-car trams that clattered past laden with Brussels citizens on their way to work. Before them the towering bulk of the Palais de Justice loomed.

'I am sorry you cannot go to the terrace, and look over the spread of Brussels. The only tourists here now are German. You would look like visitors, and questions could be asked. This way...'

Jacques led them away down in the Sablons, and through towards the centre of the city. The initial nervousness still persisted... at least in Joe and Bill Semple, who knew their lack of speech and accent would give them away. Both pinned a deal of faith on Curtis, who had impressed them not only by his language capability, but also with his general cool competence and lack of 'nerves'.

As always, of course, one could walk about a city all day, and never exchange a word with anyone. Unlike country dwellers, people did not exchange pleasantries at the drop of a hat. Metropolitan citizens tend to remain inside their own cocoons, and leave the world and his wife to their own devices.

It was on the corner of the Rue de l'Etuve, behind the Grand Place, where the first incident occurred. Jacques had stopped, and was talking quietly to Joe when a Wehrmacht corporal and two privates, burly in their grey uniforms, rounded the bend, and made for them. Joe froze in terror, and Jacques was momentarily unnerved as the corporal spoke to him in execrable French interspersed with German words. Curtis realised they were only seeking direction, and that if Jacques could not handle this situation there was little hope of them moving across Europe. He grabbed Bill's wrist, and crossed the road, talking quickly but quietly while Bill listened to the gabble he did not understand, and tried not to glance at little Joe.

Apparently all went well as they were joined later by Jacques, and a very pale and shaken Joe. In the Place St Catherine they found a small café. Jacques led them inside, and deposited them at a table while he collected the drinks.

Bill, looking desperately English in his rather upright good nature, beamed at all and sundry, whose frozen, unmelting, grim scowls implied they regarded him as a half-wit. Joe simply examined the surface of the table, and picked at a spot of dried gravy with his finger-nail until Jacques arrived with four beers.

'Cheers!' quoth Bill in best Home Counties salutation. Curtis felt the finger of doom suddenly pointing, and glared at his tall companion. The latter got the message, and hastily downed a throat-full before paling, and staring questioningly at Jacques.

'What in hell is that? It tastes like stale beer mixed with Ribena. Christ Almighty!'

Jacques merely grinned. 'It is called *"Kriek"*. It is a

Brussels drink. We like it, though it is not so good now.'

The others refrained from comment, not wishing to offend the purchaser. After all, any beer was better than no beer . . . almost. As they glanced about with a certain apprehension they were aware of four German soldiers at one table playing dominoes with devout concentration. Curtis glanced quickly at his companions. Bill and Joe regarded the enemy with nervous awareness, doing, in fact, exactly what they had been brought out to learn not to do. Someone slapped Jacques on the back as he passed, eliciting a grin and some coarse comment that made the next table roar with laughter.

Bill nudged Curtis' arm. 'They mix with the ruddy Krauts just as if they were anyone else. I don't get it.' Curtis eyed Bill and spoke very quietly. 'What the hell d'you expect? D'you think it would be very different in the Old Kent Road?' Bill's astonished eyes fixed him for a moment before realisation dawned. They sat out the next twenty minutes with a few exchanges in French between Jacques and Curtis, and then left quietly. Once outside Curtis rounded on Bill once more.

'Bill, you're not even trying! You said "Sorry" to that bloke by the door. For Chris' sake, man, *think* will you!'

Back in the loft area they went over the routine, and discussed small happenings before settling down to a tough crash-course in French-speaking. Curtis found himself, like the others, waiting for the arrival of someone bringing food or news, and hoping it was Yvette.

During the days that followed she came three times. The visits were brief, to the point, and little more than morale boosters. She intimated that they could be moved quite quickly down the first leg of the route to some undisclosed destination north of Paris, where they would again be expected to hole up for several days. She spoke of the routine in general terms, mentioning neither names nor places, but it was apparent that the pace of movement depended not merely on the availability of guides but on the moveworthiness of the evaders.

She stressed again and again how much depended upon them . . . their ability to melt into the daily scene . . . to become self-reliant in case of problems . . . and virtually to ignore the existence of their guides while away from safe-houses.

They were taken out five or six times. Always by Jacques, and never to the same places. By the end of the stay both Joe and Bill were infinitely more at ease, and no longer panicked at the sight of a grey uniform. Curtis was becoming bored and anxious. He was also beginning to live for the next visit of their mentor. Yvette remained distant but friendly. She must have realised that at least half of the evaders she helped left Europe with a candle burning in their hearts for the girl who had given them so much. Not least their life.

17

Soudon: One of the new Opel '*Blitz*' 3-ton trucks thundered into the yard followed by the Kubelwagen. As Leutnant Schippers stepped out of the car the tail-flap of the *Blitz* was already down, and his men urging the four RAF prisoners to get out. The latter were very young, like most of the Luftwaffe, but not so young as the latest Wehrmacht contingents. The war was beginning to feed on the teenagers. Soon it would be the children.

Brandt replaced the black-out curtain of the office and switched on the light once more. He had been standing peering into the dark, awaiting the arrival of his best squad with some anticipation. Now that he had a chance to inspect personally every area-unit, and bring it up to scratch purely on an administrative level, he was taking the opportunity of seeing them in action. Schippers' squad had gone out before he got there – another good point for Schippers. He didn't mess about. His unit were on the ball, and worked with enthusiasm in a job that normally excited very little.

Schippers entered, saluted, then smiled his pleasure in seeing his superior . . . especially at a time of accomplishment. His report was brief and to the point. Facts as he knew them, opinions only if they were relevant and pertinent. Fifteen minutes after arrival the first RAF man was brought into the office for interrogation. He stood with some formality and much nervousness. He was a Flight Sergeant, and probably eighteen, but looked seventeen. Brandt felt suddenly fatherly. These men were his enemies, yet he felt no bitterness or animosity. Only sorrow for the stupid game they had all been caught up into.

'Sit down, Flight Sergeant. Cigarette?'

The mumbled thanks upon taking the offered cigarette was riddled with anticipation. Brandt knew the Gestapo's reputation had preceded them (as, indeed, had been intended), and had been attributed to *all* Germans, and he was ashamed momentarily. Gefreiter Hartwig entered with a mug of steaming tea. That was a touch of Schippers'. The Leutnant had thought, with some justification, that the downed British flyer would be set at ease quicker with a hot cup of tea, than with any of the ersatz brews his own men drank (and in most cases preferred. Tea, if there was any, was not popular). The young Englishman took it with something of the surprised relief that it was calculated to encourage. Brandt suppressed a smile, and continued.

'Name... rank... number?'

'Lowe... L, O, W, E... Flight Sergeant... 014864.'

'Squadron?'

Flight Sergeant Lowe paused, gripped his mug tighter, and looked up with basic, innocent candour.

'I'm sorry, sir. Name–rank–number. That is all that is required of me. It is all you will get.'

Brandt regarded him with as much severity as he could assume. Under the gaze the Englishman flinched, more out of embarrassment at being unable to oblige than anything else. Slowly he rose and stood before his interrogator. Brandt smiled.

'Very well, sergeant. We will talk with you later. Send in the next man. Thank you.' He watched the young man breathe an obvious sigh of relief, and turn to leave.

'Take your tea with you. It may be quite some time before we can offer you another one.'

'Sir.'

The young man grabbed his tea, and left the office. Brandt exchanged glances with Schippers who sat to one side, more or less out of the light of the desk area. If this had been Gestapo the lighting, apart from anything else, would have been reversed. The next RAF man entered, tall and rangy, with an exaggeratedly jutting jaw, and an expression of rough good humour. He was not so intimidated as his Flight Sergeant.

'Sit down, Flight Lieutenant.'

'I'll stand if it's all the same to you, sport.'

The Australian accent you could cut with a knife. Brandt ignored the lack of officer-respect. It wasn't meant as an insult. He knew enough of the British and their allies to have recognised certain qualities. It was just their way.

'Very well. Name . . . rank . . . number, please.'

'Hewson . . . Flight Lieutenant . . . 016363. That's your lot, squire.'

'D'you want some tea, Lieutenant?'

'Too right, mate. Good on you. Any tucker going?'

This time Brandt could not cover the grin that the Aussie's voice and appearance provoked. Schippers, too saw the humour of the situation, and changed position on the chair.

'You are a long way from home, Lieutenant. Are there many of you in the RAF?'

'Not a lot, mate. I came over a year back to spy out the land. I reckon the Pommies know what they're doing. I told the lads back home. There's half a million on the way. They're tough boys, mate. I'd get out if I were you.'

'D'you like the new Lancaster? How does it handle?'

'I like it fine. Never flown one, though. Don't think you blokes'll go for them much. Not on the receiving-end.'

'What were you flying tonight?'

'Would you believe a Tiger-Moth? No . . . didn't think you would. Well, if that's it, cobber, I'll be getting along. Ta for the tea.'

Brandt nodded. There was nothing coming from Flight Lieutenant Hewson. The gangling pilot grinned a wide and friendly grin, and sloped out of the office clutching his tin mug. Brandt smiled at Schippers before turning back.

'They are very different from us, Schippers. It is difficult to dislike them. Next!'

18

Brussels: It was on the eighth day of his confinement in the attic that Curtis was asked to come down from the loft, and join the man with the slight limp, Jacques, in the house kitchen. The man who had originally interrogated him, the one they called 'Albert', was waiting.

'Flight Lieutenant Curtis. We would like you to assist us in something. You speak excellent French, and seem at ease in Belgium, so there is no real danger in taking you with us. Do you agree to help?'

'Ordinarily I would ask what you wanted me to do before I agreed to anything. But you are risking your lives for my sake at the moment. The least I can do is take you on trust. Of course, I will help if I can.'

'Good. First we will take you into the country. There is something I want you to see.'

They left the house, and went off through the drizzle towards the fish-market. There a tarpaulin-covered truck, with a gas-feeding mechanism on the cabin roof, awaited them. It was loaded high with old wooden fish-boxes, many broken and cornered with pieces of tin cut from soup-tins, beans-tins, fruit-tins, presumably to continue the life of the wooden boxes no longer available.

'Put this on.' Curtis was given a black jacket, stiff with dried-out damp and fishscales. It stank to high heaven of years of fish-handling. As he wriggled into the garment Albert and the man Jacques carefully loaded a galvanised tray-container onto the truck, and covered it with boxes. From the drips on the ground it obviously held water.

They piled into the cab, Albert driving, and soon were speeding down the road in the direction of Antwerp. At

Willebroek they turned to the left, and headed for the Scheldt estuary. Just before they came to the river they turned left again, and proceeded with caution down back roads until they came to the banks of the river itself. There the truck left the road, and jogged over rough clay, down the side of a birch copse, until the ground became soft. Jacques mumbled to Albert that they had gone far enough, and Albert cut the engine, and drew up the hand-brake. They sat for three or four moments before opening the doors, and climbing down. All appeared quiet.

Jacques and Albert manhandled the galvanised trough from the truck, and carried it with them, together with an eel-net, round the end of the trees away from the truck. There the land seemed to open out and breathe. Ahead was the broad river, and a great expanse of sand and mud flats. The two men put down the trough near the water's edge, glanced about them keenly, then told Curtis to follow them. East Flanders stretched out beyond . . . flat and uneventful to the Dutch border, eight or nine miles across the other side of the river.

Then he saw it. The wrecked ribs and plates of an aircraft lay in two small piles, half out of the mud, with other pieces of wreckage and one engine strewn about, half in water, half in mud. Albert led the way to the larger debris, and they stood looking at it for some moments. No one spoke. Curtis decided to wait until someone said something to him and examined the remnants of the crashed aircraft . . . a Whitley by the look of it . . . except . . .

Curtis frowned and peered closer. There was something odd about the wreckage.

'Well?' The question came from Albert. 'What is it?'

'I don't know . . . I thought it was a Whitley, but there's something wrong with it. It's just not right . . .'

Albert glanced at Jacques with a smug look on his face.

'That's exactly what we thought. It is supposed to have crashed three nights ago. Two of the supposed crew have been picked up. We think there's something not right about them too. We wanted another opinion . . . preferably from someone who knew what he was talking about. You've told us all we need to know.'

Jacques was half listening, he had the eel-net in the shallows, and was stirring up the soft mud gently, with a dragging motion.

Almost at the same moment there was a shout in German. All three turned to see four German soldiers running towards them, carbine already extended in one case, hand wrapped in the webbing-strap, covering the three of them as the corporal and his two back-ups ran towards them, their boots splashing in the shallow water.

'Halt! Verstehen sie . . . Hände hoch!'

Curtis felt suddenly cold and stupid, but Albert and Jacques merely shrugged, and put up their hands. Jacques had a single eel wriggling in the net as he held it high, dripping and flapping.

'Papieren.'

All the carbines now pointed at them as slowly they each slid one hand into an inside pocket to bring out their identity-papers and permits.

'What are you doing here?'

'Just getting some eels . . . they're good round here . . . Look . . .'

Jacques indicated the trough lying twenty yards further away with water flap-lapping round it. The corporal studied the papers and glanced at the trough, then nodded to one of his men to examine it. The man kicked off the lid when he reached it, and stared for some moments before turning back and grinning widely.

'It's full . . . dozens of the buggers. Hey, Corp . . . why don't we confiscate them? I fancy a few eels.'

The Gefreiter looked up into each of the faces in turn as he returned the papers.

'You shouldn't be here. It's a restricted area.'

Albert feigned ignorance and looked apologetic.

'I'm sorry. We didn't know that. There's no notices up. How are we supposed to know?'

'You should make it your business to know. You came from Brussels this morning?'

'Yes. We fancied a few eels. Used to come every week before the war. We're not doing any harm.'

'All right. Get back in the truck, and on your way. You can leave the eels where they are.'

Albert and Jacques put up a good display of grumbling as they shuffled back towards the truck, with Curtis in the rear looking indignant. The soldiers did not follow. Two were showing amused interest in the writhing eels while their mates watched the three of them return to their truck, pile in, and slowly drive off.

No one spoke for a couple of miles, but there was a grim satisfaction about Albert's expression. Curtis realised how thorough these people were. The trough of eels was simple and effective, likely to be useful as both cover and bribe without being obvious as either. Finally Curtis turned to him.

'I could be wrong about that Whitley. I don't think I am . . . but I could be. What happens to the two aircrew?'

Albert didn't take his eyes off the road even for a second.

'We get rid of them.'

Curtis sensed the reply before it came, but even so the cold matter-of-factness chilled him, and gave him pause.

'Wait a minute . . . I could be wrong . . .'

'You aren't. The fact that we doubt is enough. We can't risk it. They have to go. It won't be the first plant the Germans have tried, but we haven't had one in this area before. Luckily our people are thorough. Yvette will have it no other way. We cannot afford mistakes.'

There was no room for argument. Curtis sat back, and decided against any appeal for clemency. They knew their business . . . and they were right. He was realist enough to recognise that.

The remainder of the journey was passed in silence. Twice they were stopped, and forced to show their papers, but there were no incidents. They entered Brussels through Vilvoorde, and ran parallel to the canal until they turned off to Schaarbeek. Jacques took over as driver after dropping Albert and Curtis near the station, and drove off towards Molenbeek.

Ten minutes walk brought them to the Café Candide, where Curtis followed Albert through the bar to the back room. Yvette was sitting at the simple wooden table awaiting their return. Her initial questioning glance was obviously answered satisfactorily by Albert, who silently divested himself of his stinking jacket, and held out his hands to take Curtis's own.

'You won't be sorry to get rid of that. They smell rather badly. I hope it doesn't linger too long.'

Yvette looked at Curtis as he sat down opposite her.

'Thank you for your help. What is your opinion?'

Albert spoke up without waiting for Curtis's reply.

'He thinks as we do. It's too dangerous. Claude will have to get rid of them . . . now.'

Yvette nodded solemnly. 'Will you tell him, Albert? Get rid of the uniforms. There must be no trace. Burn them. I don't want the bodies to be found. Let them just disappear without trace, then the Germans can draw whatever conclusions they wish.'

Curtis found himself staring at this small, rather beautiful girl giving orders for the death of two men. Not that her attitude was callous or superficial. It wasn't that. It was only that her whole appearance ran counter to the terrible business she was directing with such cold, calm expertise. Albert returned from depositing the fishy garments in his cellar and after exchanging a few comments with Yvette went into the bar, both to phone the decision through, and to attend to his business. Yvette and Curtis sat facing each other over the bottle of red wine that Albert had put before them. Curtis poured out two glasses, then sipped the wine silently. Yvette did not touch hers until he spoke.

'You haven't told me much about "Lifeline". I'd like to know.'

The question seemed puerile the moment he had uttered it. Yvette looked at him with her large dark eyes.

'There is almost nothing I can tell you that would not put us at risk. You already know too much. More, in fact, than anyone of your evaders ever has.'

'Don't you trust me?'

'I have no choice. But it is not a matter of trust. It is a matter of *knowing*. Whatever a man knows the Germans can get out of him. They are highly expert in that field, and have no qualms about how they extract it. I am sure you know this already . . . but knowing about it is one thing. Living with that reality is another.'

'You do a marvellous job. I am not just grateful . . . I'm really impressed by the way you all go about it. It is very professional.'

'We would not be here to talk about it if it was not, my friend. That is why we cannot take chances . . . of any sort. Do you really understand that?'

'I think so.' He paused and looked into her eyes. 'I

understand you are having problems ... something to do with safe-houses?'

'Yes. We frequently have to change our route. Safe-houses become suspect, and once that happens we can no longer use them. Always we need new additional routes, and more and more trusted personnel. It is not easy to find either.'

The conversation continued for a quarter of an hour before Jacques returned, on foot, to take Curtis back to his place of concealment. On the way back he reflected that, for all their conversation, Yvette had told him nothing, and he knew as much about 'Lifeline' as he had done the previous day ..., no more.

The following day Yvette decided to follow up a lead. Reluctant as she was to take anything on trust, it was necessary to augment, and to follow through that increase. But how, and where?

Yvette knew Eugène Bergers only slightly. She had interviewed him initially, and met him subsequently once or twice. He was a very average man, late forties, balding. Unremarkable in every way but, like her uncle, apparently courageous, and determined to help a cause in which he had faith. He ran a fish shop.

'They tell me you have a suggestion to make, Eugène. I'm sorry I could not come yesterday ... there was a child on the run, and things became confused. I could not leave.'

'Please ... come into the back shop.'

Bergers expertly wrapped up a piece of bream in old newspaper and weighed it, then walked briskly into the back shop past the fat woman in the 'box' who took the money. Yvette followed. The small store was mainly occupied by empty fish boxes stacked in unequal columns. No contents filled the boxes, but each one retained the 'nose' of its previous occupants. Bergers closed the door and wiped his hands on his sack apron.

'Albert says there is a problem further south . . . I don't know where. Someone has been caught. I know some . . . people. They have their headquarters in Liège. They, too, operate an evasion line, a good one. They might be willing to work with us . . . if only temporarily.'

Yvette regarded him silently and pensively.

'You know them well?'

Bergers shrugged expansively. 'So-so. I know one of them as an old friend. He tells me things because he knows I am active as well. You could go and see them . . . find out?'

Yvette nodded after a moment's thought, and Bergers brought a piece of paper from his flannel-shirt breast-pocket and slipped it inside the fish parcel as he handed it to her.

When she reached her home she unwrapped the fish while her aunt busied herself in preparation of vegetables. Louise expressed delight in the fine piece of fish, which was slowly becoming as rare as decent meat. Yvette found her own satisfaction in the address written on the paper.

19

Liège: Lisa crossed the bridge and walked down the embankment towards the sun. On such a day Liège looked less heavy. Her mother had repeatedly told her how, in summer days as a child, she had always thought of Liège as gay . . . just as she imagined Vienna to be.

Whatever it had been then it was now drab and oppressed, with all the weight of German domination that the rich, evening light lifted only momentarily as it bathed the roof-tops and the domes in a warm, autumnal glow.

A Wehrmacht Oberst came from one of the expensive apartments that flanked the river's embankment – apartments now at the disposal of the conquerors together with their ladies of easy virtue, their furnishings and their amenities. It was toward the end of the working-day, and bikes were beginning to pour from the factories and work places. Lisa kept a close look out, for few had bells or any other form of warning. Crossing a main road at such a time was a new hazard for pedestrians. For some reason all the bikes brought out of retirement to replace motorised transport had no bells. One of the mysteries of the century... a 'Marie Celeste' of bicycle bells!

The Place Solange Rohr led off the main thoroughfare. The Hôtel de Ville was draped with huge Nazi flags, billowing gently in the soft breeze, The vehicles outside – and they were plentiful enough – were all German in origin, or commandeered by pompous or frightened officials. It was not merely contempt in Lisa's heart as she walked past... it was sadness. Sadness for her country, her people, and for all wretched, weak humanity that hoped to save themselves and their progeny by carrion behaviour engendered by their fear.

She turned into the Place, and made for the turning at the far end. The short street was a cul-de-sac with a small, insignificant garage at the end. The garage occupied an arch which passed under the railway elevation, with space enough to house four cars and little else. Jules Cassares wiped his hands, richly engrained with black grease, on a rag as he watched the approach of the petite and attractive girl with the shoulder-bag. This one would be good for a lay. Pretty too. He stepped forward and grinned, conscious that his slightly lop-sided grimace was considered sexy by the local girls, and that his dirty singlet, and tight trousers displayed his masculinity to perfection.

'Can I help you, Mam'selle?'

'I am looking for M'sieur Cassares. Is this his garage?'

'Louis or Jules ... Cassares?'

'M'sieur Louis.'

Jules sighed, and made a shrugging gesture as if to say 'your mistake, you poor child.'

'Papa!'

At the call a large, fat man in a grey, ill-fitting suit appeared in the doorway that led to the small office. He did not speak, merely glanced at his son, then at Lisa. An imperceptible glance behind her into the street preceded the soft smile and grunt of welcome.

'You wish to see me, Mam'selle?'

'If you are M'sieur Louis Cassares.' The fat man nodded quickly and waited for her to continue. 'I have come from Brussels. I am to tell you that the Black Citroen you requested in January is awaiting three tyres before it can be delivered.'

The older man stared at her for a long time before he made any movement at all, then he nodded as if to her message, and indicated with his hand that she was to come into the office. Jules grinned once more, and took the sweat-rag from round his throat, and wiped his forehead as he advanced towards the office.

'Get Leprat to stay outside, and keep his eyes open.'

The young man obeyed his father's command, and ran up the narrow wooden stairway that led to upper premises on the side of the street. Lisa entered the office, and sat in a hard and grimy chair facing the littered desk and the inevitable pin-up calendar on the wall amid a plethora of notices, and advertisements.

Blue-and-yellow Michelin posters, now dog-eared and grubby, gave tyre-pressures, and advised upon the respective merits of differing treads.

Louis Cassares grunted as he lowered his flabby torso into the Lloyd-loom chair, and never took his eyes from Lisa's face until Jules returned and closed the door. The younger man had obviously stopped before a mirror en route, and his black, shiny hair glistened and curled over his handsome face. The sweat-rag had been replaced by a red handkerchief, knotted with expert casualness. There was also an air of slight puzzlement that this young and attractive girl was not swooning at the sight of such male pulchritude. His father glanced at him under heavy lids.

'Sit down, Jules . . . Try and forget your mother thinks you are just like Gilbert Roland. Hollywood is a long way away. For you it is the other side of the moon. You are Yvette?' The last was uttered in almost the same breath, and took Lisa by surprise.

'We have been expecting you. "Le Lapin" told us about you, and that you would be coming to work with us . . . perhaps. But he did not tell us some things we would like to know.' He paused. 'What are your politics, Mam'selle?'

'I am a loyal Belgian. I will fight the Boche in any way I can. Is there something else?'

The fat man shrugged as if to say, 'Don't be a child', and regarded her once more with his heavy-lidded gaze. He picked his nose for a moment, and twisted the black hairs emerging from it, then spoke to her with almost pedantic care.

'You have . . . socialist . . . sympathies, Mam'selle? You perhaps wish to see certain changes in our country after the war is over?'

'I don't understand what you mean...'

'Don't play naïve, Mam'selle Yvette. You know exactly what I mean. You are a member of the party, perhaps? How did you meet Eugène Bergers?'

Lisa suddenly felt very alone, and quite out of her element. Something was different from what she imagined. These men were not simply patriots working to overthrow Germany. There was something else. She was, indeed, politically naïve, but not so green as to miss the drift of the conversation. Already she knew the contact was an error. The mistake she would later rectify, but it was important she now extricated herself without leaving anything behind to incriminate. When the political allegiance went, the national loyalty might falter.

'I went to see Eugène Bergers because there was some suggestion that *we* could help each other. I think he was probably wrong. You seem to be self-sufficient. We are ... and intend to remain so.'

The fat figure of Cassares shifted uneasily in his chair, and he let his eyes examine her from shoe to headscarf, though it was an examination devoid of lechery, merely assessing. The son was still grinning inanely, and picking his shining, white teeth with a quill as he devoured Lisa with predatory intent. She sat still and unmoving in her chair, and fixed Cassares with a blank stare.

At length the man nodded repeatedly and sighed.

'There is nothing you can do for us, Mam'selle. Thank you for coming. It is best that we go our own ways. My son will take you to the station, and see that you are unmolested.'

'Will someone protect me from your son, M'sieur?'

Without as much as a backward glance Lisa stood up, shouldered her bag, and walked out of the office, watched by a gaping, handsome idiot, and a cunning, rapacious old man, whose lusts were for other things than female flesh. No one followed.

'Lifeline' could manage without such friends.

20

Senlis, France: Lisa slipped her foot from the pedal and dropped neatly from the bicycle. She wheeled it to the huge, wooden doors, and rang the bell in the wall. While she waited for an answer she propped the bike against the high, stone wall, and pretended to interest herself in the contents of the saddle-bag while her eyes scanned the small square for passers-by, or itinerant watchers. There was no one. As usual the Place de la Laitière was quiet as the grave. The door opened an inch, and an eye surveyed the visitor before opening wide to admit both Lisa and bike. Berthe, the old servant, clopped ahead of her down the path, her ancient wooden sabots dragging small rivulets in the gravel.

In the great house Madeleine Chantal waited to greet her, standing before the immense, stone fireplace, her hands clasped before her, her back as stiff as a ramrod. But the formality of the stance took nothing from the warmth of the greeting.

'Yvette . . . my dear. I am so glad you could come, and grateful that it was so quickly. Did you take a taxi?'

'Of course not, Madeleine. I took the train to Chantilly, and there I borrowed a bicycle from a friend. It is safer . . . and in the long run more useful.' Lisa glanced at the firm and taut expression of Madeleine's lined face.

'You'd better tell me the problem.'

'Sophie is making coffee. When she comes I will . . . Your children are well, and upstairs in their rooms, so do not concern yourself for them.'

Sophie entered bearing a tray with Sèvres cups and saucers, and a silver coffee-pot and jug. She beamed and twittered at Lisa.

'Yvette! How lovely to see you! Now just sit still, and have some coffee. It's not what we like to serve, of course, but the best we can get these days.' Having put down the tray she turned and kissed Lisa's cheek.

'I do so hope we haven't upset your plans by asking you to call. You see, dear, we seem to have a problem . . .'

'Pour the coffee, Sophie.'

Madeleine spoke with authority, not acerbity, then turned her attention wholly to Lisa.

'Madeau is dead. No one came for the boys, then we heard there had been some resistance trouble, and made enquiries. It seemed he joined an attempt to sabotage the railway junction at Lagny — it is the main line to Germany — and something went wrong. Eight of them were shot, and died. Madeau was among the dead.'

'The fool!' Lisa's vehemence was anger at Madeau's disobeying the first rule of the evasion lines — not to take part in any other resistance activity, and thereby jeopardise the line. She was sorry that Madeau was dead, of course, but that meant a trained guide had to be replaced at a time when airmen were pouring into the main channel to be sent down to Spain as quickly as they could safely manage.

Sophie handed her a cup of grey-brown liquid. It smelt as bitter as it doubtless tasted, but Lisa stirred with an almost involuntary motion. Her mind was already racing to stop the gap, and produce a substitute guide. Natalie would have to come and take the bunch from

Lisa's hands in Paris. A phone-call would take care of that. But who could be found to replace Madeau as the area guide. Senlis was the principal safe-house for 'Lifeline', and consequently the position of Senlis guide was more than slightly important to the whole evasion operation.

'Do you have anyone in mind, Yvette?'

Lisa shook her head. 'Someone will have to come from Brussels until I can find a substitute . . . Natalie will do the route from Paris for the moment . . . she would anyway. I trust her more than anyone. I can take the present lot to the next safe-house.'

'If you tell me where it is I can take them . . .'

Sophie's offer was touching as well as futile. The idea of a seventy-year-old lady, vague at the best of times, being responsible for guiding four grown men into a hotbed of the enemy was droll, though Lisa knew that the sweet old dear meant to do just that, and saw no particular reason why she should not.

'Thank you, Sophie, but I need you here. Besides it is better if no one but the guide knows the safe-house to go to.'

'I asked if you had anyone in mind because there is someone I think you might consider.'

Madeleine, still regal and stiff by the fireplace, produced a small photograph from the purse which she wore attached to her belt . . . a visible sign that she was chatelaine, and intended that none should mistake the position.

The snap was of a freckle-faced boy of eighteen or nineteen years, smiling at the camera with a certain shyness that was beguiling.

'Who is he?'

'He is the son of our schoolmaster here in Senlis. He is nineteen and a fine young man. We have known him all his life, and would trust him completely. He has a personal reason for being willing to help. Sophie and I were making it possible for him to attend the Sorbonne when he came of age, though I hasten to say he is not motivated by gratitude to two old hens interfering in his life. No, he has a more pertinent reason to be of use. He has only eighteen months or two years at the most to live.'

Sophie's eyes had already filled with tears at the thought.

'It is so sad ... he is such a nice boy.'

'Don't interrupt, Sophie! He has a lung disease. I forget its name, but it is terminal, I am assured. One lung is already collapsed. He tried to volunteer for military service, but was refused, naturally. Even the Germans seem not to want him for their labour-gangs, or whatever they call them. I can easily arrange for him to have treatment in Paris regularly ... it would give him reason to travel. His papers are in order ... and he is keen to put the remainder of his life to use. You would be doing *him* a kindness, Yvette ... as well as a service to "Lifeline".'

'Very well. I will have him checked-out ... and then meet him, if all is well.'

'Good. Now I think you ought to see your charges. They're champing at the bit rather. Can't say I'm surprised. They've been here rather a long time.'

21

Paris: There was no doubt about it – Barry had got the hang of the place. The purloined clothing and the beret

– especially the beret – gave him a sense of occasion, as well as making him feel that he melted into the scene as to the manner born. His four weeks of moving about had given him confidence and a smattering of the lingo. It managed to get him by, despite the atrocious accent and unbelievable grammar. But Barry had effrontery. There is no more highly effective survival ingredient than effrontery. It carries all before it, and Barry was flexing his muscles.

Barry had always wanted to see Paris, and the hundred sights familiar from photographs and books were going to his head. The Arc de Triomphe, the Champs Elysées, the Madeleine, l'Opéra, Notre Dame de Paris, the Seine, the embankment stalls, the cafés . . . it was all just as he imagined. The colour was a bit greyer, but what could you expect with a couple of thousand German uniforms cluttering up the place?

He had already sat at three pavement cafés, and downed three glasses of beer when he decided that what he really fancied was a decent cuppa char, and so it was on the corner of the Boulevard des Capucines that he made for an outside table, and indicated to a waiter that despite appearances he was indeed a customer.

'*Tasse de thé*,' quoth Barry, about to add the word 'mate', and hastily changing it to 'cock', which seemed to him to have a more Gallic ring to it. Whatever he made of it the bland garçon went inside to order the brew, and Barry basked in the late morning sunshine, and savoured the air. Barry decided that you wouldn't know a bloody war was on, all those Frogs ambling about in their fitted costumes, or business-suits, or whatever. There were a few Jerries padding up and down like American tourists, flashing cameras, and ogling the girls, who, on the whole, seemed grateful for the ogling. Barry sighed philiso-phically. You couldn't blame them, whatever they said.

They were only young once, and a young bloke was a young bloke, German or not. What did anyone expect them to do? There was no such thing as patriotic biology. Thus sure of society Barry sipped his tea – which was foul.

It was then that he espied the three Jerries. Laughing and merry – possibly even slightly intoxicated – they stood before l'Opéra, on the steps, cajoling a street photographer to take a picture of them before Garnier's edifice. The man with the tripod seemed reluctant to accept either his clients or their offer, for he was gesticulating wildly, and generally being difficult.

Euphoria does strange things, and Barry Parks was euphoric. Leaving his coins by the saucer Barry rose to his feet and sauntered across the Place de l'Opéra, ignoring the few vehicles that chuffed and coughed their steamy way through the wartime streets, till he arrived beside the irritated and intimidated photographer, now reluctantly posing the three conquerors.

Barry stopped and examined the camera, then peered through the back plate, only to find the whole thing upside-down on the frosted glass. Slowly he edged his head round, and round, until the upside-down world righted itself. He considered the matter. With serious mien, and an obvious artistic flair, he joined the *maître d'occasion*, and, in truly Chaplinesque fashion, assisted in shuffling the flower of the Fatherland from side to side to accommodate the demanding plate. He then retired to view the result from the vantage of tripod, accompanying the thoroughly angry photographer, and offering comments in plain English.

After a few words the good man gawped, realised the situation, and broke into a smile of complicity, inviting Barry to do his worst. Barry stepped forward, and mumbled incomprehensibly as he edged and shifted the

Wehrmacht trio, who now appeared delighted that the stranger had brought a smile to the face of their grumbling photographer, and complied with his every request.

Finally all was to Barry's liking and, with great show of bonhomie, turned the trio into a foursome, and posed with Gallic flair under his beret. The Germans accepted the gesture of solidarity and fraternisation, and were immediately immortalised on film. Hand-shakes all round were in order, and all five repaired to the nearest café for a drink. Barry quite enjoyed the situation, and accepted it as his due, but the poor photographer, who seemed to rejoice in the joke, had difficulty in maintaining any sense of decorum, and could not keep it to himself. He leant backwards in his seat, and explained it to a neighbour, who hurriedly passed it on, and so on. By the time the three grateful Germans left with unsteady bows to their new-found friends, thirty heads were wreathed in smiles, and watching with bated breath for any new development.

Immediately the Germans left, the entire café descended upon Barry to congratulate him, and knead and slap his shoulder, declaring their intent to regale their respective families, and neighbours with the story. Thirty drinks appeared like magic, and Barry mentally decided that the war was not lost while B. Parks could inspire Europe with such fervent good humour.

What happened after that remained a mystery. Barry awoke between the bars of a rusty, iron bedstead covered with none-too-clean linen, and with a head ringing the changes. Lying some distance away on the floor, covered only with a garish piece of drapery was the tall, thin photographer of yesterday. His camera and tripod stood behind the door of the room, head bowed, and Cyclopean eye carefully shuttered. Barry sat up, and swung his legs over the edge of the bed onto the floor, scratched his head, and tasted the swollen plug of sandpaper in his mouth. It moved like his tongue. That was all that could be said.

'Hey! Gerard! ... Gerard! ...

'Oh, bloody hell, man! ...oy! Wake up!'

The last, delivered directly into the ear orifice, proved effective, and the long, stiff, object on the floor twitched twice before it raised itself on one arm, and stared unbelievingly at Barry.

'What about the old petit déjeuner, then?' Barry's eagerness seemed to have a profoundly disturbing effect upon his host, who ran from the room with commendable alacrity, and was heard vomiting in the landing loo.

When he returned, looking pale and indifferent to life, he stared at Barry with undisguised curiosity.

'You want to eat . . . now? Don't you feel even a leetle bit eel?'

'Fit as a fiddle, old luv. Whew . . . it was quite a night!'

'Please attend to your own requirements,' Gerard said with strained politeness, and returned to the floor and his blanket. Barry shrugged, and explored the tiny compartment, finding little to eat other than stale bread and wilting celery. Deciding he had better move on he scoured the flat for anything edible and portable, such as apples, bananas, or whatever, without success. Finding eighty-six francs on a shelf, obviously placed there for some specific purpose, he pocketed the money, but left a small i.o.u. to rectify the balance and place his indebtedness on record.

The morning streets were quiet . . . almost devoid of passers-by. It was Sunday, of course. A time when the German Military Police liked to carry out their frequent spot-checks . . . 'lotteries' they were called by the Parisians. Sure enough, within minutes a couple of truckloads of Germans arrived, piled out, and set up a block to stop and question every single person who moved in the area. They examined papers, persons, and female anatomy. Apart from the undoubted pleasures of the last mentioned they claimed that these raids were highly productive, and gave them many more suspects, or paperless persons, than they had previously thought likely. They were loathed. Barry, with his customary nonchalance, walked right into one at the corner of the Rue des Ambassadeurs. It wiped the smile from his face very quickly and, hastily remembering an urgent appointment elsewhere, he doubled back into the alley, only to find the German tentacles awaiting him there also. He knew it was useless to attempt escape. Well, he'd had a good run for his money, and it had been a bit of a giggle. Pity it was to end like this!

He was butted into a crude queue behind two fat and indignant ladies who turned to him for support, but Barry had run out of gallantry. Apprehension now filled his mouth, and he was drawing blanks as his mind sifted ideas of what and what not to declare. Suddenly a little three-wheel, motor-bike 'taxi' roared past the end of the lane with two young men shouting and yelling over their shoulders. This was followed a moment later by a Police car making music with its claxon, and a German army truck, all presumably in hot pursuit. This seemed to galvanise the lottery forces into action. An officer barked, the privates jumped into obedience, and clambered aboard their own trucks which set off after the miscreants, leaving the gawping and relieved pedestrians to shudder with gratitude and a mental resolve to light a candle for their deliverance.

Barry shrugged and went on his way, convinced that God was firmly on his side. Obviously He was!

22

Brussels: Oberst Gundel opened the door of Brandt's office after giving a double knock on the door. Brandt looked up from his report, and smiled at his colleague.

'Come in, sir. I'm deep in the reports you sent me, and am checking them out against my own. We seem to have some measure of agreement.'

'Good. Then we are succeeding better than we did.'

'Only in terms of numbers, sir. The percentage is still dropping. Last month we picked up only thirty-six percent of the known surviving aircrews. That is not good, and our masters in Berlin will not be very happy.'

'Are *already* not happy, my dear Erwin. I am to be replaced before the end of the summer. My "application" for active service on the Eastern front with the Waffen-SS is approved. It merely awaits a choice of successor.'

'But you have not applied, surely?'

'No. That has never stopped Prinz Albrechtstrasse. There are times when I wonder why I volunteered for the SS. I think the Luftwaffe would have suited me more . . . but I liked the uniform.' Gundel chuckled. 'We all get our just deserts in the end, my friend.'

'Then God help Germany.'

Gundel looked at Brandt earnestly for a moment, then placed his hand on Brandt's sleeve.

'Whatever you do, Major . . . never say that, or anything like that either to my successor, or in my office. It is not healthy.'

It was Brandt's turn to study his colleague. They were friendly, if not close. Gundel was the first SS man Brandt had ever met who he could consider without dislike or revulsion, but even the short acquaintance had shown that the Oberst was a troubled man. Today he was ever so slightly drunk, and his breath smelled of gin . . . Jeneva Gin from Holland. There was also an air of desperation about him that seemed to be seeking confidence. Brandt stood up and crossed his office, then calmly locked the door and returned to his place.

'Dieter . . .' Brandt's tone was earnest, and expressed more than a little concern. 'Something is troubling you. You have done me the courtesy of regarding me as a friend, even though you are my superior in rank. What is the matter? You are not the same since your leave. Is it the posting that bothers you? I could try and speak with Admiral Canaris . . . there is a chance that . . .'

'No.' The voice was that of a commanding officer expecting obedience without question. Brandt knew there was no going back along the path. He waited in silence.

'I am sorry. You meant well, I know that . . . but I do not *wish* to be relieved of my posting. It is certain death, unless I am misinformed, and that is the way I want it. There is something I have to tell you.'

Gundel sank into the chair for some minutes before his voice came again, this time deep, quiet, and without emotion.

'When I was on leave last month I visited my brother. I knew that he, too, was on leave, and I had not seen him for two years. Not since the war started, in fact. We joined the SS together. He is a member of an Einstazkommando unit under Standartenführer Ohlendorf, stationed in the Crimea. He is based at a place called Skadovsk. He told me what they do.' Gundle paused, and avoided looking at Brandt as he lit another cigarette from the stub of the old.

'There was a time when the concentration-camps, and the stories about them, were discreetly made known in order to deter political dissidents and people like that. Then they became an unpleasant fact of life, which only certain elements of the SS really knew about in any detail. The rest of us just didn't want to know.

'Nowadays . . . at least in Russia . . . they don't even bother with camps. They just kill them, and cover the bodies with quick-lime to eat them away. My brother's unit has killed over eighty thousand human beings since they arrived. The stories are not stories any longer. Suddenly I am disgusted with myself, with my regiment, with my country, and with my race. I tell you, Brandt, I think I now know why the German tribes of old had that insane death-wish that Caesar talks about. They could not stand living in their own vomit. That is why I am going to Russia to fight for the Fatherland and the Thousand Year Reich. The sooner we are all dead the sooner it will be over.'

Brandt gazed solemnly at this superior officer in the smart uniform sitting hunched in the chair. He knew the taste of those thoughts which assailed him. It was a flavour known to many people in Germany . . . one they had not yet come to terms with. The day when they would do so was not as far away as many of them hoped – among them Erwin Brandt. But the rejection was tantamount to treason.

When Gundel left him that evening it was already quite late. Brandt wanted to consider the whole question, and debate it with himself yet again, but was given no opportunity. The night raids brought a fine crop of downed aircraft, and his units were deployed to their fullest extent. Acting on figures which had become the norm, he assessed that, with his night's bag of sixteen Allied airmen, it probably meant that in this night alone between twenty-five and thirty aircrew were successfully evading capture. If they were not rounded up within thirty-six hours then they were successfully on their way back to the United Kingdom in the tender and jealous arms of one of the evasion-lines. There was no time for ruminating. There was a job to be done.

23

Jacques lifted the panel to one side and mounted the narrow ladder to the loft. Curtis, Semple and Harris looked blearily at him. Joe Harris picked up the watch that had been lent to them.

'Christ! It's half-past bloody one! You come callin' a bit late . . . or am I wrong? So it's the armistice! . . . It can wait, can't it?'

Jacques grinned apologetically. 'I am sorry to wake you, but I must tell you to prepare. Tomorrow morning we take you out of Brussels. First to France, then down to Spain. You are glad, eh?'

'You can say that again, Jacques.' Bill Semple turned to his companions. 'We're on our way! I was beginning to doubt it would ever happen.'

Curtis accepted it calmly enough. 'Then we'd better get all the sleep we can.'

Jacques talked for a few moments before he started to climb down the ladder. Just before his head disappeared Curtis leant forward.

'Jacques . . . who will be acting as guide tomorrow?'

'Natalie will take you to the next safe-house. Yvette will take you from there to the Pyrenees. Bonne chance, mes amis.'

The panel was replaced, and the three men sat silently

for some seconds.

'Might as well save the candle.' Bill Semple sniffed, careful and economical as ever. Joe beamed at both of them in turn.

'We're on our way! This time next week I could be up to my ears in salt beef and latkes. What's the matter with you two anyway? Grin, you lousy goy . . . we're on our way, for Chris' sake!'

Bill chuckled as he blew out the candle. 'Yes, Joe . . . We're on our way.'

The Way Back

1

Berlin: Sturmbannführer Ludwig Kessler stood in front of the Siegessäule, and looked up at the tarnished, gilded figure of Victory surmounting the dark, red, granite column that used to stand in front of the Reichstag. Kessler glanced about him, and checked his watch. Several people walked the Charlottenburger Chaussee despite the fading light of the early evening. Several glanced at Kessler, for once resplendent in his SS uniform. He did not often wear uniform, preferring to execute his Gestapo duties in the relative obscurity of drab civilian wear.

His assistant and general dogsbody, Veit Rennert, was to meet him beneath the Siegessäule at 18.00 precisely. It was now short of three minutes and there was no sign of the little runt on the broad walk. He was going to be late. Lateness Kessler could not abide, and Rennert would pay for it. The little man was eventually seen pounding towards him from the direction of the Potsdamer Platz. Kessler's eyes narrowed slightly as he regarded the approach of the panting corporal.

'Herr Sturmbannführer... I am sorry...'

Kessler cut him off in mid gasp. 'You are late, Rennert. You know that I do not permit such lapses...'

'Herr Sturmbannführer,' the nervous weasel interpolated with greater daring than he had ever shown on the battlefield. 'Herr Sturmbannführer – The Reichsführer has sent for you.'

Kessler halted whatever he was going to say and stared at Rennert in silence.

'You are sure it is the Reichsführer?'

'Yes, Herr Sturmbannführer. Two RFSS men came

to the office. You are to go to Gestapo Headquarters immediately. The Reichsführer himself wishes to see you.'

Kessler dismissed Rennert with the slightest of finger movements. The little man saluted, turned and breathed a sigh of relief as he walked back towards the Brandenburg Tor and the flags hanging limply in the distance. There was no telling the reactions of his lord and master. True, Kessler had never kicked him – not like some Rennert could name. Kessler had never struck him across the face. Merely used a tone of voice and accompanied it by a look of such cold disapproval that Rennert (and everyone else who experienced it) shuddered right through to his back stud. He mused uncomfortably throughout the walk back to the office. What did Himmler want with his boss? He wasn't going to be ticked off, that was certain. Kessler never put a foot wrong. Whatever he did he did well. He was loyal and devoted to the Nazi party, and had been from the early days in Munich. He had participated in the Gleitwitz raid, and frequently volunteered for unpleasant – even dangerous – duties. No. Kessler was probably getting a new job that was a bit hush-hush. That meant Rennert too!

Similar thoughts were crossing Kessler's own mind as he walked briskly towards his apartment, which looked onto the Tiergarten, and cost him the greater part of his SS salary. But, then, Kessler was parsimonious. Apart from evening meals he seldom spent any money at all. He neither smoked nor drank in excess – though he did both. He had no dependents, no hobbies, no specific interests outside his work. He had neither fiancée nor mistress. He was, in fact, alone, and cocooned in his job. The State was his family, and its purposes his purposes.

Within a quarter of an hour, still smartly turned out in his SS uniform, Ludwig Kessler presented himself at

Prinz Albrechtstrasse, and was immediately ushered to the first floor where he waited beside two black, leather-coated bodyguards who stood outside the Reichsführer's office whenever the great man was in residence.

When he was eventually shown into the large office the Reichsführer was sitting behind his huge desk, beneath a signed portrait of Hitler. He neither spoke nor acknowledged Kessler's Nazi salute.

Minutes passed. Kessler stood stiffly to attention as the insignificant man before him slowly scratched in a ledger, copying notes from a file before him. At length he put down the pen, and straightened the papers before him, closed the manilla file cover, and very slowly looked up at Kessler.

'Kessler.'

Kessler acknowledged the statement with a brief bow of the head. 'Herr Reichsführer.'

The schoolmaster's face with the weak, blue chin, and silver-rimmed pince-nez showed no emotion whatsoever as he studied the man before him.

'I want you to go to Belgium. You may have heard that Allied airmen are being spirited back to England after being shot down in Europe. One or two would not matter. It is not one or two, however. It is approximately forty-eight-point-four per cent. This cannot be permitted. I wish you to stop this.'

Kessler was about to interpolate a question when Himmler continued in the same expressionless voice.

'Officially the Gestapo is not yet concerned with such a problem. It is an area in which the Luftwaffe police operate, usually in conjunction with the Abwehr, and the local constabulary.'

Himmler's eyes glanced down at his file then up again.

'They perform their function inefficiently. You will take command of the situation. For the moment you will work alongside the Luftwaffe police without authority over them. Eventually it may be necessary to eliminate any interference, but for the moment I have no wish to upset the Reichsmarschall. You will therefore present yourself to the Tirpitz Ufer, to Admiral Canaris personally, inform him of your new posting, and request the assistance of his Bruseels cell.'

'Is my duty to be confined to Belgium, Herr Reichsführer?'

'By no means. You will have authority throughout western Europe. I wish you – for the moment – to use that authority sparingly, but you will have it. The Luftwaffe representative in Brussels, with commission to control these Allied evaders, is a Major Brandt. He is a personal friend of Admiral Canaris. His loyalties are suspect, but as yet there is no evidence against him. He works efficiently enough for the Luftwaffe – which is not efficiently enough for the SS. You will not permit ANY evaders to slip through our fingers. They are more valuable to the British at this moment than anything else they possess.'

'I completely understand, Herr Reichsführer.'

'That is why I selected you, Kessler. You have a natural grasp of priorities – as I myself have. I look to you to put an end to this evasion nonsense.'

Kessler clicked his heels, and was about to take a pace back when Himmler spoke again.

'It will not be sufficient merely to stop the gap, Kessler. I wish to capture every Frenchman, Belgian, Dutchman involved in this activity. You will question them, and extract every morsel of information you can. Use any methods that will produce results. At this moment we know of six evasion-lines operating with great success. They lead into Switzerland, or into Spain. One leads to the Mediterranean coast within Unoccupied France.

That is not so successful as the others, because the French are anxious to please us, and police their own territory with commendable efficiency. They are also unusually good at extracting information.'

Himmler regarded Kessler for one second, then opened his file once more, and began perusing the paper on the top of the small pile.

'Will that be all, Herr Reichsführer?'

Himmler looked up suddenly as if startled that anyone should ask such a lunatic question.

'Yes.'

Kessler stepped back, saluted, turned, and left the office watched by a seemingly surprised Reichsführer.

2

Brussels: Curtis looked about him quickly as they left the house. The street was almost empty. One handcart stood by the pavement unattended, and further down the street a large furniture van was being packed with last remnants, and the tail-board clapped down. On the roof of the cab a 'Heath Robinson' contrivance was already coughing and juddering as it was coaxed into providing gas to operate the turbine which would, in turn, move the vehicle. The girl Natalie walked several paces ahead, and turned the corner before Curtis finished tying his shoelace. Quickly he followed.

Soon they entered a main thoroughfare, where trams clanked past despite the early hour. The Bourse stood silent and splendid. On the far corner Bill and Joe wearing ill-fitting overcoats, and carrying cheap cases, flashed anxious looks at Natalie as she passed by, ignoring them. They let Curtis pass too before tagging-on some paces behind. ostentatiously without conversation.

The station proved easier than they had imagined. The girl purchased the tickets, beaming charmingly at the vendor behind the grill. Once in the concourse, Curtis carried out the charade as planned, and gave his 'cousin' a bear-like hug and a kiss on the cheek.

'The tickets are now in your left pocket. You're on your own until we reach Chantilly. I will meet you half a kilometre down the road to Senlis. *You* must do all the talking. Neither of the others speaks French well enough, so if you feel the need to converse make sure they need only answer "yes" and "no". Take care.'

Natalie kissed him again, and slipped away into the midst of the travellers moving about the concourse. Curtis eyed the two examining their newspapers with unusual interest, and sighed. He knew without doubt he would be safer on his own, but that was not the issue. A swarthy-faced man stared at him, then moved away.

'Bonjour, Henri! Emile!'

He greeted them as old friends about to take a journey together. They responded nervously. No Academy Awards on this trip! They fell into quiet intimate conversation, and Curtis checked his watch against the station-clock. In doing so he noted the arrival of three Gendarmes for their morning station-duty. Quickly glancing at the departure-board times – with no destination chalked up – he nudged his companions, and led the way towards the platform entrance, handing the tickets to the gate inspector, who punched them and handed them back. No trains stood at the platform.

'*Sur quel quai?*'

The guard grunted, and moved his head slightly from which Curtis assumed he meant the platform on the left.

The three men took their places on the platform, and interested themselves in their newspapers while the Gendarmerie ambled about the concourse. When the train sidled into position and they took their places in the First Class compartment, all seemed well, and Curtis began to relax. Three minutes before the train was due to leave he noted Natalie pass down the platform, and enter the coach by the preceding door. So far so good.

The frontier examination passed without mishap. It was, in any event, cursory and half-hearted, and the train proceeded down through northern France in the general direction of Paris.

It was after five when they reached Chantilly. Curtis eyed his companions, and they left the train and crossed the platform deep in conversation, Curtis doing the talking. Nothing was seen of Natalie, and when the train pulled out of the station the three evaders felt a sudden sense of loss. Their pulse-rate quickened, and apprehension loomed. They need not have worried. Half a mile down the Senlis road Natalie waited for them leaning on a bicycle, and talking to a man in faded blue overalls and black beret. He stood with one gumboot on the pedal of his own bike, then, ostentatiously refusing to see the three of them, rode away without comment.

'Your bicycles are in the ditch.' Natalie smiled. 'We should hurry! M'sieur Cuvier tells me there is early curfew in Senlis. A policeman has been knifed.'

The cycles retrieved, the three men mounted, and then followed Natalie down the road.

'I am glad you are all English. You would be surprised how many Americans do not know how to ride a bike. It makes life very difficult.'

'Don't you think we look a bit silly? I mean, business men riding bikes?'

'You do not use your eyes, Mister Semple. No one

runs a car these days. There is no *essence* . . . petrol. Everyone uses a bicycle. It is good for you.'

They fell into conversation as acquaintances might who were perforce thrown into each other's company by the exigencies of the times. The passing of other cyclists as they entered the town dispelled any fears of standing out of the crowd. Anyone and everyone was suddenly a cyclist, hurrying home through the early dark.

They entered Senlis just as it commenced to rain lightly, and were glad to be taken immediately to the Place de la Laitière where the Chantal house stood silently behind its high stone wall. The bikes were left just inside the gateway, for use, or collection, as it would turn out. Then Natalie led them down to the side entrance of the house. It was a dark evening, and the house blackout effective, but at the corner by the entrance Natalie stopped, and indicated they were to do so. In the total stillness that followed the young girl's senses were stretched to their fullest. Curtis knew that she was listening, looking, 'sensing' that all was well and unobserved before announcing their presence. They stood rock-still for something like ten minutes, all of them instinctively augmenting her perception by bringing their own senses into awareness.

All seemed well, and Natalie pulled the metal handle at the side of the door. In the depths of the old house a bell could be heard jangling with an echoing, muffled sound – apparently half a mile away – but within seconds the bolt was drawn back quietly, and the door opened. Quickly they slipped through the opening and into the house.

A curious musty smell was immediately experienced – the taste of an ancient dampness that is found in old country houses throughout Europe, this time tinged with a savour of cheese, carbolic and mouse-droppings. The door firmly shut, and blackout cloth replaced, the light was switched on by a bent, old, serving woman who did not even bother to glance at them, merely shuffled off down the passage mumbling something that Natalie obviously interpreted as instruction to follow.

They were shown into a brightly-lit drawing-room where a splendid fire burned in the hearth. Two elderly ladies half-turned to face them, one expressionless, the other beaming.

'Natalie! Come in, my dear, you must be frozen!'

The second lady stood, tall in her fine leather boots, and faced them all.

'Kindly introduce us, Natalie.'

'Not until I have kissed you, Madeleine . . .' Natalie suddenly shed her solemnity and purpose, and was a young girl embracing her favourite aunts. The affection on both sides was obvious and warming. Finally she stood between the old ladies, and beamed at her charges.

'Come here – all of you. These are two very great and loveable ladies. Mademoiselle Madeleine . . . and Mademoiselle Sophie . . . Flight Lieutenant Curtis, Pilot Officer Semple, Sergeant Harris.'

Natalie presented her charges with pride, and within minutes they were seated before the warm fire, glass in hand, making small-talk in highly civilised surroundings amid charming company. It was almost unreal. Outside, not far away, was blackout, the curfew, German soldiery, fear, and death. Over the eastern horizon Night and Fog had descended like the plagues of Egypt, bringing one unmentionable horror after another, and a new Dark Age loomed frighteningly. Here, amid the eighteenth-century surroundings of the Chantal house, all that was momentarily dispelled in the glitter of chandelier and glass, the smell and warmth of log fire, the soft reassuring richness of carpet and tapestry, and above all in the charm and serenity of these two elderly, French ladies who epitomised an aristocracy to which they had no valid claim.

Natalie left the following morning to return to Brussels, and the three RAF evaders basked in a sense of luxury and wellbeing they had never expected nor experienced for a long time. In the case of Curtis and Sergeant Harris, never at all.

'It's a different world, I tell you, without a word of a lie. My old man would do his nut, just looking at the place. You looked at your sheets? That's the very best percale mate, I kid you not. Every flippin' thing in this place is the real McCoy. It's kosher, boy, I'm telling you.'

'Don't get carried away, Joe. You can't take it with you. What d'you make of this set-up, Bill?'

Bill Semple was standing to one side of the frame, looking out of the window without being seen. He didn't turn as he replied.

'I think the old girls are very much at risk. Oh, I know the local community may well be loyal to them, even if they know what's going on. But you can't keep it dark for ever. One day it will leak out. Have you noticed where they get all their stuff from?'

Curtis looked up at him from sewing a button onto his elderly raincoat. 'I've noticed milk is delivered from a farm-cart . . . probably their own farm . . . They could claim they were making cheese, I imagine. That means they don't go into town and buy it like everyone else.'

'Don't the milkman do the rounds here, then?'

'Not in France, Joe . . . no bottles on the doorstep. What about bread? If there are, regularly, several hungry blokes like us shacked up for weeks on end they must go through a hell of a lot of it.'

'Bloody marvellous bread, ain't it? Cor, I could eat

it till the cows come home!'

'My point is that, that too, lays them open to suspicion. But they aren't fools, and from the smell on Tuesday I reckon they bake themselves . . . part of it anyway. But what about meat . . . things that they don't provide themselves from their own set-up? One day someone is going to question.'

'Two different butchers have delivered this morning already. It'll be black-market stuff. No one bothers about rationing in this house. That argues that either the old dears have a half-nelson on the whole town, or they really are not short of money . . . which I imagine is the case. You have only to look round you, as Joe says.'

Bill Semple never took his eyes away from whatever he was looking at all the time he talked, nor did he mention to the others that he was in any way disturbed, but he insisted that their directive to keep away from the windows was obeyed to the letter. That evening at dinner he was pouring the wine for Madeleine when he quietly voiced his doubt.

'Do you know of anyone in the town who might be a peeping-Tom, Mademoiselle Madeleine? Someone who would possibly want to know the comings and goings of this house?'

Madeleine regarded him shrewdly. 'Why do you ask?'

'Someone has been watching this house, off and on, for the last two days.'

Curtis swung round to him angrily. 'Why the hell didn't you say so before?'

'I wasn't sure about it . . . not completely . . . until this afternoon. He is now using binoculars. Previously he was just standing watching. Then he got himself into the house opposite – the one with the blue shutters – and very soon the binoculars appeared at the window.'

'What did the man look like?' Madeleine was unflustered and business-like. Perfectly capable of doing something about it without any assistance from them, Curtis reflected. Even delightful, twittering Sophie seemed unfearful, merely curious.

'Medium height, sandy hair, as far as I could judge – rather a bulbous, expensive nose. As a matter of fact that was what made me watch him. I wondered where he got the fuel to keep that fire going. A whisky-hooter if ever I saw one.'

'Did he have a rather feeble grey moustache?'

'Yes... you know him?'

'I think so.' Madeleine cast a quick suppressing glance at her sister lest she become talkative. 'It is La Brosse. He is the town hanger-on. Drunk half the time... spying the rest. He's done it for years. Keeps body and soul together by feeding the Préfecture de Police with scraps of information. I will speak to Inspector Daubenton.'

'Surely it is dangerous... both ways. To have the man spying is bad enough. To involve the police is even worse.'

'Do not be an alarmist, Mister Curtis. Inspector Daubenton is perfectly aware what we are doing here. He helps us regularly, and scotches rumour whenever it gets out of hand. As a boy he was intelligent and deserving of help though he was the son of a shopkeeper. Sophie and I have frequently helped the more deserving of the town children, and Daubenton has always been grateful. He finished at Police College just as the war broke out, and requested a posting to his home area rather than greater advancement in Paris. I think he understood what might happen, and wished to be in the area to assist and control his own friends and neighbours. Highly praiseworthy, in my opinion. He has been most useful to us. Sophie, you are not attending to our guests. Where is the Roquefort?'

Sophie sprang up with a little laugh, and made for the kitchen. As soon as she left the room a solemn Madeleine turned to Semple.

'Are you sure he was actually *in* the house opposite?'

'Yes – second-floor window – with binoculars. Good ones.'

'That is new. I do not like it. Old Fourcroy would never allow him into the house unless he was paying well. Where would he get such money? Where would he obtain binoculars? Mister Semple, I must ask you to observe this man carefully . . . No. Better still. I will remove it from our hands. That is too dangerous.'

Madeleine crossed to the escritoire where stood their ancient telephone hand-set.

'*Soixante-sept.*' No 'please', no request. This was a demand from Olympus, and was, apparently, treated as such. The response was immediate.

'Inspector? Madeleine Chanal. I wish to make a complaint. That wretched La Brosse has been spying again. I imagine he hopes to see my sister and me undress for bed. It is quite insupportable . . . That is no concern of mine . . . Quite so. However, this time it would seem he considers the matter worthy of outlay. I understand he has taken an upstairs room in Fourcroy's house opposite, and is doing his disgusting voyeur what-ever-it-is through expensive binoculars . . .'

Even from the table they could sense the sudden silence at the other end of the line.

'You will look into it . . . immediately? Good. I have friends staying with me who are highly offended at such things. No . . . they travel south the day after tomorrow. Without assistance, I'm afraid . . . That would be most kind. Thank you, Inspector. Good night.'

Sophie returned with the cheese as Madeleine ended her conversation.

'I asked Robert Daubenton to intervene, Sophie. He assures me he will do so immediately, and inform us of the outcome. He will also forestall any speculation by driving you three gentlemen to the station at Chantilly himself. He seems to think that, without a guide, it might prove more satisfactory.'

And so it turned out. Inspector Daubenton appeared bright and early on the morning of the tenth and personally drove the three of them to the station, standing beside them, and chatting amicably with Curtis as tickets were purchased. On the platform he turned to Curtis.

'The man La Brosse who was spying on you was charged with being a voyeur. He was released from our cells this morning at the request of a Monsieur Lamarck of the Milice. I will take all necessary precautions to safeguard the Chantal sisters . . . but I suggest you are careful from now on. Doubly so. I checked on Lamarck. He is in contact with highly suspect persons. I am not suggesting that anything is yet blown, or indeed that there is any cause to imagine they are onto your evasion-line. I think not, in fact. But please inform whoever you have to in Paris of what I said. The name is Alfred Lamarck. Now . . . here is your train. Bonne chance.'

The last thing they saw as the train drew away from the platform was the smart figure of Inspector Daubenton saluting them as it moved out.

3

Paris: In the safe-house in the Place Malesherbes Yvette met them once again. Curtis lost no time in acquainting her with the situation at Senlis, and the suspect voyeur released from custody into the hands of one Alfred Lamarck of the Milice. She was immediately deeply concerned, and left them within the hour to consult a contact in the Paris Prefecture. Monsieur and Madame Colonne, who were their gracious host and hostess in this most elegant of safe-houses, endeavoured to put all three at their ease with assurances of every kind, but Yvette's departure, coupled with her obvious concern, had set the mood as one of so far undisclosed apprehension.

When Bill and Joe retired to bed for the single night of their stay in Paris, Curtis remained up to exchange views on the progress of the war with Jules Colonne. He moved in circles that were near enough to the old guard of the Quai d'Orsay to be informed, if ineffectual. Already there were those in authority who regarded the 'Vichy' Capitulation as a disaster for France, if not the world. The others were content to sit back and resume their privileged existence, under German favour, without a great deal of material loss . . . at least in the foreseeable future. Britain, if not totally written off, was relegated to the status of a disgruntled bull-dog barking at the coasts of Europe, without making any serious attempt to assault the cliffs and beaches, or indeed, having it within her competence to do so.

It was after midnight when Yvette returned, escorted to the door by two Police Inspectors in a shining Citroen. When she entered the apartment she seemed more relaxed.

'Did you manage to sort that out, my dear?' Colonne enquired as he offered a very full glass of vermouth.

'Not really, Jules. Our friends managed to trace this Alfred Lamarck. He has no known contacts with the Germans, is apparently totally unsympathetic to the

Gestapo, but has, nevertheless some highly dubious friends and acquaintances. I don't really understand. Why should that pathetic old fool in Senlis be given binoculars merely to watch us? There have been no arrests. Nothing at all, in fact. Daubenton seems absolutely sure there is no connection with the Gestapo . . . and he is a very careful and astute policeman. I do not understand, but we have decided to leave the Senlis house unused for the next few months. We will use the alternative route.'

'Where does that go?' Curtis was merely interested, but Yvette was not to be drawn.

'The less you know, Mister Curtis, the less you can divulge if you are caught.'

Curtis shrugged and smiled wryly. She was right, of course. As ever. Colonne picked up the thread.

'I will be dining with Señor Isidro Covarrubias y Galan, who has the ear of both French and German authorities. I will try to find out about this Lamarck. I assure you our friends would know if there was real danger to "Lifeline". Now, my dear, you must rest. It is after one o'clock. Even two or three hours makes a difference. M'sieur . . . I can only offer you this settee . . . but the room is warm. I bid you good night.'

Colonne escorted Yvette to her room, and Curtis made himself comfortable on the settee. Despite the events of the day he slept easily and soundly.

It was as they crossed the bridge and entered the Place Valhubert that Curtis first felt the hairs on the back of his neck stiffen slightly. He did not look round, but entered the station booking-hall with misgiving. Yvette had given them their tickets before leaving the safe-house, so Curtis purchased a magazine at the bookstall, and flipped through it casually as his eyes searched the entire concourse, resting periodically on whoever seemed in any small way suspicious or unusual.

He came to the conclusion that anyone appeared suspicious if you wanted them to. Appearance said nothing. Movement even less. Human beings, when totally unselfconscious, did the most unusual things, and hovered or moved, frequently without rhyme or reason. It was no use. What on earth was one to look for? Professionals knew the tell-tale signs. He was a child in this game. All he could do was remain alert, and act upon his instinct. But he had enough sense to realise that telling the other two of his suspicions would only increase their tension and lay them further open to giving the game away by attracting attention to their nervous behaviour.

Yvette had disappeared. She would join the train independently and, though close by, would not appear to be with them in any way during the journey. It had been drilled into them that in the event of any trouble their guide would simply melt into the throng, or the landscape, and leave them to their own devices. That was fair enough. Guides were valuable.

The Gare d'Austerlitz was busy this morning, and the concourse jostling, and irritating. There were also far too many Gendarmes about – at the barriers, by the ticket-offices, and just ambling about generally.

Curtis felt the sudden need for air, and indicated to his comrades that he would join them in the bar/café in a moment. He stepped outside into the dull sunlight, realising his heart was pounding. He had a cool head normally, and the increase in pulse was unusual for him. He stood by the corner of the stonework as if waiting for someone, and looked across at the entrance to the Jardin des Plantes and the traffic bustling along the Rue Buffon.

A swarthy-faced man was having his shoes polished

by a ten-year-old boy. An old lady fussed and argued with an equally elderly porter.

Something disturbed Curtis. He was concerned for his own safety – only an idiot wasn't. He knew if he was picked up there would be no simple 'Name–rank–number' stuff. Ordinarily he could have shrugged that bit off with no more than natural apprehension. Being in the hands of an enemy as unpredictable as Nazi Germany was no one's idea of comfort. The Luftwaffe might treat one with certain courtesies as a POW. He was now an evader; that made him Gestapo material, and he was under no delusions as to what could happen to him in those tender hands. That put his whole mind and body at very considerable risk. It put the safety of friends, colleagues, helpers, and passing acquaintances at equal hazard. Curtis was worldly-wise enough to know that torture had its effect. People talked. Almost everyone talked, and always had. Stories of unspeakable torments being inflicted upon brave men and women who simply kept their mouths shut were very nice. No doubt it happened from time to time, but indicated more the incompetence (or squeamishness) of the torturer than the extreme bravery of the tortured. It was really a fiction put out to precondition the rank and file into an assumption of guts they might not otherwise have shown.

Something was niggling at his mind, probing his memory, and making him react with nervousness and discomfort because it eluded him still. He turned back into the station and made for the cafeteria.

Inside there was commotion. Two table-cleaners were angrily gesticulating at Joe and Bill, the latter with his hand on Joe's back. Joe was bent over with a tissue to his mouth, and a small pool of vomit on the floor between Joe's legs suggested that someone – probably Joe – had been very sick. Curtis hurried towards the small group gathering round the pale Joe and the worried, blustering Bill, who muttered a vague *'pardon'* in a very English accent from time to time.

Curtis exploded vociferously into the midst, and sent the lot packing with a few well-chosen words. Together he and Bill led Joe towards the loo.

'What the hell's going on? What happened?'

'Joe got a fish-bone stuck half-way down his throat . . . it's still there. The poor bastard's thrown up half his gut. We have to get it out.'

'Okay. We've got eight minutes before the train pulls out. Let's see if we can do it. Come on, Joe . . . I thought at least you'd violated Jewry and eaten a ham sandwich . . . Let's go, lad . . . there's some water in here.'

Six minutes later three evaders walked onto the platform of the Biarritz Rapide flourishing First-Class tickets, and took up their reserved-seats in an otherwise vacant compartment. The fourth place bore no reservation-slip, and when the train pulled out of the station it was still unoccupied.

During the first part of the journey Curtis dozed fitfully. Something still disturbed the recesses of his mind and made him vaguely anxious. No one had seen Yvette get on the train, though she was almost certainly in her place as planned. Joe, still pale and aching from his recent experience, went straight to sleep, his head on the antimacassar. Bill Semple was disposed to attempt to read the copy of *Le Figaro* in his hands. Curtis watched the countryside slip past, and, one by one, turned over every single recollection of the last few days. Somewhere there had to be a clue as to what was unnerving him, and why. It commenced to rain and the drops on the window-pane blew into diagonal hatching patterns with the slipstream as they sped towards Orleans . . . their first scheduled stop.

4

Across France: The train pulled out of the station at Tours having exchanged steam for diesel/electric, with the subsequent increase in speed and controllability, and the loss of drama and romance. The German Oberst who had snored through the journey from Orleans had left the train at Tours, and the seat remained unoccupied. Joe sighed contentedly.

'This is the way to travel, you know. I've never been first class before. It's all right, isn't it? My old Dad once said to me "Joseph" he says, "You got to be a good Jewish boy and take care of your Momma when I'm gone . . . but try and travel First-Class now and again. It broadens you." I reckon the old bastard was right.'

Bill Semple smiled, then turned to Curtis. 'What happened to Yvette? Did she get on the train, or not?'

'She's in the next coach. I saw her go past at Orleans. They keep it that way. She won't contact us unless there *is* trouble. Then I imagine we get the wink before she disappears. They do have things pretty damn-well organised.'

'Who pays for all this lot, Johnny boy? Must have cost a packet – first-class the whole length of France.'

Curtis nodded. 'That thought had struck me, too, Joe Somebody must have put in quite a bit of fund-raising The food we've been living on . . . that had to be black-market. They wouldn't have any ration-books for us. This whole operation must cost a pretty penny.'

Conversation continued intermittently. After Chatellerault Curtis got up to stretch his legs and visit the corridor lavatory. He decided to walk through the coach, and just see if Yvette was there. At least that was what he told himself. Actually he just wanted to *see* her again. He crossed through the connector, and noted a man standing in the corridor smoking. Suddenly his whole being went cold. This was the man he had seen in the station concourse in Brussels. This was the man he had glimpsed for a second in the Gare d'Austerlitz. The face had not registered in Paris. He only remembered feeling suddenly scared, as if he were being watched. Here he was on the train. For a moment their eyes met, and Curtis thought he detected a flicker of wariness in the swarthy face before the man turned ostentatiously to look out of the window. In the compartment behind him Yvette looked up, recognised Curtis, and made a move suggestive of coming out into the corridor to talk to him. He hastily gave a constrained shake of the head, and willed her to remain where she was. Yvette was alert, recognised the warning instantly, and resettled herself in her seat.

Curtis moved back to his own compartment, and closed the door after him.

He hissed at his travelling companions. 'Whatever you do don't talk to me or act as if you know me at all.'

The tone of his voice was urgent, and provoked an open mouth from Joe, and a batted eyelid from Bill, but in the main they responded splendidly, and Curtis thanked their recent training for that extra awareness that brought an almost instantaneous reaction . . . understood or not. He sat so he could watch the corridor windows and observe the reflections in the glass. It was no more than three minutes before the reflection of the swarthy man entered the coach and stood there, a double-image on top of the passing landscape. Curtis took the book from his pocket, and a pencil stub he had purloined from the house in Senlis. He quickly wrote a note on the fly-leaf and detached the page from the book, leaving it sticking out in such a way that it could hardly be missed. His fingers on the seat top told his neighbour Bill, to consult the book later.

The train was slowing down for a station. Curtis stood up, took his coat, and opened the corridor door, there to await the train drawing to a halt. The swarthy man was now openly eyeing him, tensed and expectant. The train stopped. Curtis stepped down onto the low platform. Once outside he sauntered down the platform taking good care to stand outside Yvette's compartment window so that she could hardly fail to see him. The swarthy man hovered by the train door. He had descended onto the platform but had not moved away, almost as if merely taking the air . . . exactly, in fact, as Curtis was doing.

Curtis climbed aboard again, as did the swarthy gentleman, and ambled down the corridor towards the next compartment. He sized up the exit situation calmly. The guard blew his tiny trumpet.

Curtis stood in full view long enough to ensure that his presence was noted, then hastened down the corridor, and leapt from the train, leaving the door wide open after him. The train whistle sounded, and Curtis slipped into the shadow of the platform shelter. Just prior to the engine's first burst of accelerating roar as it pulled slowly away he heard the soft clunk of the heavy door being shut. A quick glance showed no one in sight on the platform apart from the train guard at the far end. Whoever shut that door had either remained on the train, or had reason to disappear immediately he got off. Curtis assumed the latter. He waited for the train to pull away from the station before he squared his shoulders, and walked briskly down the platform to the exit.

The station ticket-collector/porter/station-master stared at the first-class ticket to Biarritz, and then glanced at Curtis.

'I just want to break the journey for an hour or so. I was feeling unwell. Is that all right?'

The white-moustached railway man nodded vaguely, not taking his eyes from Curtis, then closed the wooden door after him. Curtis stepped out into the warm, dusty sunlight, and looked about him. The small courtyard and country road were dry and pink. About half a kilometre down the road a few houses indicated that the village, or town, or whatever it was that had persuaded the railway company to build their station, was just over the rise and probably nestling in the dip beyond. A one-time railway house, built in stone to match the style of the station, and suitably ornamented, stood to one side of the courtyard. It bore a sign stating it was no longer railway property, and was, as a matter of fact, a pottery. A broken-down kiln stood in the garden, beside a stack of shattered and rejected biscuit firings, to lend credence to the assertion. But no one was about, and no display graced the window that fronted onto the station yard.

Curtis walked quietly out into the road, his whole being tense as every sense strained to hear, smell, taste, or apprehend in any way the presence of a pursuer. There was none in evidence, but every hair on Curtis's neck told him that the man was there ... somewhere.

The road sign, which no one had troubled to remove, informed the traveller that the small town about to be entered rejoiced in the name of Caserne. Curtis walked further, suddenly to be shocked out of his skin by the clangour of a bicycle-bell in his ear as he moved to cross the road. The elderly lady who had crept up on him so pneumatically stared in angry reproach as she passed on the ancient cycle, but said nothing.

Curtis found his heart was suddenly pounding and his knees trembling, which only pointed to the fact that his nerves were anticipating a more aggressive move from someone not yet seen.

Caserne proved to be a town of some eight thousand inhabitants, much like any small town in Poitou. Curtis wandered about the streets for half-an-hour before deciding upon the café where he would await the inevitable confrontation. The idea was for him to be in the commanding position, having chosen the ground, and simply see what developed. If nothing happened then he had imagined the whole thing for the last hour, and the swarthy-faced man was still on the train. That meant Yvette and the others were still in danger, but it was over-to-them. There was nothing he could do about it.

His instinct told him he was right, however. His instinct said that the man was somewhere out there in Caserne, and was probably keeping a very careful eye upon him at this moment. If he was, he was good. Curtis had used every device in the book, every possible reflecting surface, every chance to walk through water onto dry areas, then 'accidentally' double-back to check the prints before they dried out. Nothing. Not a damned thing!

He picked his café well enough. Small, with few customers. A dark interior fronting onto a side street without too much outside light to cause glare, and a conveniently vacant table set into a corner away from the door. Once at that table he seated himself, back to the wall, and ordered a demi-blonde. The beer stood before him for twenty minutes before two cars drew up outside the café, and two men emerged from the first car, followed by four gendarmes and the swarthy gentleman. Curtis had not banked on reinforcements, and realised he had played his hand badly, and unprofessionally. Well, what did one expect from a bomber-pilot?

No words were uttered on either side. The patron and his wife merely followed the entrance, the confrontation, and the silent arrest with glum, bovine stares. No handcuffs were produced. No man-handling of his arms. Nothing, in fact, save a tacit understanding that an arrest was taking place, in which both sides agreed to abide by the conventions and observe proprieties.

The car whisked him away, and drove very fast through gentle hills and green valleys, old country towns, and dusty villages. Suddenly a bend in the road brought them face to face with a make-shift barrier. The car horn blared without remission, and two French military men rushed forward to remove the barrier. The car whisked through, narrowly missing one of the men. It was then Curtis realised that the second car containing the gendarmes was no longer with them, and by a simple process of deduction understood that he was probably no longer in Occupied France.

Curtis glanced at his captors. The driver and his front-seat twin were certainly French, though to which side of the demarcation they owed allegiance was not clear. The two, silent book-ends on either side of him did not return his scrutiny. Their total ignoring of his presence suggested the Chicago 'ride', but then people have a disconcerting habit of acting in most things the way they have been shown by the movies. It was only when the car approached a cluster of buildings, and the driver hesitated for a second, that one of the silent pair leant forward, tapped the driver's shoulder, and uttered the word 'Links'.

From that moment Curtis felt he knew what it was all about. Not only had he been illegally taken across a frontier, he was being escorted by people who were not supposed to be there. Milice would not give instructions to a French driver in German. No, his travelling companions were German, probably Gestapo, and there was a pretty fair chance that the next twenty-four hours could turn out to be the most unpleasant he had ever spent. That realisation brought with it a cold sweat of terror, and Curtis could feel his stomach already trembling and reacting to the circumstances. Not to put too fine a point upon it he was trying to control a highly loose bowel and a suddenly tight bladder. Inside his shirt his heart was beating an erratic fox-trot, and he could feel the cotton shirt cold and sticky against his skin. Already he was preparing himself for the dentist's drill, the testicle crushers, and the electric currents to which they would subject his poor body, and he was mentally assessing his likelihood of standing up to the treatment before telling everything he could invent that might make them happy.

So this was the moment of truth?

He was shoved from the car across a courtyard towards the main building, once a minor château, or overblown hunting-lodge – you couldn't tell which. The thin-faced, swarthy man who had been his initial tail walked beside him, his hands stuffed into his raincoat pockets.

The last sign Curtis had noted on the way was a road sign pointing to Gueret, but the mileage was not stated. Apart from that, and a general guess at direction and distance, he had little idea where he was. Why he was there he could only surmise. Presumably, as the swarthy pursuer had left the train to follow him and not stayed with the others, *he* was the suspect . . . Fortunate for Yvette and the others, if not for himself, though at this moment ideas of nobility seemed singularly futile and highly regrettable.

The room which served as an outer office was furnished mainly with nondescript, wooden, office-furniture brought into the building from somewhere. It looked distinctly out of place amid the carved stone fireplace, the fine, eighteenth-century cornice and ceiling plaster strap-work. Even that was impersonal, without clue as to its nature or to whom it belonged. Curtis was shoved into a chair, and watched continuously by one of the Frenchmen, the one who sat alongside the driver and picked his teeth with a sharpened matchstick. Curtis's suggestion that he might visit a lavatory was ignored until fifteen minutes later, when, bursting with anxiety, he prevailed upon the tooth-pick man to escort him personally.

He sat enthroned with the door open, and the escort, still probing his cavities, stood watching the performance with total boredom and disinterest. The roll of paper bore the legend 'La Creuse' printed in Raw Umber on every sheet. The perforations were badly impressed, and Curtis mentally reflected that the product was definitely inferior to the British equivalent. The brown terrazzo flooring was cracked in several places ... one blackened rivulet running under the partition to the second cubicle. Curtis's mind seized upon any small thing to interest him and stay the thoughts that were creeping like the tentacles of a squid about his guts.

He was, quite literally, terrified, and had not yet settled into his 'second wind'. He had felt scared on his first solo flight. He even remembered being loose-bowelled the day the store manager caught him shoplifting in Woolworth's. That was a hundred years ago, when he was thirteen, and it was in a place called Leeds where he had grown up, but which now seemed on the other sided of the moon. He pulled up his trousers, and was aware of the ache under the groin, behind the testicles ... a sort of prostate anticipation of the agony to come.

Back in the anteroom he was made to wait for another two hours before a scurry of anticipation raised his pulse count once again. Something was happening. Voices behind the great, beech doors were raised, and presently the swarthy-faced man emerged, and motioned to his colleague to bring the unhappy Curtis. With faltering step and a dry mouth he entered the room, a superb large study, still retaining its original furnishings and drapes. One wall was covered by a huge, faded tapestry depicting a hunting-scene. So it was a hunting-lodge after all! At one end of the large, oak table sat a bulky, stiff figure in a dark grey suit. He sat rigid and upright, hardly moving at all. His face betrayed nothing, and his facial muscles certainly had an easy life. They moved even less than his body. The cold, grey eyes regarded him as he closed the distance between them and stood waiting.

'We have followed you for some time. You have behaved well, and given us a great deal of trouble. I hope we are both professional enough to recognise that one episode in your activities is now concluded. You have been caught . . . it is time to change allegiances. From what I hear, you have done this several times before. London will expect it of you, and automatically readjust. Your contacts are expendable. You are not. You could be of immense value to us, and we would be generous in return.'

Curtis stared at him, wholly without any clue as to what the man was talking about.

'I will assume that you are not so stupid, nor so involved, as to have personal ideologies. Your entire career has given the lie to patriotism, morality, or whatever else popular appeal indulges. You are, in other words, totally self-centred and self-motivated. Good. So am I. If I were taken prisoner in England at this moment I would change sides with alacrity, and work perfectly well for my new masters . . . until things turned out differently. I have no objection to this . . . let me make it quite clear. All good agents work from this premise.

There is, however, what I shall call an "entrance fee". You will tell us what you know of *"Operation Antioch".'*

'Look . . . I don't know what the hell you are talking about. I think you have the wrong bloke.' Curtis felt his reply sound lame as he uttered it. He almost didn't believe it himself, and it was quite obvious that his captors did not.

The stiff man sighed without opening his mouth or moving a muscle. His grey eyes never left Curtis's face. That was it! That was what was odd about him! He didn't blink. Not ever! The realisation made Curtis go at least ten degrees colder. It implied an inhumanity, a quirk that was not quite reachable.

'I had hoped you would simply accept the situation like a true professional, and make life easy for us all. This house has a perfectly good cellar . . . an excellent one, in fact. We could enjoy it together while you unburden yourself of yesterday's assignment, and prepare for tomorrow's. My friend, I do not wish to be forced to persuade you where your true vocation lies. These things are for amateurs and enlisted men. You and I have made information our personal currency. Bidders come and go . . . some pay well, some are ungrateful . . .'

'Oh, for God's sake, man!' Curtis interrupted, unable to listen to the quiet, persuasive voice any longer. 'Can't you damn well see I'm not your man? I am not an agent, a spy, an informer, or any ruddy thing. I'm a commercial traveller from Brussels. My name is Jean Linards. Your men took my papers; they will tell you that.'

The inquisitor held out his hand towards Curtis's guard without even glancing at him. The guard put a Luger into his huge palm, and the pistol was cocked and placed on the table before him. Then he nodded slightly, and the men removed themselves. The door closed.

'I will shoot you if you make the slightest move. If

that is understood, you may tell me who you want me to think you are.'

'I have told you . . .'

'Don't waste my time, my friend. I become impatient. Whatever you may be I know you are not a commercial traveller, and good though your accent is I know you are not Belgian. They speak execrable French as it is . . . yours is just slightly different. English . . . I think, possibly Welsh or Scandinavian. Please talk. This time without any attempt at evasion.'

Curtis recognised the moment had come, and knew the man was not threatening with empty gestures. He would shoot him the moment he was uncooperative. No doubt about that.

'Very well. My name is Flight Lieutenant John Curtis. R.A.F. I was shot down over Belgium eight weeks ago. I am on my way to the Spanish border to try to get back to England, home, and duty.'

'Then why did you get off the train as soon as you recognised Muron? Why did you lead him into Caserne and wait for him in the café?'

'I thought he was Gestapo. I was travelling with three others, and thought if I led your man away they had a chance of making it.'

The stiff man stared at him for what seemed all of ten minutes before he called out.

'Muron!' The swarthy man appeared. 'Telephone Gorre in Chateauroux. I want him here immediately . . .'

When Muron had closed the door Curtis's interrogator turned to him, almost relaxed for once, and looked at him with something akin to amusement.

'You know, my friend. I think I almost believe you. Your story is too unlikely to be anything other than the truth. It has a ring to it. Either you are, indeed, Flight Lieutenant Curtis . . . or you most certainly are Peter

Horswell, and as good a bluffer as they say you are. We shall see. Would you care for some wine?'

The next two hours passed in considerably greater comfort than the preceding two. The man, who turned out to be as tall as he was stiff, left him after a brief, non-committal exchange, and it was around seven that he reappeared, this time with a small, broad man. His grizzled grey beard and hair lent him a slightly animal impression which became frighteningly werewolf when he opened his mouth, as the lower-jaw projected forward and displayed teeth above the jutting.

One gathered his name was Gorre. He approached and Curtis stood instinctively. Gorre stared at him for some seconds, then began to cluck and shake his head.

'It is not Horswell. He is very like him . . . very . . . but it is not Horswell. There has been a mistake.'

The men regarded each other grimly. The short beard indicated Curtis with his head.

'What do we do with him? How much does he know?'

The big man turned to examine Curtis again, but his eyes had lost their threat, and Curtis felt reprieve was to hand.

'He knows nothing. Is Horswell the real name?' The little man shook his head.

'Then he might as well get back to England . . . if he can make it. I have a soft spot for people on the run, even if their motivation makes my toes cringe. It's everybody's world.'

They talked quietly for some moments, with Gorre glancing at Curtis from time to time and nodding. At length they returned to Curtis, and the big man spoke.

'You are free to go. I apologise for the inconvenience. Good luck.'

Curtis did not even grin. He simply followed Gorre from the room, from the antechamber, from the building. Within seconds the car was whisking him out of the lodge yard and moving towards the closing sunset. Gorre's jaw jutted over the steering-wheel in a curious grimace.

'You are lucky. If you had not been an evader you would not have left there alive. I'm not sure it is wise, but...' he shrugged and left the remainder unsaid.

'Where are you taking me?' Curtis's inquiry was not too presumptuous under the circumstances. He wanted to know.

'I dump you outside a certain house near the Vichy France border. You knock, and ask for "Darko". He will tell you what to do. Now shut up, and let me concentrate on driving... I don't know this area too well.'

Curtis did as bid, and silently watched the dark landscape slide past until they reached a small village, little more than a hamlet round an old farmhouse. During the last ten minutes of the drive Curtis had noted that something was different about the place. It was only in arriving that he realised what it was – there was no blackout. Shutters gaped into the night air, unconcerned, and at ease. The sight caused the slightest of pangs in Curtis's heart. It seemed so normal... as if the rest of life, the life he had now accustomed himself to, was constrained and ridiculous. Which, of course, it was.

Gorre stopped the car and gave a brief, curt command to get out. Then, as he drew away, he indicated the small house next to the farm. A house with one small window next the door, that was showing a light inside. Curtis waited for the Citroen to disappear down the road into the night before he turned and approached the house.

5

Berlin: The bland expressionless face of Sturmbannführer Ludwig Kessler watched the three children playing on the patchy sward. Their mother sat on the park bench talking incessantly to an acquaintance. The hooped railings that enclosed the flower beds of the park needed painting – a small detail that irritated Kessler's fastidious mind. The fastidiousness was originally a pose, something he had adopted both to please his superiors and to make him, as it were, one of them. He had come a long way since the beginning of the war and the raid on the Gleiwitz radio-station. He was no longer a trooper, no longer part of the SS 'muscle'. Kessler's muscles were housed between his ears, and they were formidable. He had played his cards well, and his present rank testified to the good opinion held of him. A Sturmbannführer in the Gestapo was 'something'. It inspired respect, and more than a touch of fear.

Oddly enough Kessler did not enjoy seeing that apprehensive look glaze the eyes of respected and high-ranking Wehrmacht officers. The power did mean something to him . . . but Ludwig Kessler expected Generals to put him firmly in his place, and not behave like frightened, fawning rabbits whenever he appeared.

The children at play fascinated him. Two leggy girls and a cherubic Aryan boy, with all the desired features of a Hitlerknabe, topped by golden curls, and pierced by two pale blue eyes still innocent in their steadfast gaze. That would not remain for long. Innocence and Germany had long been strangers, and Kessler was honest enough with himself to admit it . . . not that it mattered. The little girls' white stockings intrigued him, as did their long, shapely limbs. Yet it was a curious interest. Not overtly sexual . . . not even depraved, or merely the sensual, near-innocent thoughts of a man enjoying the unfolding promise of a young colt. No . . . as he stood and gazed – his skin pale and his hair neither quite blond nor quite silver – there was something of the albino about him. Someone without colour. His gaze had no thought, no lust, no imagination . . . nothing but a dull sensation that flooded the back of his mind. He turned away abruptly, and continued down the grey asphalt path towards the gate.

Once he left the Tiergarten he crossed the busy street and walked down the Allee towards the Landwehrkanal. The confirmation of his ascendency was apparent in the nature of the meeting to which he was heading. Not everyone was summoned to visit and exchange confidences with Admiral Canaris, head of the Abwehr. Canaris was to Kessler the most interesting man in the whole of Germany. He seemed to be a personal friend of Reinhardt Heydrich – indeed they rode together almost every morning in the Tiergarten – yet he knew that Heydrich neither trusted Canaris nor privately supported him.

He turned the corner and walked down the side of the canal. Eleven-forty. It would take him approximately three minutes to reach the Abwehr headquarters, a minute-and-a-half to walk up the stairs and present himself precisely on the stroke of eleven forty-five, as agreed. He looked at the grey, five-storey building that fronted the canal – the 'Bendler Block'. Oppressive and unfriendly, if without menace. Rather like the Abwehr itself. The Gestapo was different . . . it had Menace.

When he was eventually shown into the office of the Chief of Germany's Secret Service Admiral Canaris's face was not unfriendly, merely disapproving – if not of Kessler personally then of his function. That basic function Kessler performed as they talked, summing up the grey-haired man before him, mentally probing the thought behind the closed expression. Rumour had it that Canaris was either incompetent or actively undermining the Nazi regime . . . but whenever it had come to confrontation the canny Admiral had manoeuvred out of his position, and emerged unimpaired and vindicated. Heydrich and Schellenberg wanted to take over the Abwehr, which was far too traditional, far too non-party for anyone's liking. Kessler thought to himself as he watched the Admiral talking, and half-listened to what he was saying: 'Supposing, just supposing, that Germany's Chief of the Abwher was not merely obstructive to the Nazi hierarchy, but was actually assisting from his enormous vantage the enemies of the Third Reich. Supposing he was passing vital information which he, almost alone, possessed to the British?'

Kessler once heard talk that it was Canaris who had told the British of Germany's impending attack upon Norway, though not early enough to thwart the invasion.

'. . . so you see that my Brussels cell will not be in a position to give you much assistance. Indeed Abteilung One is both understaffed and too widely extended.'

Kessler brought his mind back from idle speculation to Canaris's comments.

'There is no need to concern yourself, Admiral. I will make use of whatever personnel are available to me, and rechannel them into more purposeful activity. I think I may say that I know my job.'

'From what I hear, Sturmbannführer, you are enviably efficient. You will be working with a certain Major Brandt of the Luftwaffe Police. He is an old friend. His father and I served together at sea during the First World War. Erwin has always been like a son to me. He is a fine man. You will like him, I feel sure.'

Kessler sensed the termination of the interview, and stood up. The men shook hands, and Kessler left as punctiliously as he had arrived. Twenty minutes exactly! Exactly what he had mentally predicated, and for one tiny moment the flicker of a smile crossed Kessler's visage.

What had he learned? No more, no less than he had expected. He was effectively on his own. Brussels would require moulding and reshaping, and Kessler's would be the hands that would do just that. The prospect both intrigued and flattered him. As he had intimated, 'He knew his job'. The evasion-lines would find that out very quickly, and to their cost. Amateur enthusiasm was no match for sheer, dedicated professionalism, and Kessler was nothing if not professional.

6

Bordeaux: Curtis stepped down from the train as soon as it stopped, and mingled with the first surge of passengers hurrying for the four or five, wood-burning taxis that would service the entire train, sharing sometimes six or seven in a cab. He managed to slip through quickly, avoided the sleepy gendarmerie, and stepped out into the hot, bright sunshine. Even the proximity to the Atlantic and the great, wind-swept, Bay could not dispel the sense of the warm south. The Gironde basked silver and wide under the afternoon glare. Bordeaux looked dusty and savoured of the smoky, pine smell that permeated all the way down from the Landes.

Curtis's instructions were precise and, as it turned out, highly accurate. The third turning on the left from the Station entrance . . . cross the road, second right, and the peeling stuccoed walls of the school were only too obvious. Right next door, approached from across a small demolition site, still boarded up, stood the new, brick annexe. Pride of the education committee, but still unused – as there was not enough money in the town coffers to complete or furnish it – it would doubtless remain as a decaying white elephant until after the war, if there ever was to be such a time. Curtis went round to the back, slipped between eight cement-bags, abandoned, and now hard and useless, and approached the green-painted door alongside what he took to be school toilets. He rang and waited.

A shuffling indicated someone's approach, and the turning of the key in the unoiled lock, accompanied by a shooting back of an obviously sticky bolt, served as prelude to the door opening. It revealed a youngish man with badly-cut, sandy hair, straight and unmanageable, that stood out at one side where it refused to obey the comb or any dictates of style. The face was scarred from years of acne, and several pustules remained to lend unwelcome focus to the face.

The grey eyes behind the fair lashes scowled questioningly.

'What d'ye want?'

'Darko said I was to call and see if his aunt was back yet.'

The red, lunar landscape twitched momentarily, and the grey eyes hardened as they assessed Curtis. Then the man moved back to allow him to enter. He shut and bolted the door immediately afterwards. A nod of the head indicated he was to follow, and Curtis padded along behind the grey sweater and the frayed, once-white plimsolls. Up two flights of cement steps, clutching a dusty, orange-painted handrail of cast metal, and down a long, echoing corridor to the end where a doorway led into the old school building. There it was immediately quieter, smellier, and lived-in. It was also like the proverbial oven.

'You'd better wait in here till the kids go home. Not long now.'

When he sat down Curtis could observe the shuffling limp his host walked with.

'What happened to your foot?'

'It's not the foot. It's the calf muscle . . . back here.'

He pulled up his trouser leg to reveal a revolting knotted lump under the pale skin. Curtis noticed the bald patch on the muscle bunching, where the trousers had worn away the normally hairy leg growth.

'The tendon snapped when I was a boy. Went crack! – like a ruddy gunshot, and it all bunched up inside. Couldn't do anything with it. Been like that ever since. Kept me out of the army, anyway . . .' He eyed Curtis narrowly. 'You British?'

Curtis nodded without giving any more away. The man stuck out his hand.

'Alain Mauriac. You came from Aublon?'

'No. Brussels. We got the train down with Yvette . . . then something went wrong.'

'Yvette! I thought you said Darko sent you.' Mauriac was immediately suspicious, and hovered from one foot to the other. Curtis regarded him keenly.

'Who is Darko? He doesn't work with Yvette – that much I learnt.' Mauriac remained silent.

'Is he a communist?'

Mauriac pursed his mouth to one side and nodded vaguely. He was about to speak when there was a sudden rush of sound from below as a hundred-odd children emerged from their rooms and crowded into the corridor to get out of the halls-of-learning as fast as they damn-well could. Both men remained still and silent until the noise and bustle subsided. A voice called out from below.

'Alain! Alain . . . you there?'

Mauriac limped out onto the landing, and peered over the banisters.

'Yes.'

'Can you possibly take the "girls–3" in the morning? Gaillard is wanted at the Hôtel de Ville at eleven. It would mean giving up your free-period between eleven and one. Is that all right?'

'Yes, M'sieur Mercier. That's all right. Au'voir.'

A swallowed farewell, and the front door slammed. It echoed inside the empty school. Mauriac crossed to the window, and peered out through the curtains, then sighed.

'They've all gone now. D'you want a drink?'

'Thanks. I could use one. I'm dry.'

The grey-eyed, grey-sweatered, colourless Mauriac took a litre bottle from a wall-cupboard, and poured out two full glasses of red wine.

'It's new, but it's a good one. Last year was a fine year for grapes. You want to buy it up when you get back to England . . . after the war, I mean. It'll stand up. Real good year.'

Curtis tasted the new wine, still coarse and fruity, but already showing unmistakable signs of full body.

'I want to get to St Jean de Luz as quickly as I can. Someone is taking a bunch of us over the Pyrenees before Friday. Do I just make it under my own steam, or is there a way?'

'Friday? You'll have to go on your own. I'll give you the route. You speak good French . . . for an Englishman.

But I can't take you.'

'I didn't expect *you* to.'

Mauriac turned to him indignantly. 'I went over once . . . with the old farmer. Don't think just because I'm a cripple I can't do things. It isn't so bad. I pretend it is worse that what it is. That way I keep out of labour-gangs, too.'

'D'you have many Germans down this far?'

'Enough. Even one is too many.' He moved to the doorway. 'I'll show you where you can sleep tonight. Just the one night. I've got two coming in tomorrow afternoon. They stay maybe a week until Ramon can take them. One night's all I can do for you.'

'One night's all I want. I have to keep moving.'

'There is something I would like to know.' Curtis glared at the man with the limp.

'Darko . . . what is his connection with the people who picked me up? And who are they? I don't understand.'

Mauriac shifted onto the other foot and avoided Curtis's eyes.

'Darko's all right. He's a dedicated socialist . . . as I am.' The last was delivered with a touch of belligerence, but as Curtis did not pick it up he continued.

'The other people . . . I don't really know them. Gorre's a sort of secret agent. Works for anyone who pays . . . most of them do. I mean they don't have any loyalties . . . any countries. They're bastards! You were lucky.'

Mauriac turned away, the conversation was terminated.

The room Curtis was shown was small and institutional. A folding-bed with one blanket; a galvanised bucket and enamel jug provided washing facilities, and there was a loo down the corridor for use before eight in the morning. After that you crossed your legs and hoped for the best.

Curtis was picked up the following mid-morning by an elderly man with a stubbly grey chin, faded blue overalls, and a black beret. He called himself Demu, and seemed friendly enough after the uncommunicative host of the night. Demu had an equally elderly open truck, piled high with bicycles. He laughed when Curtis showed his surprise.

'Everybody wants bikes nowadays. I have a source of supply. I pick up a couple of hundred, and take them out where people normally need a car to get about . . . you know. The Germans don't mind, and the authorities think it's a contribution to the community so I get extra petrol-coupons.' He grinned widely. 'I get extra petrol from the garages I sell some of the bikes to . . . part of the deal, you know? Ha-hah, I get more f— petrol than the area Kommandant.'

Demu roared with laughter as he let in the clutch, and took the truck into the main thoroughfare.

It was outside of Bordeaux that they were stopped – the first of three times. It made Curtis realise how useful the train journey was to evaders.

'How many road blocks d'you get round here?' Curtis enquired as they pulled in behind two French Army vehicles, each supervised by a single, miserable-looking German soldier, obviously hot as hell inside his field-grey uniform.

'Ever since they caught three men making for Arcachon. Last month they put one here.'

'RAF?'

'No. Frenchmen. They were going to get a boat and try to make England. Some f— hope! The stupid bastards made a run for it. Shot the whole f— lot.'

The Gendarme examining papers approached the truck, and Demu leant out of the cab window, and grinned at him. With heavily garlic-laden breath he barked at the policeman.

'You going to stay here for the duration? Every time I come through you stop me. Don't you recognise me by now?'

The Gendarme was neither amused nor irritated. Obviously fed up with the whole job, the heat, the war, his wife...

'Just give me your papers, Demu.'

The gruff driver fumbled in his top pocket, and brought out a disgracefully crumpled wad of dirty paper, and handed it to the policeman to sort out. The latter sighed, and straightened a little of it, then became fed up and handed it back. His dark eyes peered at Curtis, and the open hand requested the necessary without speech.

'You working with this rogue, or just a travelling companion?'

'They're my bikes. I want a fair profit. I come with my merchandise.'

A flicker of a smile played about the gendarme's face as he glanced at Demu, and saw slight pique register there.

'I don't blame you. All right. Get moving.' Demu needed no second urging. The truck pulled out and skirted the Army lorries in front, and chugged through between the barbed-wire-and-timber blocks. Demu glanced at Curtis and nodded approval... belched, and returned to concentrating upon his driving.

'I take you to Liposthey. You pick up the local train there. You change at Dax. If you wait at Bayonne for a couple of hours you might get a train to St Jean... you might not. They don't run too often. F—' railways!'

'Why can't I go straight to St Etienne?'

'Because you can't, lad. There's a way of doing this,

and just you bloody stick to it.'

Curtis fell silent, and watched the passing landscape for a quarter of an hour before Demu spoke again.

'Where you come from?'

'Leeds . . . in Yorkshire. That's in the north . . .'

'I know that. I've been to England once . . . when I was young.'

'You don't sound like a Gascon.'

'Heh! No f— fear! They're all bad tempered bastards round here. No . . . I come from Languedoc. Place called Ales. You been there?'

'No. I don't know the south of France . . .' The conversation continued pleasantly enough until they drew into the hot square before the station in Liposthey. Demu eyed the situation carefully before cutting the engine. He motioned to Curtis to remain in the cab, and climbed down to saunter across to the station and check train times.

'There's a train to Dax in about forty minutes. You stay in this f— cab until then. You speak good French, but nobody's going to think you are a local. You'll be all right till you get to Morcenx. After that keep an eye open. Sometimes the gendarmerie get onto the train and stay with it to Dax. They caught a few escapers that way. By the time they've got all this way they think they've made it. They f— haven't, lad. You watch it.'

The time passed slowly. For some reason Curtis was becoming nervous.

'Easy, son.' Old Demu smiled at him as he got down from the cab of the truck. 'It's not like falling off a log . . . but it isn't that bad.'

The train had quietly slipped into the station, and Curtis was anxious to get aboard.

'Bonne chance!' Curtis nodded his thanks, and hurried

229

through the booking-hall clutching the ticket that Demu had bought for him. Within three minutes the train pulled out once more, and sped on its way south. Curtis saw the bike-laden truck turn and chug away as he settled himself into the seat.

7

Côte d'Argent: Biarritz, with its 20,000 inhabitants, its smart hotels and beach, its mild climate, is really the number one spot in the Basses Pyrénées. Barry thought it was the number one spot he had ever seen. It really had the edge on Blackpool. It had class. When he got off the train he felt an immediate sense of wellbeing. The first thing he did was wholly characteristic. He decided to take the air. Not only was it a gesture highly in character with Barry Parks, it was the very thing to pin-point him as a visiting tourist, and an English one at that. Not that it mattered too much. The English had always been welcome here and considerable fortunes had, over the years, left the shores of Albion to end up in the rapacious pockets of the good citizens of Biarritz. Barry intended to rectify the balance.

He had learnt en route that Biarritz possessed two casinos, which were still open and functioning, largely for the purpose of fleecing the new European tourists – the Germans. Barry had a feeling about it. He felt it in his water. He felt it in his finger-tips. He was going to be lucky! Great oaks from little acorns grow, and all that stuff. Barry's little acorns were pathetically small. He had the price of his 'membership', and perhaps five hundred francs to play with. It would just about do.

It was still afternoon. Time enough to get organised. The first thing was something decent to wear. After all you can't just amble into a casino in a lounge suit, however commendable the cut and the cloth. There were some things that not even the war could change. He found a hire tailor who agreed to let him borrow a somewhat 'edgy' dinner jacket and gear, by leaving on deposit his grey suit and forty francs. The cut of the stiff-fronted shirt, and the size and shape of the bow-tie had a certain antiquity value, which Barry reckoned would give him just about the right 'flavour' to go through his tactics. He also reasoned that the idea of an RAF evader playing baccarat in evening dress in the Biarritz casino was just a bit unlikely for any German mind to suspect. Even the devious French might take a bit of time to cotton on. It was worth a gamble, and a gamble was exactly what Barry had in mind. After all, for Chris' sake, if you had to end up in Stalag Luft-what's-it you might as well go there rich!

Early evening found Barry, resplendent in borrowed plumage sitting on one of the benches thoughtfully provided by the city fathers for the ease and benefit of visitors, who might need to rest as they carried all their gold and jewellery to the pair of fleecing dens before losing it to the town. It was also perfectly possible simply to enjoy the evening, and watch the sunset over the sea.

It wasn't quite time for sunset when Barry seated himself, and put his omnipresent suitcase between his feet. The case was small enough to be perfectly usual at a casino, and excited no comment as he sauntered through the town to the sea-front. As the evening drew in there was a definite movement towards the casino behind him. Even Barry was struck with the sense of incongruity as females of indeterminate age, highly-powdered, perfumed and caparisoned, were escorted by stooping or portly males into the robbery-drome. Didn't anybody know there was a war on? There was the black-out, of course ... well, sort of; but the sequins and the boas were very much in evidence. Indeed the only concession to the times was the arrival of several grey or black German uniforms.

'... isn't it time Arthur gave up thinking about all that gardening nonsense? My dear, we can't even get a housemaid... as for gardeners – well!'

'It isn't a question of what one can get, Sybil. It is a matter of appearances. Arthur feels his position keenly. We are at war. Our continuation here is tenuous, to say the least. I can't imagine what Sablon has in mind...'

Barry never heard what Sablon had in mind. The voices passed and melted into the buzz round the entrance leaving Barry stunned and disoriented. English voices speaking English openly in an occupied country with bloody Krauts all round was a bit disconcerting. It threw him for at least a quarter-of-an-hour: he felt he was not quite au fait with things in the Great World. But reflection on this persuaded him that it might just give his own position a touch of credence.

Time to chance his arm.

He made for the casino. He was slightly disappointed that it was not as grand and palatial as the pictures he had seen of Monte Carlo, but it would have to do. He entered the edifice. Having picked up his carnet, he paid his fee, and deposited his case in a private locker.

Sergeant Parks made for the gaming-rooms. Ten minutes of wandering and watching allowed him to sort out the pattern before he made his first play with his pathetic collection of chips. He stuffed them into his pocket, and made for the 'cheap' table. Barry was nothing if not lucky. All his life he had fallen on his feet, and the Good Lord had not deserted him this night.

By ten Barry had left the threadbare and impecunious, and was making good time with high society at a thousand francs a time. He had borrowed a small mahogany board for transporting his winnings to higher tables, and was now about to graduate to the Baccarat room. Roulette was all very well, but somehow he felt the Baccarat shoe could serve his interests better. He joined the table, sitting next to the purple-sequined English lady who couldn't find a gardener. On his other side, and facing him across the table, were German officers. Barry had the cheek of the devil, and decided to go the whole hog, speaking in English. The lady on his left turned to regard him, as did the Germans.

'Hello! Are you British? I don't think we have met . . .'

'I don't think we have actually. I've just been having a word with Arthur and Sybil. My name's Barry Parks.'

'Oh . . . How do you do? Arthur should have introduced us . . .' A deep, gruff voice came from behind the shoe.

'Please may we continue?'

The accent was thick, and German-based, and came from a grey-haired Wehrmacht uniform encrusted in scrambled egg, with crimson bits, and gongs by the cartload.

Fortunately Barry never had to face up to a meeting with Arthur and Sybil. He cleaned up quicker than he had imagined, and, deciding that discretion was the better part of valour after all, cashed his chips, stuffed his winnings into his case, and departed with his heavy load of notes and conscience.

He spent the night on the beach clutching his case, and returned his dress suit the following morning. The idea of walking, or even taking the crude, jogging bus to the frontier did not seem wholly satisfactory to Barry.

After all he had hob-nobbed with the cream of Biarritz society. What would Arthur and Sybil say?

Barry decided that a taxi would be more suitable to his present station, and managed to find someone with a superior vehicle who agreed to drive him to Hendaye and Irun. During the first part of the trip Barry replied to the swarthy driver's questions evasively, but then decided it worth-while enlisting his help and advice. Upon Barry's admission of his identity and purpose the taxi drew up with a sudden pressure on the brakes, and the driver commenced to gabble and gesticulate vociferously. The upshot of that was that he strongly advised against their present route, and would take him to a more suitable place, at least a thousand francs further away.

He did, in fact, deposit Barry at a little place called Arette, grabbed his exorbitant fee, and scurried away in a cloud of burning gas fumes.

The Pyrenees looked close . . . and high. Barry sighed, mentally shouldered the burden of being British in such times, and set out for the mountain tops and the pass which had been pointed out to him. He would make the foothills by early afternoon, and there hide-out until night when he would make his crossing, all things being equal.

But, then, things always were with Barry.

8

The front at St Jean presented a bleaker aspect than Curtis had expected. The wind was blowing from off the sea and lifting the waves into choppy white crests. Already the warm southern charm of the Côte d'Argent had given way to the quick squalls and Atlantic greyness of the Bay of Biscay. The splendid beach, largely unmined, was quickly being evacuated. Old hands knew what the sudden squall betokened, and Curtis quickened his pace as he felt the first spatterings of rain upon his face.

The address he had been given was not strictly in St Jean de Luz. The street was just behind the Middle Quay in Ciboure, a short distance from St Jean proper, but still within the Canton. The Rue Xavier Garbon possessed a more motley collection of architecture than Curtis had seen in a long time. The blue-and-white plate at the side of the doorway to number 17 was no different from the others in the street, but the house was. Oh, dear Lord, it was! The stucco covering had been painted a curious, faded yellow – probably a decade ago – and sported faded, peeling, green shutters to the ten windows that fronted the street... all closed. In the centre of the building, on the third floor, a balcony thrust out into the street with elaborate, black-painted ironwork, and ornate, stone brackets to support the balcony. This was repeated two floors higher, under the curved and ornamental gable-end which displayed four extravagant finials, three thrusting pipe-ducts from the roof, and two circular windows, presumably giving light onto a loft area.

A painted sign, now almost faded to obliteration, suggested the word 'Hotel', but it was by no means certain. Curtis rang the bell. The door was opened quite quickly by a plump, jovial man in his sixties, with silver hair plastered down across his wide head to cover as much baldness as possible. He sported a fine moustache that suggested careful waxing, and gave a certain air of finde-siècle to the friendly, red face that beamed at him.

'My uncle suggested I call to see you. You are M'sieur Ramon, I think. My name is Linards.'

'Oh-hoho! . . . we are expecting you. Come in, come in.'

Six months ago Curtis would never have noticed the quick side-to-side glance Ramon gave the street before standing to one side and permitting him to enter. Now he did not miss a trick. Weeks of evasion sharpen your wits and observation as do few other activities. Curtis was becoming an expert evader.

Inside the house, on the first floor, the room led from a lounge of considerable proportions into a small conservatory overlooking a massive, overgrown garden. Round a low table bearing glasses and bottles, ashtrays, and every conceivable sign of relaxation sat Semple and Harris. Quietly regarding him, her hands touching on her lap, and her face smiling gently, sat Yvette.

'Our third guest, Yvette. You see? I knew from what you told me that he would reach us. I am Louis Ramon, and this is my home. You are welcome.'

'John Curtis. Thank you. Hello, Bill, Joe . . . I see you're all in one piece.'

'Thanks to Yvette.'

Curtis had avoided looking directly at her until the name was mentioned, but he could do so no longer. Their eyes met, and smiled a certain relief in finding themselves still at large in comparative safety.

'I am serving from my cellar, Mister Curtis. The Boche did not think it worth a second glance, and I did not encourage them to make one. It is large and well stocked. What would you like? Your friends are drinking Scotch, and Mademoiselle Yvette cognac . . . What can I bring you?'

'I would prefer to drink a cold, white wine, dry

enough, and cold enough, and delicious enough to make me forget there is a war on, and pretend I am enjoying a holiday with friends on the Côte d'Argent.'

'I have just the thing.'

Within three minutes Ramon returned with a bottle of Pouilly-Fumé and thrust it towards Curtis. He touched the bottle. It was cold and damp.

'I don't pretend to know anything about wine, M'sieur Ramon. It is cold, and I imagine your taste is impeccable.'

The cork was drawn, the wine poured, and within minutes Curtis had finished a second glass. Within fifteen minutes he was feeling drowsy. Within half an hour he was asleep.

When he awoke he was lying on a bed in a small, airy room. The windows were open to a warm, gentle breeze, and the sound of cicadas came from the garden below. His boots and jacket had been removed, and the crisp, white sheets felt absolutely marvellous. They gave him a sudden reminder of civilisation that choked with its simplicity and forced absence. A sudden memory of his mother and his two aunts, with whom he had spent so much of his childhood, flooded through him. Even the scent of the garden after rain, which drifted through the open window, seemed to suddenly bring back the cologne and dried-lavender that accompanied the mended, lace curtains, and the faded, Durham quilt which had covered his boy's bed.

There too, had been a suggestion of mustiness that seemed to be an integral part of wellbeing. The remembered sense of regret was still with him, part of his life. He got up and wandered down the carpeted passages, across a tiled landing towards the sound of voices. It lead him back to the same room . . . the same conservatory. Sitting – in the dark, but for an evening glow – almost as he had left them, were Bill, Joe, Yvette,

Ramon . . . this time together with a lady of some sixty years, whose dark eyes and skin suggested that she belonged even further south, probably from over the border in the Basque country.

Madame Ramon was introduced, and remained with them for half an hour before retiring, after which they got down to business. They would take the local bus from Biarritz, via Bayonne and Cambo, to St Etienne in the Pyrenean foothills, and make it to the safe-house farm on foot. They would remain concealed until later that evening, when the regular Basque guide would meet them, and lead them up and over the mountains during the dark hours. It sounded simple enough.

Thanks to the afternoon sleep Curtis was no longer tired, and remained behind with Ramon and Yvette after Bill and Joe decided to hit the hay. They talked pleasantries, French politics, and the possibility of an Allied landing from the Mediterranean, before Ramon decided it was time to make himself scarce, and leave the young people to themselves.

The moment they were alone Yvette turned to him in business-like fashion.

'What happened?'

Curtis spent the following half-hour apprising her of the happenings of the last days. At first she seemed suspicious and not quite accepting, then slowly came to recognise the truth of it all and even to show a certain, almost reluctant, admiration for his presence of mind and handling of the situation.

'The man, Darko . . . is he a communist?'

'I imagine so. Does that matter?'

'Not today, perhaps, but next year . . . who knows? Where will the loyalties lie, John Curtis? Is it France or Belgium they fight for now . . . or is it some greater loyalty as yet unspoken? I fear for my country. Sometimes I think it is an even greater fear than we have for the Germans. My uncle thinks so.'

'There are times, Yvette, when you no longer seem the cool, competent, brave and efficient girl who saves men's lives in a world gone mad. Sometimes you seem innocent ... even frightened ... You are two people ... Both of whom I respect and admire. Which is Yvette? What is Yvette's real name? Does she ever think of her charges as men ... with human feelings and desires?'

'Never! That is the first rule of success, and it never varies, Flight Lieutenant Curtis. There are no exceptions. Good-night.'

Almost with unseemly haste, as if nervous and irritated, she left the conservatory. Curtis sat back, and watched the dark sky slowly dissolve into morning.

9

The Pyrenees: The journey by local bus was uneventful. The vehicle, high and stubby, painted a faded blue, with great patches of rust blistering the coachwork, should have been retired in the mid-thirties, having almost certainly fulfilled its function along the base of the foothills for at least two decades. Now it was decrepit and uncertain, and lurched and spluttered as the grinning, fat driver crashed the gears with every single change. Curtis began to doubt the existence of any clutch-mechanism at all. At St Jean-pied-de-port the tired old thing waited for an hour before attempting the final leg to St Etienne and beyond.

In the dusty square of St Jean six peasants, two carrying a brace of fowl, mounted the bus, and occupied the middle seats with their bucolic humour and clobber, laughing and chatting through stained, gapped teeth. They were harmless enough, but concern manifested itself when, two kilometres out of St Jean, the bus was hailed by a thick-set man in khaki-drill uniform. The pock-marked face, studded as it was with blackheads, and set off by a thin-trimmed, smarmy moustache, set their pulses racing. The man had noticed Yvette as he boarded the bus, then mumbled to the driver in lieu of payment. The man sat opposite Yvette in the front, inner-facing seats, and stared at her constantly, examining her face and figure with undisguised interest. Curtis felt himself growing both indignant and concerned, and found it difficult to remain in his seat until the bus drew up in the main street of St Etienne, and they disembarked.

As he walked away he glanced back. The moustached, military gentleman was staring out at the departing figure of Yvette, then slowly turned, and regarded both Curtis and the two young men walking away from the town at which they had just arrived.

Half a kilometre out of the small town they found Yvette waiting for them by a cart-track that turned westward into the fast-rising Pyrenees, whose tips shone white in the afternoon sun. None of the Englishmen had ever been to the Spanish border before. They were initially surprised at the sheer size of the mountain range, and inwardly quaked at the prospect of the crossing. A further twenty minutes walk up the sloping track which wandered through coniferous woods brought them to a bend where, suddenly, the panorama was spread out before them. Towering peaks, now casting blue-grey shadows, seemed like a great, threatening bastion which the white edging of the range did nothing to mitigate.

'Jesus!' Joe Harris gasped almost to himself. 'We got

to go over that?'

'It isn't exactly the Himalayas, Joe . . . Six or seven hours is all it takes. There are many passes.'

'If you say so, Yvette. It puts the fear of God into me.'

Yvette chuckled delightfully, and smiled at them with her eyes in the attractive way she had. 'I have been over them myself fourteen times already. It is nothing. The Basque guides do it all the time. They live by smuggling things over the mountain. You are young, and healthy. Why should the prospect frighten you?'

Curtis turned to her without comment on the mountain aspect. 'Where do we stay until the guide arrives?'

Yvette pointed forward and upwards. 'You see that gully which runs up to the mountain . . . at the head of this valley? There is a bald patch of green, then some trees, then a big, black area of pines . . . you see? Just there; you can't see it from here, or anywhere else until you are right on top of it . . . there is a farm. Tollo will meet us there one hour after sunset. We leave around ten, and set off up the mountain. You will need to rest first.'

It took them almost an hour to reach the farm by which time the warm, roseate, evening light gave the wooded landscape an almost Canadian look, and brought out the rich red in the pine bark. The farm was stone built, ramshackle, sprawling, and lacked the care of the English husbandry they were used to. The roofs were pan-tiled and, like the pine trunks, picked up the red of the evening light, and glowed with what seemed an inner warmth.

Maria, the farmer's wife, stood foursquare in the doorway, arms folded before her once-voluminous breast, and watched them approach.

'Me alegro de verle'. More a statement of fact than a welcome in the woman's coarse-sounding mouth. She turned immediately to the men, eyeing Bill Semple with

241

a certain approval in his size, and a quick glance of acknowledgement for Curtis's good looks.

'Hambre? Hangree?' The repeated word was the only attempt at English the woman made before turning and leading them into the farmhouse.

In the large kitchen/living-room three men sat at the bare table, and gave every impression of force-feeding themselves. With bursting mouths they turned and glowered at the new arrivals. The farmer, whose name they later learned was Félicien Marques, sat and regarded them with every appearance of suspicion and dislike, until he had finished masticating. Suddenly the square, red face under a thin layer of black, greasy hair split into a grin, which revealed an astonishing set of teeth. Not two pointed in the same direction, nor were they of the same colour. Three were patently false, and appeared to be made of chipped, white-glazed earthenware, yet they shrank to obscurity beside two, flashing, metal fangs, one of cheap gold, and the other seemingly of copper.

The farmer stood up and advanced. Broad as a barn door, he had hardly gained three inches in stature by standing, but his rough handshake and astonishing grin gave no doubt of their welcome.

'Marques,' he stated, giving the word the Portuguese pronunciation of 'Markssh', then turned to the table, and indicated his enormous sons still stuffing their faces at the table.

'Raoul ... Christien.'

He shepherded his guests to the table, showing a curious respectful deference to Yvette, almost backing away from her, then stepping forward to answer a question, while his wife ladled a simple stew onto bowls for the evaders. The three men, not having eaten since leaving St Jean de Luz, attacked the food without being over polite, or too nice in their table-manners, but Yvette talked quietly with Marques in a mixture of Spanish and French. They were still engrossed when the younger of the two sons showed the RAF men outside to the stone barn, where they were to remain until collected by the guide later that evening. The three men quickly bunched some straw into a mattress, and lay down to get whatever rest they could.

Within minutes both Bill Semple and Joe Harris were sound asleep. Curtis lay on his back, and stared up onto the grey beams, and the underside of the pantiles. His thoughts would not permit such a tranquil use of the remaining time. He wondered about his crew members who had baled out with him. Had Ted Apted been picked up properly? Was young Hodges being looked after with humanity, or had the poor devil exchanged a doubtful freedom for a certain torment? And the others?

Despite this natural concern it was ultimately Yvette who filled his waking thoughts, and prevented sleep. Curtis recognised that he was in love with her. She had shown several indications of liking and trusting him, but that, he was honest enough to admit, was not necessarily the same thing. No one had ever seemed to him so beautiful, so desirable, so utterly marvellous and worthwhile. He sensed that his own emotional immaturity, and total lack of experience gave him a gauche boyishness that could only do him disservice in sexual matters once the ingenuous attraction had worn off – assuming it was there in the first place. He knew he was seeing in her a sort of Joan of Arc, which coupled oddly with her very feminine attributes. Again he sensed rather than knew, that his whole attitude was puerile, but what was he to do?

Apart from a few pathetic, embarrassed, tentative gropings his sexual experience was non-existent. He had never had a woman. He had listened to the stories in the mess, and grinned, and laughed, and volunteered no comment. His quiet and firm mien had seemingly convinced his fellows that he was one of them, and properly blooded and bedded. At this moment in time he wished to God he was. He might find the right way to speak to Yvette, and convince her of his feelings before it was too late, and they were gone from Europe, possibly for ever.

The lonely reverie was broken by sounds of footfall on the stones outside the farm. Curtis stood up and crossed to the slit window, and peered out into the night.

It was now black with the cold probings of the early moon, and a few bright, sharply-twinkling stars above the pines. The dog barked from inside the house, but nothing could be seen until the farmhouse door opened, and momentarily Curtis glimpsed a burly figure with hat and pack slip inside. He returned to his place, sat down with his back to the centre post, and toyed with a piece of straw.

Some twenty minutes later he was woken by a small, gentle hand shaking his shoulder. He looked up and found Yvette bending over him, and, without a second thought, straightened up and kissed her on the mouth. Her reaction was slow, almost sad, but not surprised or outraged, which he had feared. She merely regarded him with sad, dark eyes and smiled wanly, then straightened up and looked down at him as he spoke.

'I think I'm in love with you.'

Curtis's admission sounded ridiculous, and probably was. Yvette turned away, and crossed to the slit window, looking down at her feet as she nibbled one thumb nail.

'You must not, John Curtis. It can lead nowhere. These are not days for wine and roses. That is an English poet, isn't it?'

Curtis nodded. 'Dowson.' But he would not let her deliberately divert him once he was on course.

'Why not, Yvette? People can love in wartime, just like any other time. Are there . . . other reasons?'

'Perhaps. Perhaps others can continue their lives just the same. I can't, I know that. I have my work to do, and there can be nothing to divert it for one instant. The moment there is, we are lost. The organisation will collapse, and many fine people will lose their lives.'

'Let someone else do it.'

'That is the cry of the defeated. It is the cry of those who do not care. I *care*, John Curtis. Oh yes, I care . . . believe me! Those evil monsters will not make a cancer across the face of the earth while I am alive to prevent it . . . while you and your friends are alive to prevent it.

'Do you think this is all a game to me? Excitement for a spoilt, young lady with nothing better to do? This is my life's work, and no one could be more dedicated to it. Do not think I try to save you and your friends because you are nice young men, and it is a pity to see you die. I don't care about you other than as weapons of war who will return again, and again, and pound those disgusting Boche into submission and extermination. I love my country, and I believe in freedom and goodness, which these creatures seek to destroy for ever, but for me it is more than that. Understand, John Curtis . . . for me this war is *personal*. I hate!'

Curtis listened to her with something like awe as the quiet, modulated voice spoke with an intensity of emotion he had never heard from her before. Somewhere, sometime, she had been terribly hurt – hurt enough to dedicate her life to the expunging of that awful emotion.

His slight movement towards her was stopped in its tracks by a warning gesture of her head, and a look in her eyes. It was in that moment that he realised that it was hopeless. Yvette would never admit the possibility of a change in her feelings, nor permit the advances of any suitor. Something inside her had died, and been replaced by an all-consuming hatred.

'We leave in ten minutes. You must wake your friends.' Curtis looked at her. The abrupt dismissal of the subject was also a dismissal of him, and he knew it. Yvette met his glance for a moment, then looked away to the corner.

'There are some sweaters in the corner. I'm sorry we have not more appropriate clothing, but they will keep you warm. Each of you wear two – one on top of the other – and tuck your trousers into the top of your socks. There is little wind tonight, which is good. It will not be so cold on the top.'

She left the barn without another word, and Curtis sighed his heartfelt resignation before turning to wake his comrades.

10

On the heights: This was the third time they had rested, and the Basque guide was beginning to show signs of irritation. Curtis felt shamefaced, to say the least. Twice he had caught Yvette watching him as a shepherd watches the young lambs – to see if they could cope on their own. He acknowledged that his heart pounded against his rib-cage, and that his breath came in snatches, and from time to time his vision blurred. Each step was taking more of an effort, and he had to grit his teeth, and force himself to carry on. In contrast, Yvette – that tiny slip of a girl, slight and feminine – seemed not to notice the effort, the altitude. She had already taken the small pack from Bill Semple who was making very heavy weather of it, and looking wretched and strained. Bill let her. Joe solemnly and silently endeavoured to remain unremarked, but the curious pink pallor round his eyes and under his hairline told of the strain he was under.

Tollo, their guide, seemed not to notice anything at all. He walked as if he was taking a reluctant promenade through his native village. His eyes were everywhere, constantly flickering around and about. No shadow, no cranny, no outcrop was omitted in the scan. Neither the keen wind of the upper reaches, nor the smarting damp of the low cloud made any difference. All Curtis could see with any clarity was the pattern of stone, earth and sparse grass underfoot as he stared in a sort of drunken desperation at his plodding feet – which moved beneath him like two leaden weights encased in medieval foot-screws, growing tighter by the minute. He was already convinced of one thing: Everest was not for him. This was high enough. Another five hundred feet and your head burst – assuming always that your heart would take you that far.

The first leg of the climb had afforded them vistas, and appreciative interest made them look about, taking in whatever the cold night would permit. Not any more. Not for the last hour and a half. You just looked at your feet, and carried on like a zombie. The boom-boom-boom-boom pounding away in your head was evidence, and warning at the same time, that the human frame was a feeble thing at best, and only on loan to you while you could keep it operational. Just like your ruddy aircraft in the long run. Push it too far, and it would stall. Right now Curtis knew he was at the edge of stalling. Suddenly Tollo stopped in his tracks, and held up a hand to warn his party. Curtis and Semple staggered to a halt, but Joe didn't even notice, and bumped into Bill's rear.

Curtis clamped a hand over his mouth as he looked up, about to gasp a dazed question. Yvette stood stock still, and peered into the gloom as Tollo moved forward in several, easy, silent paces.

All that could be heard was the rush of the mountain wind in their ears, too insistent to permit one to hear any other sound through it. They watched Tollo, almost as if he were performing a curious ritual dance that had no meaning for them. He moved carefully from stone to stone, then dropped onto his hands and knees, and peered over the ridge.

They stayed stock still and silent for almost ten minutes. The pounding of their hearts did not decrease – if anything it seemed to make more noise now, with a clangerous echo inside the chest, accompanied by the conscious pulsing of blood in the temples and forehead. There was a sharp sensation in the sinuses, as if every inhalation was polluted with phosgene. Joe had to control a strong desire to sneeze, and both Bill and Curtis found their cheeks wet with discharge from nose and tearduct.

Tollo indicated they should join him cautiously. The ridge seemed to be a sort of col that looked down a full, steep slope ahead, with easier descent on either side, and the suggestion of a goat-track. Tollo's finger pointed to the right. After much peering and blinking, forcing the focus, and willing the disappearance of the all-blanketing tears, they could just make out four grey-uniformed figures with shouldered carbines ambling down the track, and chatting as they descended.

Tollo grunted '*Policía*'. . . '*Espere.*'

They all sat down with their backs to the cold grey stone. The first signs of an imminent dawn were fingering the eastern sky. Curtis leant his head back against the rock, and breathed out slowly. Tollo, his neighbour, eyed him with hard, black eyes, then grinned, showing stained teeth, and a bruised lower lip.

'Inglis . . . go back Gran Bretaña . . . make to bomb Alemania? Boom! . . .'

He chuckled, and thumped Curtis's knee with a fist of concrete.

'Were they Spanish guards?'

'*Si . . . desde luego!*' He grabbed Curtis once more, and pointed directly down and forward.

'Is Pamplona . . . Is all Navarra . . . Over there – Aragon. España. *Es estupendo* . . . eh?'

Bill Semple leant forward with a bright look on his face.

'Is that really Spain down there? Christ! I thought we'd never make it!'

Yvette smiled quietly. 'You have been inside Spain for the last twenty minutes, Mister Semple . . . Bill, I mean.'

Bill glanced at both Curtis and Joe, and was obviously about to explode into the greatest whoopee of all time, when Tollo transferred his concrete hand to Bill's shoulder.

'*No . . . demasiado ruido . . . por favor.*'

'He wants us to keep quiet . . .'

'But if we're in Spain . . .'

'You are not safe until you are in the hands of the British Consular authorities. Please do not make that mistake. There is as much danger here as over the border. The Spanish are good friends to the Germans. Do not forget that.'

The early light was beginning to pick out the surface of the low cloud below them, and even shine upon white peaks. It was time to continue, and Tollo indicated they should proceed with great care.

'At least it is down.' Bill grinned his happiness to the

others, and with a lighter heart they set off on the final leg of their escape.

11

Barry was beginning to feel the thinning of the air he was taking into his lungs. His feet were weighing at least forty pounds each by now, and there was a donkey-boiler inside him that was chugging and pounding with the same sort of noise that his little, table-model used to make when it was getting near the end of the fuel situation. That was not good. The pressed-cardboard case was weighing all of one ton – avoirdupois. He had more than once thought of chucking the damn thing away. It wasn't much use to him on top of a mountain, and if he wasn't going to make it with the ruddy thing, he reckoned it might be just worth trying for it without.

That was the thought uppermost in his mind when he reached the top of the gully, and found that, from that moment, it all went down hill. On one side of him the peaks continued upwards, snow-covered and bright in the morning light. It had to be about six o'clock by now. Danger-time for Barry. He sat down on a rock, and considered his moves, before the cold stone got through to his buttocks, and made him feel the first shivers of numbness in his nether parts. With one sighing grunt of dismay Barry realised it was now or never. He staggered to his feet, pointed himself in a southerly direction, and more or less permitted the incline to propel him on his way.

So far he had not seen a soul. Neither French, German,

Spanish, nor even the evading British who, he was told, peppered these mountains, staggering along behind Basque guides. Where the hell was everybody?

The descent took him just under two hours, and at the end of that time his knee-caps were jumping like mackerel for bread-crumbs. The trembling in his legs made it almost impossible to stand up straight without staggering, so he spent the last twenty minutes just sitting with his back against a rock, near the rushing water of a stream.

That was his mistake. Only a clown sits down near a stream. It sounded like the inside of a factory, and you can't hear anything else. Which was why he never heard Officer Robres approach, but opened his eyes to see the solemn and swarthy face looking down at him, a pair of German binoculars hanging round his neck, a pistol at his side, and a mean look about his mouth.

For one awful moment Barry thought he had made the whole three-month journey only to be grabbed right at the very end. That would be too, too cruel, and Barry just wasn't accepting it. The slowly emerging pistol, looking suspiciously like a Luger, clicked into preparedness, and generally indicated that it could be used – quickly, effectively, and *against him*.

'You speak English... *Anglais... Inglés*?'

'Littel... Up thee hands, *por favor*.'

Barry eyed his visitor shrewdly, and tried to think what he had been told about the Spanish police. This bloke was not military, he was pretty sure. Grey uniform and red hat-band. Bloody hell! Which one was that? It was the characters with the funny hats who were the *guardia civil*, and the ones to keep away from. So unless this one was from some outlandish regiment he had to be *policía armada*.

'Listen, old son. We don't have to do things by the

book, now, do we? I mean, a young fella like you needs a bit of the old ready now and again...'

Half-an-hour's constant chatting-up had reduced the Spaniard to either numb acceptance of something he didn't understand, or a mild acceptance of a substantial bribe. Barry had fished out the wad of notes in his case, and handed over one-third to the policeman. The latter didn't seem to object to the present so Barry worked on him, more by sign and implication than any verbal recognition. The upshot was that he had promised an equal sum in pesetas once he had been delivered to the British Consulate somewhere.

After an initial bemused refusal, during which Barry realised that the man was trying to tell him such a thing was not possible, for the Consulate was too far away, Barry recognised the name '*Madrid*' among the verbiage. But the suggestion of a '*telefono*' seemed to have done the trick, and they set off together towards the distant town of Pamplona.

12

Brussels: The early morning was dull and drizzling as a well-groomed man in a grey suit, with a dark overcoat over one arm stepped down from the train onto the platform of the Central Station. Without his uniform Sturmbannführer Ludwig Kessler was unprepossessing, unostentatious, yet remained very slightly sinister. It was probably the near-albino hair and eyes. He walked quietly down the almost empty platform. Other passengers were Wehrmacht officers, and four well-dressed civilians. Troops seldom travelled by that train. In any event they were largely moving eastwards these days.

Kessler had informed no one of his impending arrival. He wanted to arrive unsuspected, make leisurely enquiries, set himself up with suitable accommodation of his own choosing, and become acclimatised to Brussels before he put in an appearance at his headquarters. If they did not expect him they would not prepare. If they were off-guard they would be suddenly apprehensive, suddenly vulnerable, and his power would be established without lifting a finger or making an example.

Fear and surprise were his most cherished weapons, and Kessler knew exactly how to use them. He had had years of practice.

13

Bordeaux: Natalie Chantrens walked into the station in Bordeaux, and purchased three tickets for Biarritz. Five minutes later two young men in ill-fitting overcoats, carrying small cases, entered the concourse, and made their way to the platform entrance barrier. By the main station door another young man, who limped badly, shuffled and hovered as he bought a paper, and let his eyes reach over the top of the page to scan the platform, to check that his erstwhile charges were indeed to make their contact with the pretty girl from Belgium.

14

Spain: They had come to the end of the 'line'. The farm outside Mugaire would house Yvette until the following night, when she would recross into France, and journey back to Brussels to pick up her next batch. There was a group of six to meet somewhere on the other side of the mountains, brought in by two area-guides. Natalie would cross the Pyrenees with Tollo, and deliver them to safety as Yvette was crossing Paris on her return. And so it would continue.

A covered lorry was to take Curtis and the other two to Madrid, via Logrono and Burgos. There the Consulate would arrange for their transport back to Britain. Only when they were actually, physically, inside the British Consulate could they consider themselves truly safe, but the chances of being picked up en route were now minimal.

Curtis sat with his back against the rough stone wall of the farm, resting on the heavy, wooden bench specially placed to catch the sunlight in the morning when it was bright, fresh, and least scorching. It was still not yet eight. The farm people had been about for hours, of course, but civilised life was probably still considering its breakfast, its bath, or even whether to get out of bed or not. That life seemed to have nothing to do with Curtis any longer. He was not even sure he wanted to rejoin the club.

He was more alive and aware than he had ever been. He had found a girl who seemed to him to be everything he ever wanted. Men of twenty-odd years know very little about anything, but within his terms of reference Yvette was someone he desperately cared about.

Already he had his answer, of course. There was a simple, finite statement that was not going to change in any way. He knew it as certainly as he knew the sun would cross the heavens and set at the end of the day.

She came from the farm, and sat down beside him.

'I should have thanked you before for your action on the train. It was quick thinking and courageous of you.'

'I thought they were onto you and "Lifeline", but I somehow knew it was *me* he recognised. The only thing to do was lead him away.'

She smiled at him, a gentler, more concerned smile than any she had hitherto displayed. 'Nevertheless it was a splendid gesture. You handled it very well. Thank you.'

They fell silent. There wasn't anything to say. The faded pink paint on the lorry seemed to glow in the morning light.

'You will be in Madrid by this afternoon . . . and then England.'

'England.' Curtis breathed the word as if it were 'Atlantis' . . . not quite real . . . the place at the end of the rainbow. It was eleven weeks-three-days – ten hours since he had last felt the soil of Britain under his feet. Eleven weeks of unreality. Eleven weeks of apprehension and hope. Eleven weeks during which dozens of people had risked their lives in order that he might retain his own, and return to fight their common enemy. Eleven weeks during which he had been the guest of many; he had been fed, shod, clothed, bathed, and cared for at others' expense.

Why? What did he and his colleagues mean to these people who gave and risked so much? Were they just fellow human beings at large in the world conflict or were they the symbol of the continued fight, the hope for eventual liberty, or merely the last instrument of hatred?

The motor chugged and coughed into life as the burly, black-haired farmer swung the handle. He straightened up, and beamed at them. Joe and Bill had come to the doorstep where they turned to regard Yvette, to express the thanks that were so inadequate. What does one say? 'Thank you for my life'? 'Thank you for saving me from torture and imprisonment'?

You don't say anything, because there is nothing adequate to say. Merely a touch of hands, and a look exchanged by eyes. A look that comes from deep down, without sentiment, without tears, without words.

They piled into the truck, and without even a wave or a smile watched the farm, the mountains, and a small, girlish figure standing looking after them – suddenly very alone – growing smaller by the minute.

Then she was gone.